THE DIARY OF A COUNTRY DOCTOR

Directly the leatherbound volume fell from the box I knew that it wasn't mine but that I'd seen it before. Printed in ornate script was the word *Diary*, underneath my father's name, *Oliver Mason* M.D.

Until I saw the Jerry bomber spin down in flames, I thought I knew Lavinia. Like the land-army girls she'd been watching. Unlike them she'd kept silent. She'd stood on the edge of the cabbage patch, tall and leggy — perfectly still. I went up to her — something in her posture bothered me — and spoke her name. As she turned to me I saw tears spilling from her eyes. I asked what the matter was. A stupid question. She answered me with a question: Why do people kill one another? What could I say? I took out my handkerchief and wiped her face.

1941. My father had been a bachelor of thirty-eight, Lavinia a schoolgirl of fourteen. Some six years later the two of them had mystified the village by marrying. A few years later I too had asked myself what had induced my young mother to marry the elderly local doctor. Perhaps the diary would give me more than one answer . . .

Also in this series:

TO BE A COUNTRY DOCTOR
GOD AND THE DOCTOR

THE DIARY OF A COUNTRY DOCTOR

Alex Duncan

Star

A STAR BOOK
published by
the Paperback Division of
W. H. ALLEN & Co. Ltd

A Star Book
Published in 1983
by the Paperback Division of
W. H. Allen & Co. Ltd
A Howard and Wyndham Company
44 Hill Street, London W1X 8LB

First published in Great Britain by W. H. Allen & Co. Ltd, 1982

Reproduced, printed and bound in Great Britain by
Hazell Watson & Viney Ltd, Aylesbury, Bucks

ISBN 0 352 31268 8

One

Someone was bound to say it sometime during the day, 'blazing June', most likely one of the older farmers. He'd say it with satisfaction but he wouldn't be placid, not until the hay was safe in the barn and he could be sure that he wouldn't have to buy any at today's scandalous prices.

Eight in the morning, yet the dew on the lawn had already evaporated and the sun prised open the blooms of the Albertina – hundreds of sweet-scented shell-pink roses covering the front of the house. The Regency house, where I'd grown up and where my father's surgery had been, looked improbably perfect, a picture painstakingly painted by my Victorian great-aunt.

I parked the Ford on the gravelled path between the house and the gardener's cottage where my mother now lived, and got out. Suddenly I had a vision of my father standing in the same spot, standing quite still in the silence of a June morning.

'See this chain of hills?' He'd put his hand on my school cap. 'If it weren't for our Downs the wind from the sea would be tearing off the heads of your mother's roses.'

The South Downs, a dark blue backdrop behind the sycamores and ash trees, were blending perfectly into Dayton's valley of fields and pastures; no clouds, no mist. My father had enjoyed this view until he'd died at seventy-three, the way he'd have wished to die.

It had been on a summer day like this. We'd been lunching on the terrace in the rose-scented air. Father had mentioned, casually, that he had a touch of indigestion. After coffee my mother had gone indoors, father and I had strolled across the lawn to the tennis court with my father's two partners, Clifford Blake and Wally Truscott. We'd played doubles, father and I against Clifford and Wally.

'Should you be running around like this?' Wally had asked after we'd won the first set.

'Jack's doing the running,' father had told him.

'How's your indigestion?'

Father had laughed, 'I'll tell you after the game.'

Halfway through he'd tipped over – quite slowly. 'Well, that proves it,' he'd said to me. 'Couldn't be sure whether it was indigestion or a heart attack . . . Now I know.' He'd smiled like a man who enjoys being right, and died.

And my mother, Lavinia? Twenty-four years younger than he. She'd touched his face as tenderly as she'd stroke a horse's nose, and that was the only feeling she'd shown.

Within days of the funeral, a firm of builders had moved into our big house. While they'd put in central heating, rewired and replumbed, mother had shifted over into the gardener's cottage; and there she'd lived ever since. By the time I'd returned from London, ready to join my father's group practice, now at Dayton's new Health Centre, mother had let the house to the Blairs on a ten-year lease.

I had been disappointed. I'd envisaged making a separate flat in our old house. Yet I'd had to accept that my mother needed the income and I'd become reconciled to her arrangements. I was going to marry Liz. We'd bought the Old Mill, an irresistibly attractive ruin, which was still in the process of being resurrected. And my mother had reverted to the county life, in which she'd been brought up, and to acting in which – I suspect – she would have succeeded

6

more triumphantly than in the role of a sedate country doctor's wife.

I walked along the path to Lavinia's cottage. Her tenants had made her a present of standard roses, a line of eight flamboyant Superstar, heavily scented and longer lasting than the old-fashioned Albertina. The sunlight made the blooms shine like bicycle reflectors on a dark night.

As the cottage came in view I saw a small figure, arms out like wings, tip-toe along the guttering. With a fifteen-foot drop below her, the child looked far from safe. I stopped, afraid of distracting her from her acrobatics.

She was singing to herself, 'I'm Biggles . . . who wiggles . . . and flies through the air.' She raised her eyes, saw me, and flapped her arms. 'I'm a gull, Dr Jack.'

'How did you get up there?'

'Tree,' she pointed to the overhanging branch of an ash.

'Can you get down too?' No use telling her off, not until she was safe.

'Sure.'

'Show me.'

She wobbled to the branch, clasped it between arms and legs, and descended Koala-bear fashion. 'Easy.'

I lifted her down the last few feet. 'Don't let me catch you do that again.'

''S like flying, Dr Jack.'

'You might get hurt. If you pulled off the gutter you'd land on the gravel and . . .'

'I always get scratched. I don't mind blood.'

'Never mind blood. You could break your legs, or worse.'

'But the gutter's ever so old . . . not like the plastic kind.'

'It's metal, but it's so old that it's probably rotten. Jamie . . .'

'My name's Jamaica.' She tossed her long brown hair, small face turning stubborn.

7

'All right, Jamaica. I'm going to tell your parents . . .'

'You're not . . . not if I promise never to climb up again.' She was uncomfortably sure of me. 'You won't, will you?'

'Do you promise?'

'Well . . .'

'Jamie!'

'Oh, all right.'

'Cross your heart.'

She did.

'Why aren't you at school?'

'We've got the day off 'cause of the South of England Show, and 'cause we've got to write a project 'bout the hot-air balloons and horses and cows. We're going to Ardingly after lunch. Daddy says the roads won't be so crowded in the afternoon . . . Play cricket with me?'

'No time. I'm taking Lavinia to Ardingly. She's in the show-jumping.'

'Why do you call your mother Lavinia?'

'It's her name.'

'Can I call my mother Tina?'

'Not unless she allows it.'

'She doesn't. Maybe when I'm old like you.'

'Jamaica, I'm not old.'

'You're old enough to get married . . . Shall I tell you a secret?'

'Secrets aren't for telling.'

'I know when you're getting married,' she went on implacably.

'Then you know more than I do.'

'That's right.'

'You're making up stories again.'

'Am not,' she protested. 'You can't get married before the Dayton Horse Show 'cause your mother's jumping. And you've got to wait until she's rehearsed the new play . . .'

I recognised Lavinia's thinking. 'Jamie, where did you pick up this nonsense?'

'Isn't nonsense . . . Your mother said it to the vicar.

8

I heard . . . I did, really. I was in the apple tree.'

'Any more secrets?'

'Your mother's going to be on TV.'

'She isn't interested in washing powders.'

'She isn't going to do the snow-fairy thing. She's going to be Lady Chatterley.'

Lavinia, blonde hair tied up in a turban, tall and slim in scarlet caftan, looked like someone out of *Desert Song* rather than Lady Chatterley. Lavinia was adding a pile of books to the cardboard boxes scattered all over her living room. The boxes contained my old prep school uniforms, cricket bats, roller skates, and a collection of beat-up toys dating back to my infancy.

'Darling!' she greeted me.

'What are you doing, mother?'

'Darling, what's biting you?'

'I thought we were going to the Show.'

'You always call me *mother* when you're in a temper. I can't imagine why.'

'You're supposed to be ready.'

Lavinia glanced at the coach clock on the mantelpiece. 'It won't take me long to get changed. Plenty of time, Jack.'

'When's your jump-off?'

'Not until one-thirty. I'm in the Aga Cooker Stakes.'

'Why get me here so early?'

Lavinia swept a wide sleeve across the table. 'I want you to look through your belongings.'

'I don't want this junk. Give it to a jumble sale.'

'Darling, I've tried. Even the Brownies won't take it. Anyway, I think you should keep it. You've got plenty of room at the Old Mill.'

'The cupboards haven't been built in yet. The place is a shambles.'

'Oh well, then a few more bits and bobs won't make any difference.'

Liz came in clutching another box full of books, black hair falling over one eye, the other – bright

9

grey – laughing at me. 'Jack, my car's full. This lot will have to go into yours.'

'We're *not* going to the Show?'

'Of course we are . . . in Lavinia's Rover.' Liz dumped her burden on the corner of the table.

Lavinia, trying to make room for the box, engulfed the plaster figure of a Greek goddess in her sleeve. It went crashing to the floor and burst into fragments.

'That's the end of her.' Lavinia looked gratified. 'Such an embarrassing object. Liz, I can't tell you how ghastly it was for poor Jack . . . standing up in front of the whole school with that thing in his arms.'

'Why did he?' asked Liz.

'My dear! it was the year's classics prize. Bunny . . . Sir Lionel Bunting-Standing had donated it. He was a governor of the school. If Jack hadn't won Helen of Troy he mightn't have gone to medical school. He might have persevered with Latin and Greek.'

'And might have become a classics professor,' I concluded, 'with a nice cushy university life. Anyway, thanks for breaking Helen of Troy. I never had the guts to do her in. Now . . . Lavinia, you've done your good deed for the day. Go and put on your riding gear.'

'You will put the boxes in your car, won't you?' she pleaded. 'I'll cook you steaks when we get back.'

'You? Cook for us?'

'Darling, you heard.'

'You really are desperate to get rid of this junk. I wonder why?'

Lavinia frowned. 'Don't be so suspicious. I just need the space.'

'What for?'

'Props and things.'

'Theatre props? Anything to do with *Lady Chatterley*?'

'Well . . . yes. Who told you?'

'A reliable source, as they say in newspapers.'

'Darling, don't worry. I'm not going to roll in the hay in the altogether.' Lavinia was looking absurdly young and guilty. 'I mean, I'm sure the producer won't ask me to do anything unseemly.'

'Unseemly!' Liz and I burst out laughing.

I said, 'I've never heard you use the word before. Have you ever read *Lady Chatterley*?'

'Of course. Such a boring book, except for those gorgeous love scenes.'

'But *you* aren't going to play them rolling in the hay.'

'Certainly not.' Lavinia let her sleeves fall back. 'My arms are rather good, aren't they? And I can still get away with something low-cut. But we really shouldn't be talking about it. The producer hasn't yet got a budget for making *Lady Chatterley*. We just don't know whether the money will be forthcoming. You know what the BBC is like.'

'I don't. Off you go. Get dressed.'

'Jack, we shall need the table for supper.'

'Steak?'

'Fillet . . . if you take your stuff away.'

Directly the leatherbound volume fell from the box I knew that it wasn't mine but that I'd seen it before. Liz and I had cleared Lavinia's room and filled up our cars. The black book was the odd thing out. Back in the cottage I picked it up and opened the tooled front cover. Printed in ornate script was the word *Diary*, underneath my father's name, *Oliver Mason* M.D., written with a youthful flourish. The first entry, dated 10 June 1927, was an account of my father's graduation and a declaration of intent: he was a Sussex man and in Sussex he would put up his plate and practise medicine.

Liz and I glanced at later entries, some of them years apart. Gradually the large, masterful writing had become small and less legible until, towards the end, the last syllable in each word had deteriorated into a horizontal squiggle meandering to the next illegible word.

I said, 'Lavinia should keep this diary.'

Liz took it from me. 'She wants us to have it. She

says you might find it useful . . . professionally.'

'I doubt it. Medicine has changed a lot since my father's day. You know what he called antibiotics? *New-fangled wonder drugs.*'

Liz turned the pages. 'It may be out of date medically, but your father's written about the village. By Dayton standards I'm new here, but even I can recognise a few names.'

'I'm sure he knew all about my patients' grannies.'

'Yes, the grannies of people who come into the chemist's . . . people for whom I make up your prescriptions. I'd like to read the diary.'

'Keep it.'

Lavinia came down the stairs, looking immaculate in shining boots, light trousers, black coat and white stock. 'Ready?' She took the riding crop from a hook beside the fireplace. I'd never seen her use it on a horse. 'What are we waiting for?'

'You, of course . . . Lady Chatterley.'

'Darling, I'd rather you didn't mention Lady C. It's bad luck to talk about a project until the contract's signed.'

'You really *want* to play Chatterley.'

'Who wouldn't?'

'Your chums in Dayton Players, for a start.'

'Amateur theatre's all very well, but Cyril's always said I'm wasted in it.'

'Then why has he been directing amateur players?'

'He had a heart operation . . . thanks to you.'

'Without it Cyril would have been dead by now.'

'Darling, I agree, it was one of your super ideas. It did bring Tim running to Cyril's bedside. Quarrels between twins are absolutely devastating.'

'That wasn't the purpose of Cyril's operation.'

'I know . . . just a fringe benefit. The thing is, next year Cyril won't have time to direct Dayton Players. He's got a terrific new job in the BBC.'

'So that's how you're getting into the production.'

Lavinia put a forefinger to her lips. 'I'm not in yet. But Cyril's got me into Equity. I think it's a sort of trade union for actors.'

'It is. Got to be a union member to play Lady Chatterley.'

'I can't imagine why.'

'In case the gamekeeper takes liberties with you.'

'I thought Lady C. is all about liberties . . . though I will probably have to keep the gamekeeper in order.'

'Lady Chatterley didn't.'

'Darling, I have no time now to think about it. Today it's horses and fences.'

We walked out into the yard and I noticed that Lavinia's ancient Rover was covered in dried mud. As usual, she'd expect me to give the car its annual clean after the South of England Show. Never before – that would have been tempting providence.

'What's the village going to say?' I asked her.

'Have you seen Mrs Mason on TV, they'll say. Mrs Mason, 'err that lives in doctor's old gardener's cottage.'

'There'll be sexy scenes, in and out of bedrooms.'

'Darling, won't it be fun? I've told Cyril . . . my gamekeeper–lover will have to be thin. I'm rather good at dodging boney knees but I find plump men positively off-putting.'

'Must be the heavy breathing.'

'What *are* you talking about?'

'Horses, Lavinia.'

'Shouldn't have problems with Tommyrot.'

'Who?'

'Darling, I'll be riding Geoffrey Joseph's horse. He'll be fine if it stays dry.'

'What if there's the usual downpour?'

'You won't have to wash my car.'

'Never mind the car. How does Tommyrot react in the wet?'

'Darling, that's anybody's guess. A couple of years ago, when Geoffrey rode him, he refused to jump. Last year he bolted . . . one couldn't blame the poor horse; he just wanted to get under cover.'

*

Lavinia avoided the worst traffic hold-up by making for the blue gate of the showground. She drove into the governors' and council's car park and tucked the Rover under a tree. Was she a governor? Liz asked me. I couldn't tell her. Would she have paid £495 for the privilege of mixing with the people she'd known all her life? I doubted it. Yet somebody had provided her with a governor's badge. Not Sir Lionel Bunting-Standing. Bunny and Dot, parked in front of us, were unloading five boisterous beagles.

'Had to take the dogs,' Bunny grumbled. 'Damned nuisance. Not allowed to take them into the Queen's Pavilion.'

'It was his idea,' Dot told us. 'We could have left them at home.'

'Digging up my begonias. No fear!' His pale eyes swivelled from his minute wife to me. 'You on duty here, young Mason?'

'Not this year.'

'Word with you about my wart.' He stuck his hand under my nose. 'Still there. Unsightly. Medical profession should be able to do something about it.'

'Try your garage,' I suggested.

'What?'

'Bob Jasper.'

'Oh, Dayton Garage.'

'Right. Bob put acid from a car battery on his wart.'

'Sounds painful.'

'It was, but the wart disappeared.'

'Are you seriously advising me . . .'

'Shut up, Bunny,' snapped Dot. Entangled in five dog leads, whipped by five tails, she reminded me of a trussed chicken.

Her husband, oblivious of her struggle, contemplated his hand. 'Acid . . . eh?'

'Take your dogs!' Dot drove an elbow into her husband's bulk, 'And stop pestering Dr Jack about your ruddy wart.'

Bunny rocked back and forth on his feet, as he always did when Dot was getting the better of him.

14

'Just saving young Jack the bother of a professional call.'

'Jack's not on duty today, so leave him alone.'

'Acid,' Bunny kept rocking. 'Dare say it *would* burn the thing off. I wonder . . .'

Dot dropped the dog leads. 'Sir Lionel! Lavinia and her young people don't want to spend the day in this bloody car park. And I want to see the goats before the best get sold.'

'Dot wants to buy a goat . . . Damned if I know why.'

The beagles had discovered that they were free and belted off, heading for a small ginger dog attached to a pram. The fox-like pet yelped, the pram swung wildly from side to side and the besieged young mother laid about her with a picnic basket.

'Disgraceful!' Bunny's face reddened. 'No way to treat beagles.'

Dot planted herself in front of him. 'This is the South of England Show,' she spoke as succinctly as a radio commentator, 'and anyone stupid enough to bring his dogs is required to keep the animals on the lead.'

'Quite right, m'dear. Couldn't agree more.'

'In that case . . . hadn't you better control *your* dogs?'

'Good God!' Bunny gazed at Dot as if he were seeing her for the first time, 'Your dogs!'

'*Your* dogs.' Dot watched him break into a cumbersome trot. 'He'll give himself a heart attack, silly old fool.' She put a few fingers in her mouth and produced a shrill whistle. It stopped Bunny in his tracks and brought the beagles racing back. 'Jack, would you mind seeing him at home, perhaps next week?'

I suddenly became aware of the strain in Lady Dorothy's face. I'd always seen her as a small, tough woman who hadn't changed since my schooldays, who managed a huge and unpractical manor house plus acres of grounds almost single-handed, and still found time to raise money for the Red Cross, the League of

Hospital Friends and the Dog Rescue Society. I realised all at once that Dot must have passed middle-age long ago, that she was in her sixties. 'I'll look in on Monday,' I promised. 'If he's that worried about the wart . . .'

'No,' she lowered her voice. 'The wart's the least of our problems.'

Lavinia had wandered off to the horse lines and the practice ring. She'd give Tommyrot a gentle warm-up, study him, walk him and talk to him in the deep, soothing voice that made his ears twitch with ecstasy. If it hadn't been for the worst farm accident I'd seen, Geoffrey Joseph would have been riding his own horse. He'd severed his hand with a chainsaw. By sheer luck Liz and I had been on the farm at the time. We'd driven him and the hand to East Grinstead at suicidal speed, and a superb micro-surgeon had succeeded in re-attaching the hand. It was alive now, it was useful, but Geoffrey had conceded that he was not yet fit for handling his good but temperamental stallion. He'd said that he wouldn't be risking his horse, but he hadn't told me that he'd let my mother ride him. Yet Lavinia, who'd been exercising Tommyrot, was the natural choice.

'When's Lavinia on?' asked Liz.

'One-thirty.'

'Time to see *everything*.' Her fine, short nose twitched. 'I love the smell of crushed grass. It's another world.'

I knew what she meant. The grim northern town where she had grown up was far removed from the verdant countryside of Sussex, the spacious fields and ancient trees. She'd come to Dayton as the pharmacist at the local chemist's and even after eighteen months her wonder at rural England was undiminished.

'Jack, you never told me how large it is . . . all these stands and marquees, and people and . . .'

'Animals. It's one of the most important agricultural shows in the country.'

'And a lot besides.'

We walked through the grounds, stopping at Sotheby's display of antique furniture, at Simpson's show of country fashions, an exhibition of farm buildings and machinery, a stamp dealers', a flower tent and a dog-food stand where an artist offered instant sketches of dogs and babies. There were displays of stripped pine furniture, historic steam engines, Shell Oil T-shirts, and a marquee where the Guild of Sussex Craftsmen were demonstrating work in wood and leather, copper and silver.

We kept meeting people we knew, all keeping an eye on the gathering clouds. If it turned wet, tens of thousands – visitors and business people – would take refuge in tents and cars but the competitors would have to watch the show rings become waterlogged, their painstakingly groomed horses and cattle turn muddy and bedraggled.

We bumped into Tom Mallard. 'Sheep championship's at two-fifteen.' He contemplated the scudding black clouds.

'Your animals in?' I asked him.

'Four of the best.'

'Hope you'll win, Tom.'

'That'ud be the second winner this morning . . . My Anne's given birth. A boy.'

'Congratulations.' Liz took his hand in hers. 'How's Anne?'

'None the worse. Who'd have thought it . . . 'err in her thirties.'

Who'd have thought that the vicar's daughter would fall in love with this forty-year-old farm worker reared in an orphanage, and marry him, defying her father's snobbish and vindictive objections?

Tom laughed, 'An elderly mother . . . that's what the midwife called my Anne. And you should have seen 'err with the babe in her arms . . . a girl . . . just a slip of a girl.'

'Wish you luck with the sheep too,' said Liz.

'Thank ye kindly.' Tom squinted at the sky.

"T won't rain afore nightfall, I dursay.'

Liz watched a line of white Charollais bulls being led into number one ring. 'They look like great beasts of another age. Let's go and see the judging.'

'You'll see more from the other side.' I led her through the crowds towards the members' stand.

The ring was filling up with glossy beef cattle, shorthorn Aberdeen Angus and Sussex, belted Galloway and Devon, Hereford and Lincoln Red. The winners, if the breeders were willing to sell, might change hands from anything between £10,000 and £40,000 and finish up in places as far away as Australia or the United States.

We were halfway up a grassy bank when we saw a sight so unusual at the Show that it attracted an instant crowd. A burly farmer, whom I recognised as Len Kirby, was swinging his shooting-stick at a younger man. He'd drawn blood too. Ken Morris, who'd recently taken over his late father's farm, was bleeding from a cut on his forehead.

'Len!' I scrambled up the last few feet. 'Stop it. Have you gone mad?'

'You mind your own business, Jack,' he yelled. 'I'll teach him –'

The Dayton bobby, Sergeant Tripp, made a grab for the stick and snatched it from mid-air. 'Now, now, Mr Kirby, what's all this about?'

Len blinked. 'He hit me . . . the little swine.'

'I didn't.' Ken, pressing a handkerchief to his head, was looking bewildered. I felt sure he wasn't lying.

'I'll teach you . . .' Len Kirby charged past the Sergeant. 'I'll . . .' He suddenly doubled over, gripped his right leg and fell down in a heap.

'Police brutality!' Dayton's traffic warden, Mac Curran, appeared from the crowd. 'What have you done now, Tripp?'

'Me? It's them . . . I've stopped them murdering each other, I have.'

'That'll be the day.' Curran took young Ken by the arm. 'First-aid tent, come along. You want to make a

18

complaint against the police.'

'It wasn't the Sergeant,' muttered Ken.

'We'll see about that . . . poking his nose in where he isn't wanted . . . But where is he when the Spiller boys rip out the telephone in the High Street? Calls himself a copper . . . You okay, Mr Morris? Come along . . . soon get you fixed up.'

Len Kirby was rolling on the ground, obviously in pain.

'What is it?' I asked him. Len and I had been at school together. I'd never known him turn violent, nor was he the kind of man who'd get drunk, least of all at the Show.

'My leg,' groaned Len. 'Jack, I swear he kicked me . . . back of the leg.' He struggled into a sitting position. 'Help me up.'

'Stay where you are. Better get a stretcher, Sergeant. And ask first-aid to find a duty doctor.'

'Jack . . .'

'Keep still, Len.'

'I'm not letting Morris get away with it.'

'Now why should Ken want to attack you?'

'Chip off the old block. Crazy as a coot. Did himself in with sleeping pills and . . .'

'Shut up, Len. I know more about it than you do. I won't have you blame the kid for what his father was. This isn't like you. Give the lad a chance . . .'

'I lost two lambs on account of him. Told him to mend his bloody fence . . .'

'Ken's got a lot of mending to do. You know his father left the farm in a mess.'

'Or maybe he helped the lambs through the hole.'

'Rubbish. No farmer in his right mind would steal from his neighbour, and well you know it.'

'Who says Ken's in his right mind?' Len Kirby's face was a grimace of pain. 'In the old days they used to hang the likes of Morris.'

'Glad it isn't the old days.'

'Jack, I never thought *you'd* turn against me.'

'And I never thought you'd be stupid enough to

19

pick a fight with a young neighbour who's doing his damnedest to save the family farm.'

'You didn't see . . .'

'No, I didn't. First thing's to find out what's the matter with your leg.'

'He bust it good 'n' proper, sneaking up from behind.'

'Len, be reasonable . . .'

'I am being reasonable,' he yelled.

'You can break a bone just walking . . . or sitting at a table doing your tax returns. When I was at Guy's . . .'

'I'm telling you! Morris was right behind me. I'll kill him if it's the last thing I do.'

Two

We were standing outside the first-aid tent, the parade of cattle forgotten. Flora Blake, eldest daughter of my senior partner, was worried. She'd been a fully fledged doctor less than a year, a trainee general practitioner with a Millers Common firm less than a month. There was a family resemblance, though none too obvious, between Dr Clifford Blake – who was pink, egg-shaped and tall – and his offspring who was blonde, lean and tall. At the moment she was looking like an overgrown schoolgirl about to fail her A-levels.

'I couldn't find a mark on Mr Kirby.' Flora glanced over her shoulder into the tent. 'I don't understand it. I mean . . . you'd expect something. A contusion . . .'

'Not if Morris didn't kick him,' said Liz.

'But he swears . . .'

I said, 'He's been swearing a lot today. Don't pay too much attention. What with the harvest to come, June's a bad time for a farmer to be laid up.'

'I don't think he's fractured a bone, do you?'

I didn't, though Flora hadn't given Len anything like a proper examination. He'd been in such a state that it had been more sensible to deal with the pain. Quite rightly, Flora had given him a subcutaneous injection of pethidine.

'What next?' she asked me.

'Forget I'm here.'

'Isn't Mr Kirby on your panel?'

'Your father would call this, *passing the buck*.'

'I could call an ambulance,' said Flora doubtfully.

'Rush him off screaming and kicking, and wash your hands of him?'

'That's unkind,' objected Liz.

'Not really.' Flora grinned. 'Actually, Jack's right. My father's always preaching that there are too many family doctors who hive off their responsibilities . . . push their patients into hospital at the drop of a hat. Honestly . . . I don't want to do that.' She glanced at her watch. 'I reckon he's over the worst pain by now; he'll stand up to some poking.'

'He may have to go into hospital,' I conceded.

We went back into the tent. Len, still on the stretcher, had relaxed.

'Feeling better?' Flora asked him.

'I'm all right, thanks. Sorry I made a nuisance of myself.' He sat up.

I took him by the shoulders. 'Where do you think you are going? Dr Blake hasn't examined you yet. Lie back.'

He grunted but he didn't object. Flora worked on the leg gently and expertly. She knew what she was looking for. When she palpated the area above the ankle Len flinched though he didn't complain.

'I think it's the plantaris,' Flora told me.

'What's that?' asked Len.

'A tendon . . . Wait a moment.' Her thumb felt around. 'The Achilles tendon's ruptured.'

'Oh well . . . never mind,' said Len cheerfully. 'So long as no bone's broken. I must go and find my family. April will be looking for me.'

'Keep still,' I told him. 'A torn Achilles tendon's an injury that's got to be dealt with.'

'You can't ignore it,' Flora agreed. 'Mr Kirby, would you let Jack examine the leg? I'd be glad of his opinion.'

'Go ahead,' he answered her appeal.

I confirmed the area of tenderness. There was the typical knotting of the calf muscles, and after a while I too found the break in the tendon.

Flora, who had been looking through the first-aid box, held up a bottle. 'Should we give him an injection of Hayalase?'

'I think so.'

'Another injection?' Len was getting impatient.

'Dr Blake isn't doing it for fun.'

'Sorry. Shove the stuff in if you think it'll cure the thing.'

'It's no cure,' I explained, 'though it'll ease the leg. You might have to go into hospital. Not now. Let April drive you home, and rest.'

'I'm not leaving the Show. April's in the hackney driving class. She's worked hard at it. I'm not going to spoil it for her.'

'You can stay in here.'

'No. I'll manage.'

I knew he wouldn't give in. Flora injected the Hayalase into the tender area and then strapped the leg with a crêpe bandage. We helped him to his feet, and I gave him his shooting-stick.

He limped a few steps. 'Good as new. Thanks for patching me up.'

'You'll do for now,' I told him. 'I'll call in to-morrow.'

'No need.'

'That's for Dr Mason to decide,' said Flora. 'You'll have to be seen by an orthopaedic surgeon.'

'At the hospital?'

'Yes.'

'I don't have the time . . . The pain's almost gone.'

'Dr Blake's right, Len. I'll see you tomorrow.'

'If you say so.' Len was probably remembering that I hadn't advised him too badly in the recent past. I'd solved a troublesome allergy problem for him. 'Jack, tell me the worst.'

'You'll live.'

'Seriously.'

'The ruptured tendon might have to be stitched together.'

'An operation?'

'I think so.'

'By God! I'll get Morris for this!'

'You'd better leave Morris alone. In fact you owe him an apology. He didn't touch you.'

'I felt . . .'

'Not a kick. What you felt was the tendon tearing . . . which sometimes does seem like a kick. It's the kind of thing that happens to footballers. They too believe they've been attacked and tend to turn nasty.'

'Well, it's a queer thing but . . .'

'I suggest you find Morris and explain why you went berserk. If he doesn't believe you – and it wouldn't surprise me – tell him I can confirm your story.'

'You don't know,' muttered Len. 'The Kirbys' land's been adjoining the Morris's for generations.'

'I know one thing: Ken Morris is just out of agriculture college and he's been thrown in at the deep end. He's about the hardest-working farmer in the district. Give him a chance and you'll find out that he's a good man.'

'Chip off the old block. But have it your own way.'

The rain had held off and the Show was speeding up. Activity everywhere. At the blue gate the sheepdogs, due to perform in the afternoon, were being unloaded. Nearby the foxhounds, awaiting their turn, were barking their heads off, making their box shake like a jumping bean. At the red gate the Royal Regiment of Artillery Motor Cycle Display Team were polishing their already silver-bright Suzuki machines.

In the south grounds red and yellow hot-air balloons, still tethered, were wagging their giant heads above the crowd. Over all drifted the zestful music of the Regimental Band of the 5th Inniskilling Dragoon Guards, on special leave from Germany.

Liz, beside me, was unusually silent. 'Too crowded for you?' I asked her.

'Just thinking.'

'About what to do with the junk Lavinia's wished on us?'

'No. It's Len Kirby . . . why he hates Morris.'

'He's got a temper, but he doesn't hate. The pain must have been quite bad.'

'There's more to it,' insisted Liz. 'I've been trying to remember. There's something I know, but I can't put a finger on it.'

'There was no love lost between Len and Morris senior. He was a sloppy farmer and a drunk.'

Liz frowned. 'Why should Len hold that against the son? It isn't like him.'

'No, it isn't,' I had to admit. 'Come on, let's find seats. The show-jumping's about to start.'

Though I can communicate with a horse to the point where it won't try to crush me against a tree, roll on me or deliberately throw me, I wouldn't call myself a horseman. Yet I could understand why Liz was enthralled by the spectacle in the ring. In a sense I had the horses to thank for meeting the one girl I'd ever wanted to marry. It was Lavinia who had discovered, heaven knows how, that Liz had *good hands* and initiated her into the equestrian set.

Liz was sitting forward, fists on cheeks, watching each jump with eager concentration. She made small noises of regret when a horse knocked down a bar and showed her pleasure at every clear round. I didn't get caught up in the excitement of the crowds around us but I enjoyed the speed of the animals, the ripple of muscle as the horses tucked in their legs and sailed over the fences. To me it seemed quite a feat. Unlike my mother I didn't believe that horses were born to leap over obstacles.

Lavinia, on Tommyrot, had survived the first round without a fault and was about to tackle the second, over raised fences. Tommyrot was a big chestnut with a nervous rear. He came into the ring, tail swishing, throwing his head. Lavinia allowed him a minute's playtime, letting him side-step and dance, before

25

calling him to order. At the sound of the bell he leaped forward, rushing at the first fence – a high gate. For a moment it looked as if he might put on the brakes and refuse to jump. Then, from an almost standing position, he suddenly rose on his hind legs and eased himself across. The gate rocked, but it didn't fall.

Watching Lavinia take the second and third fences, I could see daylight between her and the saddle. She was standing in the stirrups, appearing to lift Tommyrot over the obstacles, willing him into another clear round. It struck me that she might have made the Olympic team more than once if she hadn't opted for marriage with a much older, demanding general practitioner and for motherhood. I was grateful that she had but I still didn't understand her reasons.

'She's in the jump-off against the clock,' said Liz excitedly.

'Good, but I wouldn't put my money on Tommyrot.'

'He's jumping well today.'

'He isn't fast enough.'

'The six-foot fences will slow down the other horses,' Liz consoled herself.

First in the ring was Muriel Standing, daughter of Bunny and Dot. She was riding White Savage, a small but nimble horse as determined as his rider. He obviously wanted to be rushed and Muriel let him have his head. I could hear his hoofs knock bricks and bars, but at the end of the round he'd collected no more than four faults.

Lavinia was next. Liz looked at the sky. So did Tommyrot. A dark grey cloud was churning overhead. Big, lazy drops were beginning to splash down.

This time the chestnut decided against dancing. He stood quietly until he heard the bell and Lavinia let him go. He'd rolled lazily but safely over the first fence when the rain came down in earnest. Suddenly his ears went up and he rushed the double like a demented war-horse. No question of Lavinia controlling his stride. Tommyrot's intention was unmistakable; he was racing for cover.

'Ground's slippery,' muttered Liz, anxiously.

'She'll make it!' shouted someone beside us. 'He's over! They've done it.'

He'd slithered too close to the wall, yet Lavinia had somehow got him over the top. He'd dislodged a brick, but it hadn't fallen. The treble was coming up, fences too close together for comfort. Tommyrot plunged, with Lavinia hanging on like a Cossack. I just hoped she wouldn't end up clinging to Tommyrot's belly. And then the horse cleared the last fence, his time so tight that it would be hard to beat.

Liz and I got up, ready to congratulate my mother, when Tommyrot reared and bolted to the exit, something Lavinia had not anticipated. She fell off backward, hitting the ground hard. While we ducked under the barrier Lavinia picked herself up and came to meet us.

'Are you hurt?' I didn't like the way she was clutching her left arm.

'Buggered up *something*,' she said angrily.

'Your shoulder.' There was a distinct droop. 'We'd better take you to first-aid. Can you walk?'

'Darling,' her language, at any rate, was reverting to normal. 'I'm not crawling, am I? I must see to Tommyrot.'

'A steward's looking after him.'

'I've got to make sure . . .'

'I will,' said Liz.

'All right. See Geoffrey gives him a good rub down. He hates the wet.'

The shower had passed. The next competitor had gone into the ring and was waiting for the bell.

Lavinia shook her head. 'Ground's soggy,' she said, not without satisfaction. 'Fiddler won't be as fast as Tommyrot.'

'Come, mother. I want to examine your shoulder.'

'Not now,' she brushed me off. 'Must watch. I think I've won – unless Jo Budd knocks a second off my

27

time.'

'Your shoulder . . .'

'Keep your hair on, Jack. You can take a look at my shoulder here.'

'It'll hurt.'

'I'll survive.' She was already unbuttoning her coat.

Lavinia's shoulder looked oddly flat at the top, the typical appearance of dislocation. I told her what she'd done to herself and that she was in no condition – provided she *had* won the Aga Cooker Stakes – to remount Tommyrot and collect her cup.

'Then put the bloody joint back where it's supposed to be,' she snapped. 'Now.'

'Don't be silly mother.'

'That's what your father did. I put out the same shoulder when Tosca threw me . . . Get on with it.'

'How did father do it?'

'Now you're talking.' She gave me a pained, lopsided grin. 'He stuck his knee in my back . . . or somewhere.'

'That must have hurt.'

'What if it did? Don't dither.'

Clearly there was no budging her. I looked around for something, any tool that would make the operation as unbrutal as possible. An open picnic basket looked promising. I approached the elderly owners.

'May I borrow your milk bottle?'

'What for?' The old man looked me up and down.

The truth seemed best. 'You saw Mrs Mason come off her horse?'

''T were great. Come off with a wallop, she did. Like I said to the wife; shouldn't wonder if 'err's broken 'err back.'

'Not her back,' I told him. 'But she's hurt and I want to give her first-aid.'

'Knock 'err out with the bottle?'

'Not quite. You're welcome to watch.'

'I'll help.'

'No thanks. The bottle will do.'

The old woman emptied the remains of the milk into a cup and gave me the bottle. 'She must be 'urrt bad . . . we always enjoy the jumping, me 'n' Charlie. Never know what's going to happen, do you?'

I thanked the old people and returned to Lavinia. She was looking pale. 'Darling, do hurry up.'

'Keep watching the horses, will you.' I took off my sweater and wrapped it around the bottle. 'Relax.' I put the package under her arm, as high as it would go. Then, using it as a fulcrum, I gave her arm a hard down-pull. There was a crack, Lavinia yelled, but the shape of the shoulder reverted to round and normal.

Lavinia took a deep breath. 'Well done, Jack.'

'Well done yourself. Sore?'

'To hell with that. Tommyrot, the son-of-a-bitch, has won. See you later. I'm going into the ring.'

'Don't fall off again, for God's sake.'

Three

Lavinia's shoulder must have been painful, yet she was going to cook our supper. Liz, taking over the kitchen, settled the argument. We fixed Lavinia's left arm in a sling but let her lay the table with her right.

I looked around for the day's paper, didn't find it, and scanned the bureau bookcase instead. What with my father's old medical books gone, the shelves were denuded. Mother never had been much of a reader. There were sets of Jane Austen and Dickens, presumably kept for their attractive leather bindings, a few racing annuals, standard volumes on stable management, a few Noel Coward and Rattigan plays and – of course – a paperback edition of *Lady Chatterley's Lover*.

I went out into the yard, took my father's diary from the car, and sat down at the bureau beside the one and only reading lamp in the cottage – an antique angle-poise which blinked like a traffic beacon and tended to fuse all the lights in the house.

Father seemed to have used his diaries for all purposes, from recording black spot on his Princess Elizabeth roses to a disastrous day on the golf course, from the problematic birth of handyman Earl Plum-Ascot to a wartime duel above the Downs between an RAF Spitfire and a Messerschmidt.

A strange year, 1941. The inexorable throb of engines as the German bombers droned across the

Channel towards London. The excitement of watching our little fighter planes burst through the clouds and dive upon the enemy. How well my father conveyed the savage satisfaction of seeing a flaming bomber spin out of control. Waiting for it to strike the ground; feeling as much as hearing the impact of the explosion.

Sometimes, father admitted, *it is hard to remember that some poor young dupe has just been blown to smithereens. Couldn't really blame the land-army girls in the cabbage patch for cheering their heads off, stupid young bitches. A death is a death, or isn't it? But they wouldn't understand that. Not enough imagination.*

I turned the page. *There was one bystander who didn't behave like a demented jumping bean – young Lavinia. She was the first baby I delivered after I started practice in Dayton. Must be fourteen years ago. I can't imagine how the Chiltern-Browns, a county family long past its glories, could have produced such a clever and vital child. The mother never gave a damn for anything but horses. Fatal hunting accident. Broke her neck about four years ago. Father, Captain C-B, is a horseman too, the kind that supports the bookies. His estate is mortgaged up to the hilt and he'd be bankrupt by now if the land-army girls didn't keep his home-farm going. In this war, growing food is a priority. The war has given the Captain a new lease of life. In uniform again – though nothing more exalted than an air-raid warden – he appears to have cut down on the liquor. I'd say his liver is beyond redemption, but he looks less bleary-eyed and might just survive to the end of the war.*

The daughter has also been bitten by the horse-bug, but Lavinia's passion is informed by intelligence. She understands the essential character of each horse much as she divines the nature of other forms of life. Her other interest is the Dayton Drama Society. For her age she is no mean actress. I find her useful in the practice. She functions as my early-warning system, knowing everyone in the village, therefore knowing whose injury has become infected, who is developing jaundice or whooping cough.

Until I saw the Jerry bomber spin down in flames, I thought I knew Lavinia. Like the land-army girls she'd been watching. Unlike them she'd kept silent. She'd stood on the edge of the cabbage patch, tall and leggy – perfectly still. I went up to her – something in her posture bothered me – and spoke her name. As she turned to me I saw tears spilling from her eyes. I asked what the matter was. A stupid question. She answered me with a question: Why do people kill one another? What could I say? I took out my handkerchief and wiped her face.

1941. My father had been a bachelor of thirty-eight, Lavinia a schoolgirl of fourteen. Some six years later the two of them had mystified the village by marrying. A few years later I too had asked myself what had induced my young mother to marry the elderly local doctor. Perhaps the diary would give me more than one answer.

After supper I offered to wash up, but Liz and Lavina declined help. I guessed they intended to enjoy a post-mortem on the nature of Tommyrot and his performance at the South of England Show.

I returned to the diary, leafing through the pages, reading at random until the name Arthur Kirby stopped me. Something about Len's father. The entry was dated July 1940.

The war is having a stimulating effect on social life in the village. The Saturday night hop has been revived. At first girls were dancing with girls. Then the army camp on the other side of Millers Common discovered our nightlife. So now we have a surplus of teenage soldiers making up for the local boys who have gone into the Forces. I expect there will be a few unscheduled pregnancies before long.

There is a strange atmosphere at the dances. The village hall windows are draped in sombre black-out curtains and the weak coloured bulbs keep the place in semi-darkness – which doesn't deter Captain Chiltern-Brown from putting in official appearances. He stands at the front entrance, three steps above us, peculiarly para-military in his air-raid warden's uniform, waits until the three-man band stops playing, then barks, 'Put that light out! Don't you know there's a war on?' There is laughter and cat-calls but someone always tugs the curtains tight. And on with the dance, 'A Nightingale Sang In Berkeley Square' and 'Deep Purple Blue', 'Pack Up Your Troubles', 'I'll See You Again' and 'Daisy, Daisy, Give Me Your Promise True'.

No trouble until last Saturday. I took Mary and Ethel Pauling and Arthur Kirby to the dance. Old man Kirby had recently died; three of his men had been called up, and Arthur was running the farm with the remaining couple of old age pensioners. I thought he needed a break. The Pauling sisters are nice girls, good-looking too. Ethel, the red-haired one, is a good dancer and quite a comic. Mary, who has just started teaching at the local school, is more serious but equally popular with the boys.

We were dancing 'The Dashing White Sergeant', Ethel and I, Mary with Arthur, when the commotion started. Bill Morris had come in and was staggering about the floor, blatantly drunk. His uniform jacket was unbuttoned, one sleeve ripped out. He stumbled up to Mary and tried to wrest her out of Arthur's arms. Arthur shielded Mary, but Bill kept pestering her. Eventually a couple of Bill's army chums dragged him away.

When the four of us left the hall around midnight he was waiting for us. Mary, he bawled, was his girl and he was taking her home. Mary said quietly that she was nobody's girl and that she was going home with her sister and friends. Bill yelled obscenities and lunged at Arthur. It was an ugly brawl which did not finish until Bill passed out – not because Arthur had been rough. It was the booze that got the better of him. On Sunday, Arthur told me, he kept away from the boundary between his farm and the Morris's. He did not wish to revive the unpleasantness. On Monday his cowman told him that Bill had gone back to barracks. That evening Arthur's sheepdog, Hector, was missing. After a long search he found Hector whimpering in the ditch between the two farms. The vet said the dog had been poisoned. He died that night.

I closed the diary. Forty years have passed since the fathers of Len Kirby and Ken Morris fought outside the village hall. Yet the seed of bitterness was still alive. *Chip off the old block*, Len had muttered as he'd limped out of the first-aid tent. I'd failed in convincing him that Bill Morris's son had not attacked him from behind.

Lavinia doesn't believe in taking pills. Her normal limit is a couple of aspirins a year, washed down with rum-laced tea. The fact that she went to bed when told, and accepted her annual pain-killer ration, told me just how sore her shoulder was. Yet when I looked into her bedroom some ten minutes later Lavinia was asleep, her snores sounding like softly clicking castanets.

Liz and I, relaxed after the day in the open, lingered over coffee. I told her what I'd read in my father's diary.

As usual she went straight to the heart of the matter. 'What kind of man, a farmer at that, would poison his neighbour's sheepdog? He must have been a real bastard.'

'Morris was an alcoholic. Knowing that his wife was the better half didn't help.'

'Why did Mary choose him of all people?'

'Maybe she believed that marriage and a family would make him settle down. Pity it didn't.' A year ago Bill Morris had died of alcoholism and an overdose of Mary's sleeping pills. I remembered the relief I felt when the coroner had brought in a verdict of *suicide while the balance of his mind was disturbed*.

'Mary's had enough trouble,' said Liz. 'I hope Len Kirby will give her son a chance.'

'Ken will have to do a lot better than his father. Morris was a rotten farmer. Never mended his fences. His animals were always causing damage on the Kirbys' farm.'

'Ken *is* doing better than his father . . . you said it yourself.'

'Len wasn't denying that. But it isn't so easy to get rid of long-established prejudices.'

'I know.' Liz put her head on my shoulder. Her hair smelled of crushed grass. 'All the same I love the village . . . and your pig-headed Sussex farmers. They don't forget their quarrels in a hurry, but they're also kind and loyal. To listen to them you'd think that your father is still alive, taking care of their health. And whatever happens in the rest of the country, *they* aren't going to change their lifestyle.'

'Well . . . they no longer use horsedrawn ploughs. They've got quite sophisticated milking machines and combine harvesters.'

Liz laughed. 'Did I say they were backwoods men? You know what I mean, Jack.'

'Yes. You like living in a traditional community.'

'Listen!'

I too heard running feet. A moment later someone was banging on the door. I moved fast. Didn't want them to waken Lavinia.

Jamaica came tumbling in. 'Dr Jack . . .' She was out of breath and looking even more improbable than usual in a frilled nightdress and grubby tennis shoes. 'Uncle Jack . . .' she tugged my hand, 'come quick . . .'

'Jamie, why aren't you in bed?'

'You're always asking silly questions. Why aren't I at school . . . why aren't I in bed? Don't you want to see me?'

'I do, Jamie. But not late at night when you should be asleep.'

She stood up straight, legs together, arms pressed to her side, the picture of a child about to recite for granny. 'Mummy's sent me. I'm to say, please come to

35

the house 'cause Pippa's baby's gone wrong . . . We can't switch him off.'

On the way to the house I persuaded Jamaica that a consultation between doctor and patient was private, even when the patient happened to be a nine-month-old baby boy. Eventually, head bowed in protest, she made for the front door while I went along to my father's former surgery, now the staff flat. Pippa's baby really was making a lot of noise, screaming in short sharp gusts.

Jamaica's mother, Tina Blair, was waiting for me in the lobby. 'Dr Jack . . . am I glad to see you! We've had hours of this. Pip was perfectly all right when Pippa put him to bed. Then he started . . . about eight. He hasn't got a temperature. I just don't understand it; Jamaica used to have tantrums, but Pip's such a placid little character.'

Pip had been lucky. If Pippa's grandparents had had their way he wouldn't have seen the light of day. The Tippets had been prepared to look after their orphaned granddaughter, but not her illegitimate baby. At first they'd refused to believe that their Pippa, aged fifteen, could be pregnant. Then, when I'd made them accept the fact, they'd tried to badger the girl into seeking an abortion. Pippa had been adamant; she'd have her baby and keep it. She'd embarrassed and angered her grandparents by calling in Vivienne Allen, our local social service. Vivienne was, of course, well known for her partiality to one-parent families.

The social service had stormed into action, procuring dingy digs for the pregnant girl – a temporary home in Millers Common where Pippa felt isolated and unhappy. Then Lavinia had conceived one of her more improbable plots. Rufus and Tina Blair, trying to run the big house my mother had managed when maids were easy to come by, certainly needed domestic help if Jamaica wasn't to run completely wild, Lavinia somehow convinced the Blairs that they'd be helping themselves by providing a home for

Pippa and the baby. A logical plan, but I hadn't believed that such logic would work. It had. Young Pip was doing nicely within the kindly Blair family, except that something was now bugging him. As Jamaica had put it so succinctly, he wouldn't be switched off.

We found Pippa, babe in arms, pacing the floor of her bed-sitter. She was in tears, Pip was wailing.

Tina Blair put her arm round the girl. 'There, there. Dr Jack's here. He'll be all right.'

I took Pip and put him on the bed. Out of his shawl he beat the air with legs and arms and stopped crying. Not for long. He looked at me with that curious deliberation of intelligent infants, gulped in air and let out a piercing scream. As I stood contemplating him, wondering where to begin the examination, he gripped his left ear as if trying to pull it off.

'Has he done this before?' I asked Pippa.

'Well . . . he's been playing with his ears.'

'Both of them?'

'I don't know . . . He's always waving his arms about.'

I took the auroscope from my bag. 'I want you to hold him . . . keep his hands away from his head. All right?'

'Yes, Dr Jack.'

'You hold his hands,' said Tina, 'I'll stop him wriggling.'

Pip didn't like the confinement. His screams filled the room, and as I inserted the auroscope they rose to an even higher pitch. I expected to see signs of otitis media or mastoid. Certainly, the external ear looked red and inflamed, but I was unable to see the drum. Instead I got a bright green reflection which made no sense whatever. Pip kept yelling and I kept studying the green area. I'd looked into hundreds of ears but I'd never seen the likes of it. It passed through my mind that I should send the baby to hospital, yet I kept looking through the auroscope, mesmerised by the green phenomenon.

Suddenly I noticed a minute dot in the centre. Something in my brain clicked. 'What's Pip been playing with today?' I asked.

'Well, he always has his bunny,' said Pippa.

'Nothing smaller?'

'No . . . except his rattle.'

'Anything green?'

'Oh . . . he was playing with my beads while I was feeding him. Pulling hard, he was.'

'Did he break the string?'

'He did, the little devil. The strength of him!'

'Oh . . ,' Tina looked up. She'd understood.

'I need an awl,' I told her, 'or something like it. Have you got such a thing?'

'I think there's an awl in Rufus's tool box. I'll get it.'

Pippa knelt beside her infant, trying to comfort him. She was too stunned to take in what was happening. Tina returned with a box of small tools, including needle files and an awl. I asked the women to hold Pip again and showed them how to keep his head still. It was not easy. As I inserted the awl into the infant's ear the whole of his body squirmed and twisted.

'It won't take long,' I tried to reassure Pippa. With luck, it wouldn't. If I failed Pip would have to go into hospital.

I probed until I felt the awl meet a smooth, hard surface. Presently the point stuck fast. I turned very slowly. Time seemed at a standstill. Another turn of the awl, and another. Hand steady. And again; not too fast. Suddenly I felt the point bite. Pull – though not too hard. The object inside the ear appeared to be moving. Or was it an illusion? Another twist. I stopped for a moment, postponing defeat – if it was to be defeat. Then I braced myself. A fast, decisive tug. The awl came out, a green plastic bead stuck to its point.

I held it up for the women to see. I guess I felt like a soccer player who'd scored the winning goal.

'Oh doctor!' Pippa picked up her baby; the screams subsided. 'I don't know how he did it . . . silly boy.'

'You've been the silly one,' I told her. 'You must never let a baby play with any object he can swallow or put inside himself. Luckily we managed without an operation.'

'Thanks ever so much . . . and Mrs Blair too.'

'Anything we should do for Pip?' asked Tina.

'Just put him in his cot. I'll put antibiotic drops in his ear. He's almost asleep.'

'So am I.' Tina smiled and went out.

When I put in the drops Pip was too drowsy to react. I told Pippa to bring him to the surgery next day for a check-up.

As I let myself out I collided with the social service. Vivienne was looking even more pseudo-ethnic than usual in a floating Indian cotton dress which hung uneasily from angular shoulders and bobbed around her big feet.

'What are *you* doing here?' I asked more sharply than necessary.

'Calling on my case,' she snapped. 'Jamaica was so worried that she couldn't sleep.'

'She phoned you?'

'She did. She said you were here, but . . .'

'Then there was no reason for you to make a midnight call. Go home Miss Allen.'

'Pippa and Pip are my one-parent family. It's my duty to –'

'You're not going to fill in forms at this time of night, are you? Be sensible.'

'I must make a report for the survey.'

'Not now, for heaven's sake.'

'There are no surgery hours for social problems, doctor,' bitched Vivienne. 'I have to deal with emergencies twenty-four hours a day.'

'I know; without you the district would grind to a halt and the disadvantaged would overrun the pastures. But a green bead jammed in a baby's ear is a medical problem, not a sociological one. To put your mind at rest, the offending bead has been extracted, the patient's comfortable.'

39

'Disadvantaged people are *my* responsibility. And your lack of cooperation, Dr Mason, is making it difficult for me to work on my survey.'

The survey was an elaborate scheme evolved by Vivienne herself. It produced mountains of charts, reports and forms and I suspected that it was meant to prove that Vivienne was too useful to be made redundant. Poor thing, she was scared of the unemployment figures which were climbing towards the three million mark; so she was fighting the creeping shadows as best she could – with an empire-building exercise. If her paper mountain grew large enough she'd feel justified in asking the administration to employ an extra secretary for her. Well, the eighties were not an easy time for sociology graduates in their thirties.

Vivienne turned her back on me, ethnic dress billowing. 'I'm going to visit Pippa first thing in the morning.'

'You'd be wasting your time.' I opened the car door for her. Pippa had told me that she was fed up with the social service's frequent visits; all those questions and cups of tea. 'I think you should let Pippa and Pip take care of themselves. If you promise to leave them alone I'll provide you with new material for the survey.'

'Who?' She was suspicious. 'The caravan people on Josephs' farm?'

'Certainly not.'

'I can't think of anyone else, doctor.'

'You can't be expected to know what's stewing in every pot between Dayton and Millers Common.'

'I *would* know if you didn't refuse me access to your patients' records.'

'Miss Allen, the records are confidential . . . as you well know.'

'How can I work with my hands tied behind my back . . . no cooperation from the doctors.'

'I've just offered you cooperation. Stop visiting Pippa and I'll provide you with a whole selection of new disadvantaged people.'

40

'One-parent families?'

'Two. I might even have a battered wife for you. Is it a deal?'

Four

On a sunny morning the Old Mill is all I like best about Sussex. From the top of the house I can see fields and pastures stretch south to the foot of the Downs. The evaporating dew, drifting over the hills, veils contours and colours in gossamer mists. On the east side of my land the sunlight leaps on the stream which once drove the mill wheel, flames the burgundy leaves of the copper-beech beside the pond and shimmers on the white trunks of the silver-birches. That's how the world must have looked on the first day of creation – new, clean, fragrant.

I had moved into one room of the Old Mill some three weeks before the South of England Show, and still each morning seemed like a new beginning.

Sunday. The Dayton church bells were mingling their carillon with the songs of thrushes and skylarks, and the twittering of the housemartins which had built their nest under my stone roof.

Since I'd bought the place, wreck that it was, a blackbird had watched me slash the brambles, cut down a jungle of sycamore seedlings, dig the heavy clay soil and transform the wilderness into the rudiments of a garden. The senior blackbird – Liz's name for him – was remarkable for voicing my innermost feelings. *Hurry hurry, quick quick*, he'd call when I was slacking beside the pond. But whenever I thrust the spade into the ground – muscles aching, sweat running into my eyes – he'd swear *bloody hell, bloody hell*.

Get on, get on, he hustled as I went down to the kitchen.

'Don't rush me,' I answered out of the window. 'Let me have my breakfast.'

I was filling the kettle when I saw the long, lean figure of Earl emerge from the trees. He was tanned a dark coffee colour, wearing nothing but plastic sandals and a red loincloth. As he strolled over the bridge across the brook he drank from a bottle of milk.

Liz had now come to terms with the fact that Lavinia had wished Earl on us, that the village idiot had taken up residence in the log cabin which he and the scouts had built in our copse. Except that Earl was something other than a village idiot. He'd lost his long battle to get himself admitted to a psychiatric unit on a permanent basis. But he'd somehow achieved the next best thing – a home and a handyman's job with his doctor.

He materialised in the kitchen, looking like a fakir, and put his empty milk bottle on my draining-board. 'What are you going to do with this wood, doc?' He picked up a length of pine.

'Box in the sink.'

'Planks need chamfering.'

'I know.'

'It'll take you all day.' Earl gazed at the plaster-boarded ceiling. 'You'll never finish the house before your wedding, doc.'

'You know when I'm getting married?' He was probably better informed than Liz and I.

'Won't be before the Dayton Horse Show.'

'My mother's in it.'

'Nor while she's rehearsing the new play.'

'It's not my mother who's getting married.'

'Well . . . you never know.'

'Earl, if you have picked up some silly gossip . . .'

'No, doc; I was only thinking . . . You could be

43

getting married early in October,' he plodded on, 'before the Players start on the Christmas show. Don't you worry, doc, Mrs Mason will fit in your wedding somewhere . . . Give you time for decorating.'

'I thought you were going to do it for us, Earl.'

'Depends on my health. Never can tell when I'm going to have trouble with my work-application. Decorating's a special job. You need to be able to concentrate properly.'

'You were perfectly able to concentrate on building your own place.'

'I was, wasn't I?' His face broke into the loose-mouthed grin that had earned him the reputation of being simple-minded. 'That's why I reckon my work-application won't last much longer.'

One just couldn't win over Earl Plum-Ascot. Too many generations of shrewd, perfidious politicians had gone into the making of him. I took a mug from the one and only kitchen cupboard I'd managed to put up. 'I suppose you want a cup of tea.'

'I wouldn't say no, doc. It'll take the taste of milk out of my mouth.'

'Why go on drinking milk if you dislike it so much?'

'My sainted mother believed in milk.'

'Sure, when you were an infant – thirty-five years ago.' I made the tea, poured for us both, then broke a couple of eggs into the sizzling frying pan.

'There was a full moon last night, doc. The moon always makes him go funny. He didn't half go for Maisie.'

He was Earl's father, whom he accused of being a witch; *her* was the young barmaid he'd married about a year ago. Maisie had seen me at the surgery, exhibiting bruises, but when I'd offered to speak to her husband she'd asked me not to.

'What do *you* know?' I asked Earl. 'You don't live with them.'

'I went over there . . . wanted my wire-cutters from the shed . . . He threw his boots at her. Took off his belt and all.'

Maisie did seem an ideal case for the social service. Young wife, ill-tempered old husband. If anyone could subdue Richard Plum-Ascot it was Vivienne.

'And father,' Earl was enjoying himself, 'he had big scratches all down the side of his face. Blood everywhere.'

Was Maisie sinning, not just being sinned against? Better think twice about letting Vivienne loose on the Plum-Ascots.

There was a knock on the back door. Earl went off and presently returned with Ken Morris.

'Hope you don't mind,' apologised Ken.

'You're welcome,' I waved him to a chair.

Earl drained his cup. 'I'll be going, doc. Come evening I'll bring you the hare.'

'What hare?'

'Been watching him for weeks.'

'I've told you to keep off Sir Lionel's land. I won't have any poached . . .'

'Me, poach!' Earl looked hurt. 'It's Sir Lionel's dogs that put the fear of God into the poor bunny. He doesn't know where to turn . . .'

'So he escapes to our copse? Earl . . . no poaching.'

'Not me, doc. Never.' Earl made a fast getaway, leaving me in no doubt that Liz would be cooking jugged hare before long.

I offered Ken a cup of tea.

He refused. 'Sorry to bother you so early on a Sunday morning, Dr Jack.'

'Is it Len Kirby?'

He nodded. 'I hear he's going into hospital for an operation.'

'That's right.'

'On account of what happened at the Show?'

'Yes. I tried to make clear to him that you hadn't touched him . . . that one can rupture a tendon just crossing the High Street.'

'Len believed you?'

'Not sure.'

'I never bothered him. Don't know what he has

45

against me.'

'It could be a very old story.'

I went to the living room, where I'd stacked the school gear and books Lavinia had off-loaded, and fetched my father's diary.

I found the passage about the brawl between Arthur Kirby and Bill Morris. 'Better look at this.'

Ken read, then turned back the page and re-read my father's account. 'That happened before I was born.'

'It's how the trouble started, I imagine.'

'My father wasn't an easy man,' admitted Ken, 'but I haven't upset the Kirbys. I'm doing all I can . . . mending the fences . . . filling the holes in our part of the road . . .'

'That's what I told Len.'

'How is he?'

'Well, he's making no secret of it; Mr Stormont's going to operate on the ruptured tendon . . . stitch it together.'

'How long will he be off work?'

'Six weeks or so.'

'He won't be fit in time for the harvest.' Ken looked concerned. 'Maybe I should go and see him.'

'What's the point? He's in a bad mood. Wait until he gets back from hospital . . . a week or ten days. In any case, don't expect a friendly reception. Knowing Len, this damned feud won't stop overnight.'

'It's got to stop.' There was in Ken's young face something of his mother's firmness and courage. 'If it's a fight he wants, he won't get it.'

'That's something else I told Len.'

'Without making much impression on him?'

'Too soon to say. He's in pain. Anyway, April doesn't believe that you attacked her husband.'

'She wouldn't. She used to be nice to me when I was a kid. Okay,' Ken got up. 'I'll keep away from the Kirbys until her old man's out of hospital.'

'He owes you an apology.'

'I'm not expecting it. Thanks, Dr Jack. You've told me what I needed to know.'

46

'What's that?'

'Just . . . how to sort things out.'

I wasn't sure how he'd do that, but he seemed confident.

By late afternoon the sky had clouded over and it was cool enough for cutting the grass. When I got back to the house there was a light on in the kitchen. Earl, now in shorts and a butterfly-patterned shirt, and Lavinia were drinking tea at the table. Between them reclined a large dead hare.

'So you've done it,' I blamed Earl.

'Poor creature; it was a happy release,' Earl assured me. 'The way Sir Lionel's beagles were carrying on he wouldn't have lasted another day.'

'Let's take him to Liz,' suggested Lavinia. 'Darling, you haven't forgotten? We're going to Brighton. Liz has booked a table at the French restaurant.'

Earl doubled up. 'I've dislocated my stomach.'

'Stomachs can't get dislocated,' Lavinia sounded dubious. 'Surely . . .'

'My head's falling off my neck,' Earl persevered. 'You can hear it creak, can't you? Mrs Mason, I want the doc to send me to The Close.'

'Out of the question,' I told him. 'We've been through all that. And don't you sling a tankard through the pub windows again. It won't get you into any psychiatric ward.'

Earl shambled to the door, muttering, 'The pond . . . mud, nothing but mud. Never get it cleaned up. Not even trying . . .'

He left, making me wonder – not for the first time – whether he wasn't in fact a fit subject for a psychiatrist. Would any sane man have fought battle after battle to gain admission to a mental hospital?

'He'll grow out of it,' said Lavinia, 'provided you don't give him too much work.'

'He's doing damn all, except kill edible animals.'

'He's rather good at it, isn't he?'

'I don't need a bloody gamekeeper.'

47

'I like pheasants best. They are gorgeous . . . We used to get a lot from your father's patients, before shooting became so commercialised. Now I certainly wouldn't buy them at the butchers . . . not at twelve pounds a brace.'

'I see.'

'What do you see darling?'

'Why our local pheasants have become so accident-prone. They seem to be hurling themselves at cars, including yours.'

'Two birds in one year, darling. It isn't much.'

'You should trade in your car for a Land Rover.'

'Don't be unkind, Jack. I just like good food. I wonder whether Lady Chatterley did. I don't think it's mentioned in the book.' Lavinia collected the teacups and put them on the draining-board. 'Bunny's sick.'

'Mother, this animal is not sick. It's dead.'

'Not the hare, darling. I mean Sir Lionel.'

'The warts, is it? I'm going to call on him.'

'Darling, I've just remembered. I think I know why Earl's been fussing about your pond. He's absolutely mad about swimming.'

'Not in the pond.'

'Of course not; it needs cleaning up. Earl wants to get into mental hospital . . . specifically The Close . . . because it's where they've built this new indoor swimming pool.'

'God help us!'

'I wouldn't rely on Him. The scouts will give you a hand, if you go about it the right way. If the pond's clean enough for Earl to swim in he'll probably drop the idea of going into that hospital . . . Of course, you've got to get your priorities right.'

'Mother, you've lost me.'

'But darling! isn't it perfectly obvious? There's Earl, who needs somewhere to swim . . . preferably on his own doorstep; and there's the Bunting-Standings. You'll have to look after Bunny first. He passed out in church this morning. It wasn't a bit like Bunny . . . flopping like a guardsman on parade.'

48

Five

The animal, cropping the coarse grass between the flagstones of the terrace, looked like a forest deer rather than a goat. It had a shining brown coat, big sad eyes and viciously angled horns. I managed to pass the goat without turning my back on her. Though she followed me at a dignified pace I didn't trust her. Yet she was obviously doing some good to the terrace at Standing Hall; it looked less overgrown and neglected than usual.

The french windows opened and an onslaught of dogs came belting out.

'Heel! Heel!' Dot was rushing after the beagles. 'Keep away from Cordelia! Bloody hounds! Bunny's got no control over them.' The goat stood still, head down, ready to deal with any dog unwise enough to tackle her.

The beagles, getting the message, formed into a pack and went racing off after an imaginary hare.

Dot put a soothing hand on the goat. 'Cordelia's a perfect dear,' she told me. 'We got her at the South of England Show. Wonderful buy. Gives Bunny all the milk he can drink, and a lot left over. My goat's cheese hasn't been a wild success.' She walked back to the house, a little figure in dungarees, short grey hair blowing in the breeze. 'Next time I make cheese I'll put garlic in it. That should get rid of the goaty flavour.'

'Does Bunny like the taste of the milk?' I asked her.

'He hates it.'

'Then why . . .?'

Dot led me into the drawing room. The furniture was shrouded in dust-sheets, the stucco ceiling draped in cobwebs. As Dot sank down on a sofa, particles of dust went dancing into the sun. 'Bunny hates goat's milk, but it's good for him.'

'Is that your idea?'

'Well . . . I've got this old book on natural remedies. In the sixteenth century Sussex people used to cure tummy pains with goat's milk. So I thought it couldn't do Bunny any harm. Of course he made a fuss when I wanted to buy a goat, but he's become quite attached to Cordelia.'

'And he's actually drinking her milk.'

'Morning, noon and night. No protest . . . that's what worries me.'

'There are more modern medicines,' I reminded Dot. 'Tell me about Sir Lionel's stomach pains.'

'Very well,' Dot lifted her head and listened, 'I don't think he'll come in here. Haven't used this room for years . . . The trouble with him is, he won't ask for *real* medical advice. He'll happily waste your time about his warts – he's as vain as a virgin – but he will not speak of anything more serious. And the tummy pains are nasty. I know they are. When they come on he goes green. Then he totters out of the room – silly fool – and when I ask him about these turns he bites my head off. Dr Jack, I really am worried about the old idiot.'

'How long has he had these pains?'

'I'm not sure, but I noticed the blood about a year ago.'

'Blood?'

'He passes blood . . . and some slimey stuff. I've seen it, because he often forgets to pull the lavatory chain.'

'Have you spoken to him about it?'

'Once or twice. He says he's got piles . . . nothing

50

important. He's read up *piles* in a medical dictionary. Dr Jack, I think he's got it wrong. He's lost a lot of weight this summer.'

'How much?'

'I don't know, but his clothes are hanging on him . . . The paunch is gone. I wouldn't mind that if he hadn't lost so much energy. If he's been keen on one thing it's his work as a magistrate and on God knows how many committees. He loved those committee meetings. Now he keeps asking me to phone the secretaries and give his excuses. *Pressure of work*, my eye! He sits in front of the television, newspaper in hand . . . and snores. Then he doesn't sleep at night. In and out of bed.'

'Does he go to the loo?'

'I suppose he does . . . though sometimes he stays up an hour or more.'

'I'd like to examine him. Will he let me?'

'I think so . . . provided you tell him you've come to see his warts. It's how your father would have tackled him.'

'My father would have told Sir Lionel that he's looking *run down*.'

'That's a useful one. The state he's in, Bunny will accept it. He won't refuse to be examined if you mention his warts . . . and a *tonic*. Bunny will swallow any bloody thing in liquid form.'

On Lady Dorothy's instructions I went out by the french windows, sidled past Cordelia's nasty horns, stood up to the concerted assault of the beagles and made a noisy entrance through the back hall into the morning room. It was the one place in the big manor house which looked lived-in and almost clean.

The pitted oak refectory table served meetings of the Red Cross and the Dog Rescue Society; I'd seen it used as a desk, a dining table and a work-bench. This centrepiece was surrounded by chairs designed for various degrees of discomfort. On the far wall was a Dutch dresser loaded with crockery and a Victorian sofa covered in dog hairs. The whole lot was

51

dominated by a couple of huge pictures painted by the Bunting-Standing's daughter, Muriel. Her giant horse's head, executed with tubes of paint squeezed straight onto the canvas, had a kind of demented intensity. And Muriel's still life was anything but still; her flowers had the quality of voracious monsters reaching out murderously for human victims. The pictures, painted with such ferocious energy and displayed with parental pride, appeared to have no effect on Bunny.

He sat facing the savage flowers, an unopened *Farmer's Weekly* before him. Aroused by his barking dogs he told them to shut up and greeted me with a vague nod. One of the beagles jumped on a chair, mounted the table, and began to devour a remnant of cheese.

'Sit down, m'boy.' Bunny swept the dog to the floor. 'Bloody dogs. Dot's no good at controlling them. Not fit to live indoors . . . Ah yes; Dr Mason's boy, aren't you? What can I do for you? Trouble at your Health Centre?'

'We have no problems at the Health Centre,' I assured him. 'Thought I'd take a look at your warts.'

'Acid from a car battery you said, didn't you? Well, I funked it.'

'Good. It wasn't a serious suggestion.'

'Didn't Bob, down at the garage, use acid?'

'He did, but certainly without my approval.'

'Got any better ideas, Dr Jack?'

'Yes. Let's do things properly. You look run down, Sir Lionel.'

He chuckled. 'Sort of thing your father would have said. Clever fellow; couldn't pull the wool over *his* eyes. Knew the village inside out. Even sorted out my troubles with Claudine . . . kept it from Dot. Hell to pay if Dot had found out about Claudine. You know what women are . . . Well, I suppose you want to examine me.'

'That's right.'

'Go ahead, m'boy. Your father used to start off by

telling chaps to drop their trousers.'

'So do I,' I lied.

Bunny got up shakily, went to the door and locked it. 'Don't want Dot busting in, do we? Man doesn't like to be caught with his pants down.'

The lumpy horsehair sofa was not an ideal place for examining a patient. And the dogs, who took it for granted that their master was lying on his stomach for their benefit, made it no easier. They kept leaping up beside him, pawing his back, expecting him to play. By the time I'd finished with Sir Lionel I had developed a technique of using my hands on the patient and my elbows on the dogs.

Bunny tottered to his feet and began to dress. 'Run down,' he stated. 'Known it all along. M'daughter's coming over this evening. Get her to pick up the tonic at your Health Centre . . . What's this?'

I had taken a hypodermic syringe from my bag. 'I want a bit of your blood.'

'Whatever for?'

'For tests.'

'You mean, I might be anaemic?'

'Possibly.'

'So that's why I get so damned tired. Don't like people sticking needles into me.'

'I won't hurt you.'

'Principle of the thing.' It was a mild enough protest. Bunny watched the syringe fill with his blood, an expression of detached curiosity in his eyes. 'What are you going to do with this stuff?'

'I'll take it to the hospital laboratory for analysis.'

'What then?'

'I'll know how to treat you.'

'Like your old man, aren't you?' Bunny smiled. 'Hope you're as discreet as he was.'

'What do you mean, Sir Lionel?'

'Bunny to you, lad. I mean that your father never let the cat out of the bag.'

'It's quite normal for doctors not to gossip about patients.'

53

'Understood. But I was thinking of Claudine . . . not medical ethics. Your father knew all about Claudine . . .'

Why was the old man suddenly talking of his past private life? The only reason I could think of was that sick people did occasionally act out of character. Knowing Bunny as a pillar of church and bench, Dot as the queen of Dayton's most worthy charities, it had never occurred to me that another woman might have entered their marriage.

'Man's got to have a dream, y'know,' Bunny put a hand on my shoulder and walked me to the door, 'or call it a challenge. Don't mind telling you . . . my wife thinks I've finished with Claudine. But I haven't given up yet, not by a long chalk. I'm going to debud Claudine if it's the last thing I do.'

Debudding. I hadn't heard the expression since my adolescence, when Dayton's young farmers had used it as a euphemism for bedding a virgin. It didn't surprise me coming from Bunny; what did astonish me was his confession of the long-lasting attachment to Claudine, whoever she was.

'You'll be calling again?' asked Bunny.

'Of course. I may ask you to have tests done in hospital.'

'That's out. Never been in hospital in m'life.'

'You'd go as an outpatient.'

'Ah . . . that's different. Don't mind dropping in at Millers Common. Been in there often enough when I was chairman of the Hospital Friends . . . Well, thanks for looking at my bum. Uninteresting part of the human anatomy, don't you know. No character about it . . . Oh, by the way,' he peered down the hall through the open back door. 'I expect Dot will be lying in wait for you . . . splendid little woman, but nosy. Don't mention Claudine to her, will you. No sense in stirring up old scandals, is there?'

Dot, the goat on a dog lead, was waiting beside my car. 'What do you think of him?' she asked.

'He isn't well. I want him to see a specialist.'

'Nothing to do with his warts. It's his inside, isn't it?'

'Yes. But until I get the results of various tests I can't make a proper diagnosis.'

Dot nodded. 'I understand . . . Did Bunny mention Claudine?'

'Who?'

'Of course, you wouldn't tell me. Medical ethics and all that. I wish the idiot would talk to me about Claudine. But I suppose he doesn't realise that I know. He's absolutely obsessed with the bloody Claudine. Debudding, indeed! Nothing but stupid male pride, raking up the old scandal.'

There are a lot of reasons why I go to our Health Centre before my partners and the staff arrive. In the early morning my mind is clear and uncluttered; it is a good time for planning my letters to specialists, later to be dictated to Angela, and for preparing my visits to individual patients, to the hospital, old people's home and schools.

In our practice the bulk of work is done outside surgery hours. In London there are lock-up practices where the doctors work office hours. When a patient falls ill in 'unsocial hours' an answering machine advises him to go to the casualty department of the nearest hospital. It certainly wouldn't do in the country, where the doctors become an essential part of the close-knit community.

On the morning after I'd asked the lab to do blood and liver function tests for Bunny I found it hard to concentrate. I wandered around the consulting room, losing myself in the view of the Downs, the familiar rise and fall of their curves smudged in a heat-haze. I noted that someone, a generous patient or nurse, had weeded the flowerbed in front of the Health Centre and cut the nettles at the fence. I watched the sun break through the mist and light up the scarlet snap-dragons and the many shades of pink and yellow mari-golds, geraniums and nasturtiums.

When the church clock struck eight I stopped

resisting the impulse that had made me take my father's diary to the surgery. I sat down at the desk, pushed aside the paperwork I'd meant to deal with, and opened the diary. I'd read the first forty pages, from 1929 to the early thirties, but after that I'd merely dipped in at random because father's handwriting had become progressively harder to decipher.

I recalled telling him, when I was at medical school, that his letters were almost illegible. His reaction had been typical. He'd always hated admitting that he might be in the wrong and he'd been brilliant at concocting instant answers proving that he was right. As he could think faster than most, it took his critics some time to spot the weakness in his argument and by then Dr Oliver Mason would be engrossed in another subject.

His answer to my complaint had been in character. If I was going to be a doctor, he'd said, I'd better get used to the fact that medical people deliberately evolve a style of writing which looks like ancient Hebrew to non-medicals. Patients tend to open the letters their GPs give them to take to specialists; therefore family doctors have to ensure *somehow* that those letters cannot be read by laymen.

Since then I'd read a good many letters and case histories written by my colleagues but I found my father's handwriting, so deceptively neat, as near illegible as ever. Lavinia, I felt sure, had never attempted to tackle the diary. I couldn't blame her.

I began to leaf through with purpose. If I spotted Sir Lionel Bunting-Standing's name I might discover something about the mysterious Claudine. Bunny, I didn't doubt, was a very sick man. There was little I could do for him until I had the test results except deal, if possible, with the circumstances which were preying on his mind – the Claudine affair.

I came upon two entries concerning the Bunting-Standings, the first in April 1943.

Dot Willis has had news of Bunny. He's a prisoner of the Japanese. Some clever dick has told her that the

56

*conditions in the Camps leave much to be desired, but
fortunately Dot has a one-track mind where Bunny is
concerned. Bunny is strong and courageous, he loves
her and he'll come back to her. I hope to God he will.
Dot is a funny little thing, poker-faced, with an
abrasive sense of humour. She certainly didn't make a
song and dance about Bunny being shipped to Malaya.
But if Bunny died I'd worry about Dot more than all
the other servicemen's girls of Dayton put together.*

And in October 1946:

*Dot has won. Today she became Lady Dorothy
Bunting-Standing, though not without further trials
and tribulations. Bunny, who must be six foot three,
came back from the Far East weighing seven stone, his
guts infested with bugs and worms which have so far
defeated medical science. His spell in hospital put up
his weight to nine stone – Dot observed that his bones
no longer cut but merely bruise her – but the tropical
diseases experts haven't yet succeeded in ridding him of
the parasites. Bunny assured me that his good con-
stitution would put him right, repaired the greenhouses
at Standing Hall and got down to hard and serious
gardening. Hence Bunny and Dot were too busy to
marry before the autumn horticultural show. I was
quite annoyed that they didn't carry off more prizes. In
my opinion Dick Plum-Ascot, who's been sitting at
home on his bottom throughout the war, didn't deserve
three first prizes; or if he did the judges should have
bent the rules. However, the village is glad that Bunny
and Dot have succeeded in upholding the proprieties
and that their child will be born inside wedlock.*

All very well, but where did Claudine fit in? I had no
time to continue deciphering. Damning my father's
eccentric style I put the diary in my bag.

It would have been much easier to wade in and
question Bunny and Dot about Claudine. As it happened, both had made a very common mistake in
taking it for granted that their listener knew what
they were talking about. Because Claudine was an
apparently important aspect of their lives they'd

automatically assumed that I knew as much as my father before me. Some instinct, nothing more positive, had prevented me from probing. Now, in the clear light of morning, I realised why. I'd been chary of showing ignorance – any kind of ignorance – because I'd subconsciously realised that Bunny and Dot would soon need to have full confidence in me – as Bunny's doctor and as their friend.

'Can you spare me a minute?' The health visitor looked into my surgery.

'Come in.' Mrs Cherry, having been licked into shape by my father, never wasted my time. I'd been thirteen or fourteen when she'd joined the practice – a round, pink, wholesome woman of uncertain age – and she hadn't changed at all, except that she'd become less chatty and better at her job. 'What can I do for you?'

'I'm a bit worried about Maisie.'

'Richard Plum-Ascot's wife?'

'That's right. I used to call on her years ago. She had tuberculosis. Father infected the whole family. Mother and son died. Maisie kept house for the father until he went. Then she was found to have tubercle. I know it's past history – her tests have been negative for years – but she isn't looking at all well. I saw her in Millers Common supermarket the other day. She's lost weight.'

'What do you suggest?' I asked Mrs Cherry.

'I'd like to call on her.'

'I don't see why not. She'd be pleased to see you, wouldn't she?'

'She would, doctor. But I'm not so sure about her husband. He's a bit of a snob . . . what with his father and uncles having been members of parliament. I bet he thinks health visitors are people who look after the dregs. You know what he's saying about his son? It would seem that Earl's an estate manager.'

'Well, if it makes him happy.'

'I hope Earl doesn't hear about it. He'd go

bonkers.'

'Mrs Cherry, Earl *is* bonkers . . . or almost. He's still hankering after retiring into a mental hospital.'

'Not just *any* mental hospital, doctor. He wants the newest and the best. He's improved since he's been working for you. But I hate to think what he'd do if his father gets his back up again . . . Probably take off his clothes in church.'

'He did that last year. Earl doesn't usually repeat himself. Don't worry about Plum-Ascot. You call on Maisie, if you feel you should.'

'Very well. I won't go in uniform, though somebody's sure to recognise me all the same.' Mrs Cherry looked at her watch. 'Mustn't keep you Dr Jack. There'll be patients waiting for you.'

She was on her way out when I called her back. 'Mrs Cherry . . . Do you know anyone by the name of Claudine?'

'Claudine . . . it rings a bell. Does she live in the village?'

'I don't know. Could be someone at Millers Common.'

'There's Sister Claudine, one of the teachers.'

'At the convent school?'

'That's right.'

'A nun?'

'Yes . . . She's the tennis coach.'

Six

The first patient of the morning limped in, a man of about forty with a fleshy face and a medium-sized beer-belly. I knew what he was about to say, and say it he did.

'It's me back, doctor.'

I looked at the card Angela had put on my desk. 'Sit down Mr Bright.'

He lowered himself into the armchair with a groan. 'I been lifting those boxes of spares, see, and me back gave way. I could feel it, I could. Now . . . well I can't move, not proper like.'

'When did it happen?'

'Yesterday.'

'At work?'

'That's right.'

'What's your job?'

'Storeman.'

'Lifting boxes is part of the job, I suppose. How heavy are they?'

'Well, they got metal in them.'

'Twenty pounds?'

'No, nearer thirty.'

That didn't seem a great weight. 'Where's it hurting?'

Mr Bright waved his hand across his lower back.

'Will you lie on the couch; on your back.'

He lumbered across and made himself comfortable.

'Keep your knees straight,' I told him, 'I'll lift your legs, one at a time.'

I'd raised his left leg about twenty degrees when he groaned. 'Stop it . . . stop it, doctor. You're hurting me back. Oooh . . . it's a disc, i'n't it? Must be a disc, doctor.'

I raised his right leg. As before, he complained.

'Very interesting,' I told him.

He looked at me, blue pop-eyes alert. 'Disc . . . that's what it is, i'n't it?'

'I'd better examine your back, Mr Bright. Sit up, so I can get a good look at your spine. Upright. Keep your knees straight. That's it.'

'You finished?'

'Yes. You can get down.'

'But you didn't do nothing to me back.'

'No need.'

He was tucking his T-shirt inside his jeans. 'Yeah . . . well . . . it's a disc, i'n't it?'

'Who do you work for, Mr Bright?'

'Jones, the contractors.'

'I thought you people were on strike.'

'No, not yet. We're coming out next week.'

'I see.' I did see why Dan Bright wanted a certificate declaring him unfit for work. He'd be getting national insurance payments during the strike, making a lot more money than his mates who hadn't gone sick. 'Mr Bright, you'll be happy to know that you're perfectly fit.'

'But me slipped disc . . .'

'Your discs are exactly where they're supposed to be.'

'Yeah?' He looked sulky. 'How do you know?'

'Simple mechanics. I'm sure you can work it out for yourself.'

Bright studied the examination couch. It didn't take him long to realise where his performance had gone wrong. He'd moaned when, lying flat, I'd lifted his legs. But there hadn't been a peep out of him when I'd made him sit up with his knees straight, which

61

amounted to the same as lifting his legs to ninety degrees.

'Well, I never!' His face broadened into a grin. 'Live and learn; that's what the missus always says. Now she'll make me break me back in the garden. Dead keen, she is, on them little button chrysanths. We'd have got first prize for them in the horti-show last year if it hadn't been a fiddle.'

'You don't say.'

'Yeah . . . well.' He saw that he was in no position to complain of *fiddles*. '"S like this . . . everybody knows as how Mr Plum-Ascot's a nurseryman . . . professional like. Sends his chrysanthemum all over the world, see. Reckon his wife shouldn't be allowed to exhibit at the Dayton show. I mean, it's for amateurs, in't it? Doctor . . . about me national insurance . . .'

'No certificate, Mr Bright. Consider yourself lucky that there's nothing wrong with you.'

'What I mean is, maybe you want some decorating done. I'll have time, when we're on strike.'

'Very kind of you.'

'I mean, it won't cost you like what you'd have to pay a builder.'

'I thought you were offering your services free. Matron at the old people's home is looking for someone to paint the outside woodwork.'

'Lots of windows,' Bright shook his head. 'Big old place, the senior citizens' home. It'll cost them.'

My fifteenth patient was another I hadn't seen before. She was a tall woman with red frizzy hair, dressed in a white trouser suit. A green scarf, which matched the colour of her toenails, trailed from her neck, her wrists jangled with bracelets. According to the card Angela had filled in, she was Ms Sybil Dawn, aged thirty-six, living at Rook's Cottage, Dayton.

'Isn't that the Wellington's house?' I asked Ms Dawn.

'It is, actually. Maggie's my sister. I'll be staying

with the family until I've found somewhere to live. This is such a gorgeous part of Sussex. Much better than London for bringing up a child . . . Actually that's why I've come to see you, doctor. I've decided to have a baby . . .' Her announcement trailed into a silence that threatened to become dramatic.

'Fine. What's the problem?'

'You think thirty-six is too old for having one's first child.' It was a belligerent statement rather than a question.

'It depends on the woman.'

'I am on the old side though?' she persisted.

'Yes. How does your husband feel about starting a family?'

'I'm not married. I don't particularly want to marry. But I think one of my friends would make a suitable father. He's ten years younger than me . . . gorgeous-looking man, awfully clever. He's in public relations; so am I, actually.'

'Babies tend to interfere with the mother's career, Miss Dawn.'

'Oh, I've worked it out. I'd go freelance.'

'The prospective father's happy about your arrangements?'

'I wouldn't expect him to move from London. He could come down weekends . . . Jasper and I have a really great relationship right now. But it probably won't last. I mean . . . one changes, doesn't one.'

'You might change your mind about producing a child. Why not think about it a bit longer?'

'Doctor, I've thought about it for years. There's always been something that made me put it off. My career . . . I wanted to establish myself as an executive. Then . . . well, my men wouldn't really have served the purpose. But now there's Jasper. I believe he'd be just ideal.'

'How does he feel about fathering your child?'

'I haven't mentioned it to him.'

'Shouldn't you discuss it with him before you make any more plans?'

'I don't see why. He won't be paying. I've got enough to buy a cottage. Afterwards – as I said – I'll try freelance work. I've got my connections in London. And there's social security. I mean, one-parent families aren't left to starve, are they?'

'You wouldn't be able to live in executive style on state hand-outs.' I got up. 'You must excuse me. There are patients waiting to see me.'

Miss Dawn remained seated. '*I* am a patient. I want to know whether I'm fit to have a child; I mean, physically fit.'

I asked who had looked after her in London. Whether or not she'd needed medical care, she wouldn't have done without a doctor. Predictably she'd gone to Harley Street, privately, not that she'd suffered ill health; nothing worse than a mild flu and a sprained ankle.

'I take care of my health. I'm on Antannos, of course,' she said. 'Antannos Inc. have been my biggest clients. I expect you know all about Antannos products.'

'I don't.'

She looked at me as if she'd just met someone from outer space. 'You haven't read the advertisements? They're absolutely brilliant!'

'Sorry, I never pay attention to adverts.'

'But you must have seen my Antannos commercials on TV!'

'I don't think so.'

The outrage in Ms Dawn's eyes suddenly reminded me of a remark in my father's diary. *The world is like a honeycomb, and each cell is an isolated miniature world. There is little connection between the inhabitants of the separate cells: farmers, dockers, bus-drivers, builders – each group alien to the other, each group possessing its own values, priorities, super-stitions and gods. The only common link between the cells of this fragmented world is the human body. As a physician one must familiarise oneself with any body from whichever part of the honeycomb it happens to emerge.*

Miss Dawn had emerged from a public relations cell in which Antannos appeared to be something of a god.

'Antannos are herbal products,' she explained. 'Natural foods which protect the body against unnatural environments. I'll get my secretary to send you the literature. You, as a doctor . . .'

'Thank you,' I stopped her. 'Meanwhile, I suggest you see a gynaecologist. Privately.'

'I only want a check-up. Couldn't it be done under the Health Service?'

'Not if you're in a hurry.'

'You mean, I'd be put on a waiting list?'

'You would. The specialists in this area are busy; obviously, urgent cases must have priority.'

'It *is* urgent. I'm thirty-six years old and . . .'

'Miss Dawn, I will not refer you to a gynaecologist under the National Health Service. If I did a patient might be kept waiting who should have immediate attention . . . for instance, a woman with an early cancer.'

'Yet I can *pay* for seeing a specialist right away. I think it's disgraceful.'

'There are specialists who do mainly private work.' Miss Dawn was wasting my time, but I couldn't let her go with twisted ideas on how the system operated. 'As we're not yet living under a dictatorship in this country, doctors have a choice between Health Service or private practice or part-time work in each. And the patients are free to choose the service they want. However, the Health Service – which exists for the whole population – must give priority to the most urgent cases. Is that clear?'

'I see your point,' she got up, at last, 'but it makes no difference in my position. I still want . . .'

'I'll give you a note for a gynaecologist who takes private patients. You can phone his consulting rooms and make an appointment.'

I wrote a three-line message. *Public relations advertising executive, female aged thirty-six, wants to start one-parent family provided reproductive organs are in working order. Suggest you persuade Ms Dawn to communicate her intention to unsuspecting father-to-be.*

I put the note in an envelope and sealed it perfunctorily. Ms Dawn was sure to open it.

My next patient was Joclyn Runciman, a man in his fifties who had moved to Dayton recently and bought a flat in the converted vicarage.

I'd seen him for the first time some three weeks earlier. He'd complained of nagging pains on the inside of his thigh and he'd told me that his doctor in Surrey had treated him for rheumatism. The pills his GP had prescribed were – in his words – playing merry hell with his guts without relieving the pain. I had sent him to the hospital for X-rays.

I put the most puzzling of the pictures on the viewing box. An abnormality was clearly visible but it didn't look like anything I'd seen before. If it was an injury it was an uncommon one.

Mr Runciman walked in, stiff-legged, and hovered until I offered him a seat. He chose a high, hard chair. I asked him how he was.

'Surviving, doctor.' He had a smile that made him look a lot younger than his age. 'Fact is, since you stopped the pills my guts have settled down.'

'How about the pain?'

'Neither better nor worse. I can live with it, but I'd rather not if anything can be done to relieve it.'

I consulted his card. 'Your medical history is good. No serious illness. No accidents?'

'No, nothing that put me in hospital.'

'Any mishap at work?'

'I'm a publisher.' Again the friendly smile lit the grey eyes. 'In my profession one doesn't strain anything, except one's mind . . . on very rare occasions.'

'What about leisure activities? Squash? Tennis? Golf?'

'I'm hopeless at ball games. Riding's my only sport.

66

But I haven't been on a horse since I moved from Surrey.'

An idea kept nagging at the back of my mind, an annoyingly vague thought which flickered and faded and failed to form. 'What decided you to move, Mr Runciman?'

He realised that I hadn't asked out of idle curiosity and talked freely. He'd been born and brought up at Hickstead, not far from Dayton. His family had been farming county people for generations and there were still Runciman cousins dotted around Sussex. In a sense Joclyn had come home.

The house in Surrey had been his wife's choice. Then, after twenty-five years of marriage, Mrs Runciman had fallen for the master of the local hunt and there'd been a divorce.

'No one was to blame,' said Joclyn, 'except me. The slump in publishing kept me working all hours. I spent too much time in London or rushing around the world. Gillian became bored . . . we had no family. A year ago I gave up the management of my firm, but it was too late to save our marriage. Well . . . at least we settled the miserable business amicably. All Gillian wanted was our house. I let her have it.'

'So now you're retired.'

'Not quite. I'm still a director of my company. I do a fair amount of editorial work, but I don't have to go up to London more than one or two days a week. I was hoping to help at my cousin's stables . . . train horses. That's my main reason for troubling you, doctor. I don't want to let Brian down.'

'He's keen on having you work with his horses?'

'Yes. Well, it's one of the few things I seem to do quite reasonably. But I wouldn't be any good to him if my leg packed up. Thought I'd better know the worst.'

'You did say you've had no accidents?'

'Oh, none worth mentioning. Broke the same collar-bone twice. And I had concussion; Merlin's Son bounced me over a fence at Hickstead. Lucky he didn't break a leg. Bit lame, that was all. My mother would have shot me if Merlin's Son had come to grief.'

'It happened a good many years ago.'

'I must have been seventeen . . . eighteen.'

'No other injuries?'

'Just the odd bruise. I don't fall off easily.'

It meant that Joclyn Runciman was making much use of his thigh-muscles in controlling his mounts. All at once I recalled a paragraph in my father's diary. Soon after he'd married Lavinia he'd accompanied her to the local gymkhana and – much to her annoyance – criticised her style of riding.

As I am no horseman, he'd written, I should have been more tactful with my Lavinia. Having put her back up, there was nothing for it but to give her a lecture in anatomy. I produced the book, showed her pictures of the leg-muscles and eventually convinced her that she was squeezing her horses too tightly with her thighs. Typically, she felt concerned about the horses, never mind the eventual damage to her thighs. But her reason for listening to my advice is of no importance. I, on the other hand, have learned a little more about my spirited and quixotic spouse.

I put Joclyn Runciman's X-ray back on the viewing box. 'There's no reason why you shouldn't go on riding,' I told him, 'provided you can put up with some pain or discomfort.'

'You mean, just ignore the rheumatism?'

'You haven't got rheumatism. That's why those anti-inflammant pills didn't help you. Look at your X-ray. Can you recognise the bones?'

'I think so. That's the knee . . . and the hip joint.'

'Right.' I picked up my pen and traced an area on the thigh. 'Do you know what this is?'

He shook his head. 'Didn't know I had a bone there.'

'You shouldn't have. What you see here is a thing called a rider's bone. In fact it isn't a bone at all. It's a calcification of your adductor muscle. You've been holding on to your horses too tightly. It might have saved you from falling off, but – as a result – you've done structural damage to the muscle.'

'You said it won't stop me riding. Will I need an operation?'

'No, there's nothing surgery could do for you. It's a static condition . . . meaning, it won't get worse.'

'That *is* good news.' Runciman looked as pleased as if I'd told him that his condition was curable. 'I'm most grateful to you . . . No more pills?'

'Not the Ibuprofens which upset your guts. Ever tried a mild painkiller?'

'My wife gave me paracetemol once or twice. It helped a lot when I had toothache.'

'Right. Take paracetemol when you feel the pain's more than you can put up with.'

'It wouldn't be very often.'

'Good. You might also find that something like turpentine liniment will ease the leg.'

'Horse liniment . . .' he laughed. 'There is poetic justice for you.'

The receptionist had gone to lunch. Crossing the waiting room to Angela's office, I almost overlooked the small woman who sat beside the rubber plant. The tawny colours of her dress and hair melted into the background. Her large, dark eyes watched me anxiously.

'Dr Mason?'

'Yes. What can I do for you?'

'I am late . . . I think,' she got up. 'I can come back another day.'

'No need Mrs . . .'

'Goldstern . . . Martha Goldstern.' There was a faint foreign accent to her low voice. Not unattractive. 'You were going to lunch perhaps. I don't want to detain you, doctor. It isn't important.'

'It must be, or you wouldn't have come to see me. Come in, Mrs Goldstern.' I held the consulting room door for her. 'I don't have a meal at lunchtime.' Anything to help her overcome her shyness. 'We eat in the evening. Much more enjoyable, especially after cutting up wood or gardening.'

'I love working out of doors.' She was more at ease. 'But I can't make much impression on my garden.'

'Where do you live?'

'At Marsh End.'

'Won't you sit down?'

She perched on the end of the armchair.

'I believe my father sometimes called on you.' Father had talked of the German couple who lived at Marsh End and kept themselves to themselves.'

'Dr Mason senior looked after my husband in his last illness. He was very kind when Sandor died.'

'Must have been eight or nine years ago.'

'You remember.' She seemed glad that we weren't total strangers.

All I remembered was hearsay; that the couple had been refugees from Nazi Germany, that Sandor Goldstern had been a well-known artist and illustrator of nature books, and that he'd been a recluse. His widow still lived behind high hedges and was rarely seen in the village. Offhand I couldn't think of anyone who'd mentioned her as a friend, which was strange in a community like Dayton. Isolation must have been the Goldsterns' choice.

'Will you be exhibiting at the horticultural show?' I asked her for want of a better neutral question.

'I don't have green fingers. Also, there's so much to do in connection with my husband's work. I'm trying to complete the books he planned, a whole wildlife series. But I mustn't waste your time, doctor. You see . . . I'm not really ill but I . . . I can't swallow food . . . solid food.'

'How long have you had this difficulty?'

'About three months. It seems to be getting worse.'

'You've lost weight?'

'Yes. My clothes are hanging on me.'

'Can you swallow liquids more easily?'

'Liquids are no problem. It's just solid things like meat or bread.'

'I'd like you to have some tests. Would you go to the

hospital at Millers Common?'

'Whatever you say, doctor. I have a car . . . What kind of tests?'

'I'll arrange for a barium meal and X-rays.'

'Please, I'd like to know why.'

'I want to make sure that there's no obstruction; take a look at your oesophagus – here, below your throat – your stomach and duodenum.'

'What if there is an obstruction? Please, doctor . . . I'm not afraid. I wouldn't be troubling you if it weren't . . . well, if I became seriously ill I'd be a nuisance to people. My son would have to know, I suppose. He lives in Australia. And there's the work on my husband's books. I'd rather know the worst.'

'Surgeons remove obstructions in any number of cases – successfully. But at the moment I have no reason to think that there is any obstruction that prevents you from swallowing solid foods. It would merely be a routine investigation to help me make the correct diagnosis. I'll be arranging it for you within a week or so.'

'I do nothing?'

'No, except make yourself nourishing soups or any meal you can swallow.'

'I don't feel hungry, doctor.'

'You mustn't lose any more weight, Mrs Goldstern.'

I didn't expect my mother to make lunch for me, but she always had a good collection of cheeses in the fridge and didn't mind if I helped myself. I'd just settled down in her living room with a plate of Stilton, crackers and the newspaper when she came in, wearing stable gear – jeans and a shirt that I had outgrown at fourteen. Her sun-bleached hair was tied back in a convenient ponytail.

'Hello, darling.' She flung herself on the couch beside me. 'What a morning! Betsy's had a son.'

'Who?'

'Tommyrot's sister.'

71

'Oh, the brown mare.'

'Isn't it wonderful? And Lady Chatterley's in the bag. I've signed the contract. We'll start filming early next year. You do realise what it means, don't you?'

'Publicity. And you'll get more free meals than ever.'

'It's you I'm thinking of. Now I'll be able to do your wedding in November, before we start rehearsing the Christmas play.'

'Liz and I want hot sun on our honeymoon. Where are we going to get it in November?'

'Darling, you'll just have to go a bit further than Europe . . . Bangkok's supposed to be absolutely wicked.'

'Don't think Liz would appreciate that kind of wickedness. My bank manager wouldn't like it either.'

'Darling, are you broke?'

'I've taken on a hefty mortgage. Remember?'

'You really shouldn't worry about such details at your age. If Bangkok's out, why not make it a skiing holiday. You can get quite cheap package tours.'

'Too cold. Mother, one of these days Liz and I will sneak off to a registry office . . .'

'Not on your nelly! Liz has a right to a proper wedding. And you . . . The village would never forgive you. Anyway, what's your hurry? You two are almost living together now. Keeping up appearances *a little* can't be such a hardship.'

'Getting up at five in the morning is wearing.'

'Why bother to do it? Your father would have appreciated your rather inept attempts at observing the proprieties. But who cares nowadays? Our farmer friends are up early too. Nothing's said, naturally, but your car *is* observed and obviously not *all* your patients call you out at crack of dawn. Jack, you will let me organise your wedding in November, won't you?'

'You will, whatever I say.'

'That's settled then.'

'Yes, provided Liz agrees.'

'She does. I asked her first.' Lavinia picked a chunk of cheese off my plate. 'What's biting you?'

'Nothing . . . nothing at all.'

'Darling, you wouldn't be eating my Stilton for lunch if you didn't have something on your mind.'

'Does the name Claudine mean anything to you?'

'Ah . . .'

'Well?'

'Tell me more, Jack.'

'Connected with Bunny and Dot.'

Lavinia bit into a cracker. 'Claudine . . . Sister Claudine at the convent school. She's the only one I can think of. Why are you asking?'

'Idle curiosity.'

'Confidential?'

'Yes . . . I've met Mrs Goldstern. You know her?'

'Nobody *knows* her. The Goldsterns never mixed.'

'I wonder why.'

'Perhaps they were over-sensitive – coming from Germany; though people wouldn't have been unkind to refugees. Your father didn't care for Mr Goldstern, but he liked the wife. Now that she's free, I don't know why she's hiding herself away in that gloomy wilderness.'

'Does she live on her own?'

'As far as I know. The son emigrated to Australia.'

'She told me she's working on a series of wildlife books planned by her husband.'

'Your father said she acted as his secretary, and that he was very demanding. Jack, do you want me to include her in my next party?'

'Would she come?'

'Could be; if *you* invited her. She thought a lot of your father.'

'When's your next party?'

'No plans. But if you want me to sort out problems for you I'll organise a Sunday booze-up.'

'I'm not keen on midday parties.'

'I know, darling. But they're nice, short and less expensive than evening ones. Besides, Sunday noon's

73

convenient for the Bishop . . . if one happens to need him. Or perhaps I should rustle up a rabbi for Mrs Goldstern. Anyone else you're sniffing at?'

'Lavinia, show *some* respect for my medical research.'

'Research with cheese.' She took the last piece off my plate 'Just like your father.'

'Next time I'm in London I'll buy you garlic sausage.'

'Not like your father. Darling, do get the real thing from Fortnum and Mason. How about tea?'

'No thanks. I'll have coffee at the hospital.'

'I must change.' Lavinia uncurled herself. 'Playing golf.'

'Enjoy yourself.'

'Of course. I won't forget your questions . . . though you pick up as much as I do nowadays. Can't say I'm too happy about your interest in Bunny and Dot.'

I'd barely mentioned the Bunting-Standings, yet Lavinia – true to form – had divined the drift of my chief concern.

Seven

There was a message for me at the hospital. Dr Teller, the pathologist, was in London but would be back at the laboratory by five o'clock. It seemed he wanted to see me as urgently as I wanted to see him. I decided to stay in Millers Common and make a couple of calls I'd scheduled for the following week.

Walking past the scatter of long, one-storey buildings I wondered whether my father's dream of a new purpose-built hospital would ever be fulfilled. Queen's had started as a GP hospital in a thirty-roomed Georgian country house. In the two World Wars it had been enlarged with those barrack-like wood or concrete blocks, temporary buildings which had never been replaced. What saved Queen's from looking like a refugee camp were the trees, shrubs and well-tended flowerbeds.

Year after year the local doctors reminded the relevant government department that a new hospital had been approved, and sent in a list of alterations and repairs to be carried out if the old Queen's was to go on functioning – even temporarily. Year after year essential repairs were sanctioned, new inconvenient bits added.

Trevor Chailey, the senior surgeon, had chalked up one victory in his battles with the bureaucrats. He had at last convinced the powers in London that unconscious patients should not be wheeled from ward to operating theatre through rain and snow. As a result several blocks had been connected with a spider's web of covered walks. Those long, open corridors had proved ideal for supporting climbing roses and clematis. Patients and porters arrived in the operating theatres dry, unless the prevailing sou'-wester drove the rain sideways through the covered walks.

On this warm day one could forget the snags. Crossing from the laboratory to the car park the whole complex looked a well-integrated part of the countryside. Outside the original house, which the administration had turned into comfortable offices, a man was busying himself in the flowerbed. It was Len Kirby, on his left knee, the right leg stuck out at an improbable angle.

'What are you doing?' I asked him.

'Afternoon, Jack.' He picked up his crutches and levered himself up. ''T was time for planting the chrysanths. Good exercise for me.'

'Yes, provided you don't dislocate your hip. When are you going home?'

'Tomorrow . . . and not afore time. Jack, have you been working on my farm?'

'Whatever gives you that idea?'

'Wouldn't be for the first time.'

'April's been managing all right.'

'So she says. I don't know what's come over her. Can't get any sense out of her. I've given her a list of things that need doing and all she says is, everything's taken care of.'

'You should trust her.'

'I do, but there are things on the farm I wouldn't expect her to handle . . . Surgeon says it'll be another month afore this leg's right.'

'You're not doing too badly now.'

'There's the combine harvester . . .'

'You won't be able to work it, not yet.'

'Drat.'

'Don't try to drive the tractor either.'

'Surgeon's told me.'

'Then be sensible.'

'I had a card from Morris . . . the nerve of him.'

'Time you stopped being stupid about him, Len.'

'Doctors here said the same as you,' he admitted, 'that the leg could have gone without any help from Ken Morris. So I gave April a note for him. Pester me, she did.'

'You apologised, I hope?'

'In a manner of speaking. I said I was giving him the benefit of the doubt.'

'You might have been more generous.'

'They've been a thorn in the Kirbys' flesh, the Morris tribe . . . for many a year.'

'And you're making bloody sure that nothing changes between you . . . I'll be seeing you at home.'

'Don't waste your time on me, Jack. You look after the sick.'

The Mother Superior certainly didn't look sick. Her face reminded me of last year's apples – cream, pink, wholesome but richly wrinkled. Her study looked like any headmaster's office except that the shelves along one wall were filled with religious books and a small alcove contained a crucifix.

'How kind of you to come so soon, doctor,' she greeted me. 'I felt a little guilty for telephoning your surgery, because – strictly speaking – we have no health problems.' She approached a pie-crust table with a silver tray. 'May I offer you a sherry?'

'That's a wicked suggestion, Mother Superior.'

'Should we have put out the whisky?'

'You seem determined to make an alcoholic of me.'

'Oh dear,' she laughed. 'I quite forgot. Dr Mason senior never accepted a drink before sundown. We're so used to Father O'Neil . . . he always enjoys a little refreshment. You will take tea with me?' Before I could stop her she'd picked up the telephone. 'Would you prefer Earl Grey or Lapsang?'

I chose Earl Grey, fairly sure that she would not talk

until I'd accepted her hospitality. While we waited she asked after my mother, who had once acted in a nativity play with the pupils of the convent school. I hoped Mother Superior wouldn't discover that Lavinia was the star of the forthcoming *Lady Chatterley* production.

A young nun brought in a tray set with Georgian silver. Mother Superior poured the tea into paper-thin china cups and offered me cookies baked by an American novice. The beat of a lawn mower came throbbing through the open windows bringing the heady scent of cut grass.

'So peaceful,' Mother Superior was savouring the bright afternoon. 'The new term starts next week . . . and this place will sound as if it were invaded by flocks of starlings. Occasionally girls stay with us during the hols, boarders whose parents are abroad or separated. This summer we had Katie . . .' She gazed into the garden. 'Such a nice child, but I am worried about her, doctor. She and Pippa were great friends . . . There are certain unfortunate similarities in the backgrounds of the two girls. Pippa lost her parents, Katie's are separated . . .'

As the noise of the lawn mower increased we both looked out. The mower came chugging down the lawn, followed by a nun. And the nun, using the machine as a kind of partner, was leaping into the air and spinning like a ballet dancer.

'Really!' Mother Superior laughed. 'Such goings-on. Father O'Neil wouldn't approve at all . . . Of course Sister Claudine is very physical.'

'Sister Claudine?'

'She's the sports mistress . . . I hope she isn't going to perform cartwheels. Pay no attention to her, doctor. She's an excellent tennis coach; just a little unseemly in her energy.'

Unseemly was the wrong adjective for the little nun. Her unselfconscious joy and fun were so infectious that even her superior couldn't bring herself to stop the dance. I could imagine Sister Claudine being mischievous but not causing mischief in Bunny's life or anyone else's. Yet such a surplus of energy might find unexpected outlets; and what better outlet than sex? Hadn't Mother Superior said that Sister Claudine was *physical*? Sir Lionel Bunting-Standing and a nun? Watching those whirling black skirts it seemed preposterous though not impossible.

'. . . and Pippa will always be on our conscience,' Mother Superior was saying. 'Though she was a day-girl – not constantly in our care – we failed her. We even failed in tracing the Spanish barman who fathered her child.'

'She wasn't sorry when he disappeared. She told me she doesn't want him. Pippa has a good home, and she's enjoying her child.'

'Even if we'd wanted to keep her here, the school governors wouldn't have permitted it. Sir Lionel Bunting-Standing – who is a kind man – felt that we couldn't make an exception.'

I might have guessed that Bunny was a governor. Bunny never solicited voluntary jobs but, belonging to the dying breed who were trained to give their services to the community, he'd become involved in most local institutions.

'I made it clear to Pippa,' said the Mother Superior, 'that I would always be interested in her welfare and that she may visit us. But I certainly didn't expect her to hold . . . clandestine meetings in the sports annexe. Late at night, doctor.'

'Would you explain?'

'One of the sisters has seen her. The first time she merely noticed three people on the verandah of the sports annexe . . . two females and one male. When they saw her, they ran away. We assumed they'd been potential vandals. After that we made regular checks. On the second occasion Sister Mary found the three by the toolshed – she had a flashlight with her – and she recognised Pippa and Katie. She didn't know the man . . . Once again, the young people escaped. Of course she immediately went to Katie's room . . .'

'I expect Katie was in bed.'

'Indeed she was . . . in her dressing gown. Sister Mary should perhaps have questioned the girl then and there. But she had doubts; Katie appeared to be fast asleep. If the child's family life weren't so . . . unsettled I'd have tackled Katie. As it is, I considered it best to look upon those meetings as a prank . . . possibly a midnight feast. As a girl I myself was guilty of such escapades . . . Pippa and company haven't been seen since, but I have observed . . . certain changes in Katie. She is looking heavier . . . rounder.'

Another pregnancy at the convent? 'How long has this been going on?'

'The first meeting took place in June.'

More than three months ago. 'Have you spoken to Katie?'

Mother Superior nodded. 'Perhaps I've been too circumspect. I told the child that she wasn't looking well – she isn't, in fact, and I suggested that we should seek your advice. She refused to see a doctor.'

'Did you tell her that she'd been seen out at night?'

'No. You see, Katie's become very withdrawn since her parents' divorce. I considered I'd be wrong in making her doubt that I was on her side.'

'How old is the girl?'

'Sixteen . . . an immature sixteen.'

'But a young woman of child-bearing age.'

'Dear God! I hope we're wrong.'

'One should know one way or the other.'

'Of course, you're right, doctor. Would you be prepared to see the child?'

'Certainly, if she consents.'

'She'll have to be persuaded, somehow. It would be right to have the mother's cooperation, but I am still hesitating. The mother has re-married; I believe Katie is blaming her for the break-up of the family . . . The father is in Canada.'

'Are there any brothers or sisters?'

'No, she's an only child. Doctor, I'm at my wit's end. What is to be done?'

'Pippa might be able to help.'

'I've been wondering. I wouldn't blame Pippa for looking upon me as the headmistress who expelled her.'

'I think Pippa understands that you had no choice. Let, me talk to her.'

I was looking for a place in the hospital car park when the social service's Mini came shooting out. The sight of an obviously angry Vivienne reminded me that I hadn't yet kept my promise to her. I hadn't fed her cases for the survey that might save her from redundancy for the simple reason that the practice happened to be short of *disadvantaged* people. Both one-parent families, Pippa's apart, were managing without Vivienne's intervention. One girl had landed a job at Millers Common playschool, where the baby could be with her, the other had become reconciled with her parents. And Maisie, the potential *battered wife*, had learned – if Earl's information was accurate – to give as good as she got.

Vivienne thundered past without seeing me. As I eased my car into the gap she'd left, Pat Low, the District Community Physician, waved to me from his. He waited for me beside his Volvo.

'I was going to phone you,' he said. 'Have you heard from Shastri?'

'Shastri? The owner of the Indian restaurant?'

'That's him.'

'No, he hasn't been in touch.'

'Mr Shastri's just imported another eight members of his family from Pakistan. I'll get my health visitor to chase him up.'

'Vivienne's been chasing you?'

'Relentlessly, no doubt praying that the new Pakistani lot turn out to be disadvantaged. Well . . . not if I can help it. I'll make sure Shastri takes care of his own, if it's the last thing I do.'

'He can't be poor.'

'Coining it . . . employing his relations as slave

labour.'

'After a while the worm turns.'

'Jack, don't speak to me of worms. It's a touchy subject. I'd just about dealt with hookworm in one lot of immigrants who arrived at Gatwick when the new one landed. This time it's tuberculosis. I suppose we're lucky that the latest Shastris came before the new school term, or we'd have to test several hundred kids. So far, so good; everything's under control . . . except that the new arrivals haven't yet registered with a GP. They'll be registering with you, seeing that Shastri's on your panel.'

'Right. I'll be expecting them.'

'Have you any influence with the social service?'

'No. She regards doctors as her natural enemies. We're the people who keep our patient's records from her.'

'I want to keep the housing committee from her. Every time a new batch of immigrants arrives she drives the housing people nuts. She pesters me for certificates declaring that the Indians or Pakistanis must have better accommodation . . . then demands instant allocations of council houses. Who wouldn't like to see them in better premises?'

'They shouldn't be sleeping in under-stairs cupboards or six to a room.'

'Who says they should? But the housing committee can't ignore the existing waiting list. In this area there are too many local people who've been waiting for years for a council house.' Pat sighed. 'You know what it's like . . . There must be *somebody* who can get it into Vivienne's fat head that the immigrants must wait their turn or we'll have bloody riots in Millers Common . . . I was hoping to have a word with the chairman of the housing committee, but he hasn't been attending meetings recently. I hear Sir Lionel hasn't been too well. Perhaps you'll be seeing him. He lives in Dayton, doesn't he?'

'Yes.'

'I'd appreciate it if he explained the housing

situation to Vivienne. He seems able to manage her. Nothing like a title for coping with revolutionaries . . . Must have a game of golf soon.'

'It's my partner who plays . . . or my mother.'

Pat didn't hear me. He'd flung himself into his Volvo and was making off, narrowly missing the ambulance coming in at Keystone Cops' speed.

James Teller's office beside the laboratory was quiet. We sat at a table littered with X-rays and reports – James, the pathologist, Helena Tate, haematologist and Trevor Chailey, the senior surgeon. We all felt tired, but Helena – until recently the glamour girl of the medical staff – was looking sallow and middle-aged.

She said, 'We haven't considered Positron Emission Tomography.'

'What for?' said Trevor. 'What can PET do except investigate the disease process. It's unlikely to tell us anything new . . . in this case.'

'We could refer Sir Lionel to the Hammersmith,' said James Teller.

'Nuclear Magnetic Resonance? It might produce one or two more details, but is it worth dragging the poor man up to London? I don't think we should subject him to more tiring investigations. What do you think, Jack?' asked Helena.

'I don't think so either. Any other suggestions?'

'I could operate on the bowel,' said Trevor. 'But it wouldn't improve the end result. There are secondaries in the liver and the right lung; the man is riddled with cancer. If I operate he'll die in pain, if I don't he'll die – more comfortably – from terminal anaemia. He isn't in a great deal of pain, is he, Jack?'

'He's complained of discomfort rather than pain. He feels he wants to move his bowels, but can't, and he's convinced that the mucus and blood he passes is due to piles.'

'I'd let him go on believing it,' said James, 'unless he starts asking the direct question. But in my experience patients who're dying of cancer don't often ask, *doctor, have I got cancer.*'

Trevor picked up an X-ray and held it to the light. 'What surprises me is that he's still alive.'

'Not me.' Helena smiled, 'Sir Lionel's got something to live for. He told me he's president elect of the Horticultural Society. He's tickled pink about it. He said he'd held heaven knows how many offices but he'd never before made the top of the Horticultural Society. He's hard at work on his inaugural address.'

'He's always taken trouble,' agreed Trevor. 'When he was chairman of the League of Hospital Friends he raked in more money for Queen's than anyone before or after him. At one stage he raided the attics of his county friends and organised a sale of antiques . . . he even requisitioned a Sotheby's auctioneer. That's what paid for number three operating theatre. Remember?'

'Not likely to forget,' James chuckled. 'It was before your time, Jack.' Trevor and Helena were beginning to look less harassed. 'We'd been agitating for this operating theatre for years but – as usual – the administration deemed it more important to have the offices fully carpeted and centrally heated . . . and to paper over the cracks. Then Sir Lionel produced the lolly, specifically for the new operating theatre. A specialist architect came down from London and building went ahead. The medical staff organised a formal opening and a buffet supper. And – for a bit of slapstick – the nurses were to stage a mock operation . . .'

'The night of the event,' continued Trevor. 'A lot of distinguished guests crowded into the theatre . . . glasses of sherry in hand. The patient – matron – was on the operating table. Patel – my registrar – and I, in cap and gown, were supposed to go into action. And then there was a funny noise . . . like a Victorian mothers' circle swooning. Patel managed to take his place beside the patient – he was only five foot four.

84

But I banged my head on the lamp. In fact the only way I could have operated was . . . on my knees. The architect had made a small miscalculation . . . he'd forgotten the depth of the operating lights.' Trevor joined in the laughter. 'So . . . eventually the builders literally had to raise the roof.'

'Sir Lionel was quite a man,' said James.

'He's still alive,' Trevor reminded him. 'It'll be hard on you, Jack.'

Eight

'You don't have to tell us, m'boy,' said Bunny. 'We know it's piles, don't we, Dot. Medical dictionary makes it perfectly clear. Classic case . . . mine. Inelegant complaint, but harmless. Join us for lunch?'

The ham and salads on the table looked good, the way two of the Bunting-Standing dogs were helping themselves to the scraps on Bunny's plate was less appetising.

'Thanks, I don't eat lunch.'

'That's bad, Dr Jack,' said Dot. 'No wonder you're so lean. Now, help yourself. I insist.' She pushed her plate and used cutlery across. 'You don't mind, do you? Saves washing up. Tuck in.' She brushed one of the dogs off the table. 'Bunny, I wish you'd control your dogs; ham is expensive these days.'

'You shouldn't allow them on the table at all.' Bunny pulled a piece of bread out of the dog's mouth and put it back on the board. 'Try our home-made loaf, m'boy. Dot's a good little baker . . . very fussy about the flour she buys.'

I rationalised that Dot didn't have foot and mouth disease, that she certainly wasn't the kind of animal owner who'd allow her dogs to have worms, and helped myself to ham and tomatoes.

'Know what's given me the damned piles,' announced Bunny, 'Been sitting around too long. Committee meetings, y'know. The nearly unacceptable

86

face of democracy . . . meetings. Should do more real work . . . garden . . . greenhouses. Not leave it all to the little woman.'

The little woman glared at her husband. 'Wipe your chin, Bunny. You've got goat cheese stuck to it. Makes you look positively senile.'

'Less of your spunk, m'dear. How about getting us a drink . . . lager?'

'Dr Jack doesn't drink in the middle of the day, as you should know. I'm going to make coffee. And it's goat milk for you.'

'Hate the stuff.'

'Bunny, you're not making a song and dance about it.'

'No, m'dear. I'll shut my eyes and imagine I'm back in the POW camp and the Japs are giving me a treat . . .' Bunny watched Dot's departure. 'Somebody in this house has to drink the stuff. Dot won't. Tried to palm it off on m'daughter. No luck. Goat was damned expensive; can't waste what the brute produces . . . Well, m'boy, what's the score?'

'How are you feeling?'

'Weak as a pup; that's the worst of it.'

'You're very anaemic.'

'Thought as much. Stands to reason. Piles make one lose blood. Iron tonic, that's what I need. Right?'

'Yes.' I felt a fraud, yet thankful that Bunny had read the medical dictionary and arrived at his own conclusions. 'I'll give you a prescription . . . Are you still chairman of the housing committee?'

'I am. Not been at the last couple of meetings though. Something on your mind?'

'I saw the District Community Physician yesterday. The Pakistani population in Millers Common has gone up again. Dr Low anticipates pressure on the housing committee, from the social service.'

'Oh yes . . . that girl. What's her name?'

'Vivienne Allen. Dr Low would appreciate it if you had a word with her about the waiting list for council houses.'

'Ah yes . . . remember. Girl reckons immigrants and one-parent families should be given accommodation before anyone else. Had plenty of letters from her. Can't say I understand her type. Always dressed in loose garments; no idea whether she's fat or thin; no figure one can remember. Greasy, long hair . . . tosses it about like a tail. Had a donkey who swatted flies that way.'

'Dr Low would like you to make her see sense. He believes she'd listen to you.'

'Can try. Did rather well last time I had a go at her. Cost me the best part of a bottle of sherry though. Never mind . . . all in a good cause.'

'I was at the convent yesterday. Sister Claudine was mowing the lawn.'

'Oh yes . . .' Bunny's reaction was noncommittal. 'Claudine . . . Must get down to her. Much on my mind . . . the exuberance of her . . . the incredible delicacy. Living work of art . . . that's my Claudine.'

Dot returned with coffee and a jug of milk, more dogs swirling round her legs. Bunny, who'd suddenly turned grey, used the diversion for leaving the room. As Dot fussed with cups and saucers, both of us pretended to be unaware of Bunny's painfully slow progress.

We sat in silence until Dot felt certain that Bunny had gone some distance from the morning room.

'Unsteady on his pins,' she said, at last. 'Dr Jack, I cope better when I know the truth. He's dying, isn't he?'

'I'm afraid he is.'

'And there's nothing anyone can do.' It was a flat statement.

'I'm sorry, Dot.'

She nodded. 'Will the pains get worse?'

'No; we'll be able to control that.'

'Thank God. The drugs . . . will they make him whoozy?'

'Eventually.'

88

'He needs time, Jack . . . to achieve what's been perhaps his greatest ambition. It would be damned unfair if he didn't make the horticultural show.'

'I heard he's next year's president.'

'Yes, but that's only part of it. There's a cup he wants to win. He's never been what you'd call a pot-hunter, but he's dreamed of winning the Lady Corbett cup ever since he rebuilt our greenhouses after the war. He got pretty close once; then Richard Plum-Ascot pipped him at the post. It was a dirty trick.'

'What happened?'

'Bunny roundly accused Plum-Ascot of stealing his plants and there was an almighty row. The libel action went against Bunny. Plum-Ascot used that ding-dong for keeping Bunny out of the presidency . . . It's a long story. The best of Bunny's plants were in fact stolen, but I don't think Plum-Ascot took them. Putting two and two together, I believe that Earl stole the plants without his father's knowledge. Earl's mother was still alive then . . . and Earl's mother won the cup. There was nothing one could do . . . Earl being a nutter. It's old history, but if Bunny won this year it would make all the difference to . . .'

'It would make him happy.'

'Yes. Though I say it myself, he deserves this one small triumph.'

'Not so small, to him.'

'Thanks for being so understanding. We've got to keep him alive somehow.'

'When's the show?'

'Third of October. Six weeks. It's not much to ask for, is it?'

'We'll try, and that includes the doctors at the hospital. Make sure Bunny doesn't exert himself. He must take it easy.

'He does during the day, pretending he's got to catch up on his reading. But the minutes of the committee meetings send him to sleep.'

'They'd send me to sleep.'

'Bunny puts on a show for visitors, but I know how

89

weak he is. It's the nights that worry me most. As you've seen, he can hardly drag himself to the loo. Yet he gets up in the middle of the night and goes out. I've watched him crawl across the lawn twice in the past week. Should I have gone after him? Stopped him? I couldn't interfere. I think I've known for some time that it's curtains for Bunny. I watched him struggle across the garden and did nothing. Somehow I couldn't bring myself to keep him away from Claudine.'

The state of Mrs Goldstern's property made me realise how bravely Dot had been struggling to preserve the Bunting-Standing grounds. Somehow Dot was keeping the lawns cut, fruit trees and roses pruned and dead wood cut out of the trees. Martha Goldstern had let her five acres revert to nature. Along the dank path I was following, sycamore seedlings were killing off what had been good conifers, brambles and convolvulus were strangling the wilting remains of lilac, plumbago and other flowering shrubs. The wilderness I'd been clearing at my Old Mill had been bad enough but the so-called garden of Marsh End was infinitely worse.

However, the birds didn't mind. They were giving an end-of-day concert such as I hadn't heard for years. On my comparatively short walk to the house I saw a family of green woodpeckers, several species of tits, bullfinches and chiffchaffs, a barn owl and a long-eared owl. In front of me ran a reception committee of surprisingly tame black and white wagtails.

By the time I'd reached the house I was almost convinced that Martha Goldstern had deliberately turned the property into a bird sanctuary. The state of the house persuaded me otherwise. The paint was peeling off doors and window frames. The mansard windows were broken and patched with cardboard, and several tiles had slipped and were resting precariously on the rusty gutters.

Of course the bell was out of order, but the cast-iron

knocker in the shape of a dolphin made enough noise to bring Mrs Goldstern to the door.

'Doctor!' She looked surprised to see me and a little embarrassed. 'How kind of you to call. Please, come in.'

She led me through a long, chilly hall with a floor of ancient octagonal tiles. The whitewashed walls were crammed with excellent watercolour paintings, mainly of birds and wild flowers. Her husband, if it was his work, had certainly deserved his fame.

Mrs Goldstern showed me into a large studio brightly lit by several rails of spotlights. 'Do you mind coming in here, doctor? The temperature drops such a lot in the evenings and the studio's the warmest room in the house.'

'It must also be the most interesting one.'

'If you're interested in pictures. Most of these are the originals of my husband's book illustrations.' There were a number of paintings I liked but many more which were well below the standard of the watercolours in the hall. I was struck by a half finished picture of blue tits on an easel. It showed three birds clinging to a brick wall and looking into a window. Unlike so many nature paintings I'd seen this one impressed me with its wonderful sense of fun.

An idea began to form in my mind. 'How long will it take you to finish this picture?' I asked Mrs Goldstern.

'A week or ten days. Some of the details . . .' she broke off in confusion. 'I just dabble . . . This is nothing.'

'I don't agree . . . The pictures in the hall are yours, aren't they?'

'You're an art expert, doctor?'

'No, but I can recognise the style, Mrs Goldstern. Even the unfinished picture is destinctive enough.'

'I learned everything I know from my husband,' she said, almost harshly. 'Will you have a drink?'

I was about to turn down the offer when an idea in my head became clear. 'I'd like a cup of coffee.'

'I can offer you whisky, gin . . . the usual selection . . .'

91

'I'd prefer coffee, if it's not too much trouble.'

'Of course not . . . It won't take a moment.'

She expected me to stay in the studio, undoubtedly, but I followed her. Unlike the outside, the house was neat and well kept. We walked through a rectangular hall and a dining room, which had an unused feel, into a kitchen with attractive pine cupboards and shelves full of copper pans. I noticed that the Aga cooker was not functioning and looked too spotless to have been in use recently. Mrs Goldstern put on an electric coffee-pot.

I said, 'You have a beautiful kitchen.'

'My husband designed it. He thought the kitchen was the most important room in the house.'

'Hence the Aga cooker. My fiancée tells me it's the perfect one for people who care about good food.'

'My husband did.' It was a flat statement.

'You'd recommend an Aga?'

'Oh . . . any modern cooker would do me.'

Or no cooker at all? I took a copper pan off a shelf. It was heavy and expensive, also polished to perfection. But when I wiped my hand over it there was dust on my palm.

Mrs Goldstern set a tray and I carried it back to the studio for her. While she poured the coffee I told her of the birds I'd seen in her garden.

'It's kind of you to call it a garden,' she smiled. 'I think it's a jungle, but that's how my husband liked it.'

'And you?'

'I keep thinking of having it cleared, but I don't know how the birds would react. I don't want to frighten them away.'

'If the job's well done – with the nesting places in mind – you wouldn't lose them. There's a good man in the village . . . Hugh Stenning.'

'That's what I need . . . someone to tell me who to get and where to go. I will ask Mr Stenning to call.' She offered me a biscuit and helped herself. 'There are also things I should do about the house . . .'

'I noticed. I expect you've been too busy working on your husband's books to look after this place . . . too busy and too tired.'

'I could do with more energy, doctor.'

'Then you should eat properly, Mrs Goldstern. You seemed to have no trouble swallowing the biscuit.'

'No . . . I washed it down with coffee.'

'I've had the results of your tests. There's no obstruction anywhere; oesophagus, stomach, duodenum . . . all perfectly normal.'

'I didn't want to ask . . .'

'And I didn't want to tell you until I'd seen you eat . . . which you managed without difficulty.'

'Is that why you asked for coffee?'

'It was one reason. I hoped you'd find us something to go with the coffee. I also wanted to see whether you're in the habit of using your kitchen. You're not, Mrs Goldstern, are you?'

'Not much. I hope you don't think I've been making it up . . . It is true that I can't swallow solid things like meat.'

'I believe you.'

'But you say there's nothing wrong with me.'

'I said that the tests have been perfectly satisfactory. You have no disease but you do require treatment. Nothing unpleasant. You need regular meals and a well-balanced diet. If you find solids difficult to swallow you'll have to emulsify the meat and vegetables. I noticed you have a mixer that'll do the job in minutes.'

'That's true.' She didn't sound over-enthusiastic.

'I'll send you a diet sheet listing the food and quantities you need.' I finished my coffee and got up. 'When did your son go to Australia?'

'Three years ago.' She accompanied me to the door. 'Now he's planning a business trip.'

'Then you see him from time to time?'

'He hasn't been back so far. But by next year the journey should be worth his while . . . I hope.'

As I tracked through the jungle, back to my car, I

pondered Lavinia's scant information about the Gold-sterns. My father hadn't liked the dead artist. And the widow? Yes, he'd found her sympathetic. How had Lavinia put it? *Now that she's free, I don't know why she's hiding herself away in that gloomy wilderness*. A recluse? Yet she wasn't my idea of a hermit. I hadn't learned a great deal about Martha Goldstern, except that I'd have to unearth facts and more facts if there was to be any kind of future for her.

Nine

The dinner Liz had cooked to celebrate the completion of our dining room left nothing to be desired; Lancashire soup, made with the first cabbage and potatoes I'd grown at the Old Mill, roast duckling with all the trimmings and zabaglione. The only thing that spoiled it for Liz was that the celebration was premature. Earl had not kept his promise of completing the room next to the kitchen.

I had used dozens of disposable hypodermic syringes, collected for me by my colleagues at the hospital, filled them with Rentokil, and made war on the woodworm. Having eliminated the pests I'd stripped the woodwork down to the original honey colour of the oak beams. Liz had similarly dealt with the refectory table and the ladderback chairs which she'd bought in a junk shop near her parents' home in Stockton-on-Tees.

Earl had undertaken to paint the walls and ceiling between the oak beams plain white. When Liz had arrived she'd found the plasterboard ceiling untouched, two walls painted a dreary grey. Her search for our handyman-gardener had proved unfruitful. He'd left the doors of his log cabin open, a pair of trousers and sandals under a bush by the pond, the paint brushes – unwashed – on Liz's cooker.

'Perhaps we should call the police,' said Liz for the umpteenth time. She put the sundae glasses through the hatch into the kitchen and put a half bottle of brandy on the table.' If Earl is found at the bottom of the pond we'd never forgive ourselves.'

'Wherever he is, it won't be in the pond. Swimming's his chief joy in life. He wouldn't misuse water for killing himself. Stop worrying, love. It's not the first time Earl has taken off.'

'But he's our responsibility now.'

'A good many members of the medical profession have pronounced him sane. Earl is thirty-five years old, responsible for himself . . . and even allowed to vote.'

'He's been strange lately.'

'Liz, when isn't he strange? Look, if Earl doesn't want to be found, Sergeant Tripp wouldn't stand a chance. Forget it. He'll turn up when it suits him.'

'Well . . .' Liz began to waver. 'Perhaps he couldn't face us; he has made an awful mess of the walls. I should have listened to him when he said his work-application was dropping.'

'That's Vivienne's jargon. All it means is that Earl's decided that he doesn't feel like doing any work.'

'I know you're right, but . . .'

I went and kissed the top of her head.' Time to go to the meeting. We'll check Earl's cabin when we get back. Where's the notice?'

Liz fished in her handbag and produced a manila envelope. 'Why have they invited me?'

'Because you're a pharmacist . . . though I don't expect Colonel Maverick has any idea where you'd fit into his plans.'

I re-read the Colonel's notice. *In deference to popular concern regarding the probability of nuclear war H.M. Government has taken the decision to strengthen Civil Defence throughout the country. In line with Article XXXVI of the Defence Act 1854 local government is obliged to initiate Defence Committees, initially at Parish Council level. Special importance is being attached to the active participation of medical and ancilliary Health Service personnel. Your atten-*

dance is requested at an exploratory meeting on Friday, 10 September, at 8.30 p.m. Venue: the private bar at The Crown.

The evening was so warm and pleasant that we took the long way to the centre of the village. In the front gardens of Meadowfield Road the roses were having a last fling before the frosts came, flowering profusely beside some early chrysanthemums.

'Who is this Colonel Maverick?' asked Liz. 'Is he a local man?'

'More or less. There's a bit about him in my father's diary. His parents had a farm the other side of Millers Common. In the war he served in a cavalry regiment . . .'

'Such a thing still existed?'

'The cavalry fought in tanks, I think. After the war Maverick went into politics and got into parliament as a labour member. He collected a lot of directorships, made a lot of money and bought a large estate in East Sussex. He lost his parliamentary seat in the last election.'

'Good,' said Liz. 'I don't believe in rich socialists.'

'Neither did my father. He wrote some scathing things about millionaire reds in hunting pink.'

'I wonder why he's been chosen to start up a defence committee.'

'He volunteered, I expect. Some people collect directorships and committees, others – like Bunny – have them thrust upon their shoulders.'

The private bar at The Crown, normally used for Scout or conservative party committee meetings, had been adapted for its new purpose. Someone had put up a raised platform, backed by a map of the world, and various screens with complicated-looking pin-up graphs. At the far end Ron Dicker, the landlord, was serving drinks to a small handful of people, including my mother. Lavinia was looking trim and glamorous in a grey flannel suit befitting the occasion. Not until we'd joined her did I recognise the school uniform I'd outgrown at the age of sixteen.

'Have I seen this suit before?' I asked her.

'Darling, of course. Super tailoring . . . it was wasted on you pimply boys.'

'The jacket fits, but how do you manage to get into the trousers?'

Lavinia turned and lifted the back of the coat. 'No problem for a theatrical costume maker.' Someone, presumably Dayton Players' wardrobe mistress, had inserted a triangle in the centre seam. 'We had to sacrifice the coat pockets, but it's been worth it . . . Liz darling, I've got an earlier suit of Jack's. It might fit you. In Fortnum's you'd pay four hundred pounds for it.'

'I wouldn't,' Liz was enjoying herself.

'Nor me.' Lavinia touched the lapels with sensuous pleasure. 'Divine quality. I'd say *they don't make the likes of it any more*, but that would date me . . . Here's the Colonel. Wonder why he's invited me to this meeting.'

'Perhaps he wants to draw on your experiences of the last war.'

'Darling, I was twelve when it started. I do remember odd things though. We were given gas masks. I left mine at home, but the case was perfect for carrying lunch . . . And the nuns at the school were given permission to wear shorter habits, so they could move faster. We were supposed to run to the cellar when the air-raid sirens went off.' Lavinia followed us to the chairs in front of the platform. 'Rather odd, planning for the next war. I'm sure if they didn't show all this violence on television the Russians wouldn't waste their money on those ghastly rocket-things.'

It was a small gathering; Joclyn Runciman – so new to the village and so courteous that it would be easy to impose on him; Mac Curran, the traffic warden, chewing his beard in frustration because Sergeant Tripp had been chosen to sit on the platform; health visitor Mrs Cherry; Earl's father, Richard Plum-Ascot; and – inevitably – Vivienne, the social service. Colonel Maverick, on the platform beside our local policeman, unpacked a briefcaseful of papers.

'Hrrrm,' Sergeant Tripp opened the meeting. 'I'm here as secretary of the Defence Committeee . . .'

'Who elected you?' sneered Mac.

'And my first duty,' the Sergeant ignored him, 'is to say a few words about Colonel Maverick. You all know him, in a manner of speaking. He was the only Labour Member of Parliament in the whole of this area . . .'

'Yes,' interrupted Mac, 'it means they're building too many factories at Millers Common.'

'Thank you, traffic warden . . . You've all seen the Colonel on TV. Now I'm pleased to introduce him as the newly adopted parliamentary candidate for the Dayton and district constituency.'

'Which party?' asked Mac in an audible whisper.

'Labour.' Sergeant Tripp remained poker-faced. 'Considering the successes of the Communists in the party, it's a triumph of good sense that the local lads have adopted such a moderate candidate . . . I'll now ask Colonel Maverick to proceed.'

'Ladies and gentlemen,' Maverick didn't get up. Small, smooth and round, he looked like a pink-painted Easter egg. 'Let me first answer Sergeant Tripp's remark about my party. The rumours of a Communist take-over are vastly exaggerated. Indeed my personal experience of my own constituency party people has been a very happy one. I found them most understanding. They even held their meetings on dates that fitted in with my hunting commitments . . .'

Vivienne, misunderstanding the amused applause, clapped her hands too loudly and too long.

'However, tonight I'm wearing my civil defence hat, ladies and gentlemen . . .'

'I move,' called the Sergeant, 'that we herewith elect the Colonel as chairman of the Defence Committee. All in favour?'

'Why not?' murmured Mrs Cherry, beside me. 'Who else would do the job?'

'Carried,' said Sergeant Tripp.

The Colonel beamed white dentures at us. 'Thank ye . . . capital . . . capital. Now, the point at issue is that the government wants the people of this country to be prepared for war. That is, to face facts, to learn how to protect ourselves in case of a nuclear attack.' He held up a luridly coloured pamphlet. 'A grant of one million pounds has been set aside for civil defence. Of course, spread over the whole country it's a smallish amount, but it will pay for clerical assistance, telephone – provided we don't use it wastefully – and postage. It's our initial task to send recommendations to the Ministry in London . . .'

'Deep shelters,' said Mac Curran, 'that's my advice.'

'Capital, capital. 'Fraid the government can't afford that.'

'Government's spending *our* money. If we didn't spend it on them new missiles we could build deep shelters.'

'Unrealistic,' Maverick answered. 'But there must be *something* we can suggest, on a more modest scale.'

'Nothing modest about nuclear bombs,' said Mac.

'Doctor,' Maverick turned to me. 'Perhaps you'd tell us what we'd be up against in an attack.'

I took from my pocket the xeroxed copy of an article in the *Lancet*. 'I have a lot of facts and figures here, but I'll sum up. America and Russia now have one and a half million times the destructive nuclear power of the Hiroshima bomb . . . enough to kill the world's population either directly, by heat, blast or by radiation and pollution . . .'

'Nasty,' said Mrs Cherry.

'Doctor,' Maverick drummed his fingers on the table, 'are you in fact saying that there is *no* defence against nuclear war?'

'I'll read you the conclusion of this paper. *Modern preventive medicine reaps many benefits from diagnostic and therapeutic experience. Such knowledge would not be available in the event of a nuclear bombardment, which would not discriminate between joggers or smokers, clean water supplies and sewage, in its devastation. Medicine would be swept aside in an instant. The medical profession must devote its time and effort to ensuring prevention before the threatened event.*'

'You mean . . . doctors are actually doing something?'

'Doctors, even in Russia, are constantly telling their governments that nuclear war would put everyone out of business, including politicians, including the presidents of Russia and America.'

'Yes, capital . . . capital.' Maverick's fingers became more agitated. 'But we really must stick to the point . . . return to the business in hand, *civil defence*. I think we should keep firmly in mind that war is a continuing challenge to progress in medicine and in other fields . . . Now, do we have any practical suggestions?'

'Brown paper.' Lavinia looked so earnest that I knew she was about to dynamite the meeting.

'Brown paper?' The Colonel frowned. 'I must admit, it rings a bell.'

Lavinia produced a battered booklet. 'A civil defence manual of the last war. You may borrow it, Colonel. In it there's a bit about saving oneself from blast . . . Or is it heat? I can't remember which. Anyway, the advice is to wrap oneself in brown paper.'

We walked across the playing field.

Liz said, 'It's no laughing matter, but . . .'

'The minutes of the meeting will be even funnier.'

'Did anyone take minutes?'

'Vivienne, of course.'

'It's one great big confidence trick . . . government pretending that there is protection against nuclear bombs. Wasting a million on it too.'

'Don't let it depress you, love.'

'It may never happen?'

'Let's think of now.' I took her in my arms, kissed

101

her, and remembered the first time we'd made love in the high grass on the edge of the cricket field. Liz was my immediate future and I'd think no further – not on this Indian summer night.

'Listen!' Liz pulled away. 'Hear it?'

'Probably a fox.'

'No . . . there's someone at the cricket pavilion. Another break-in?'

We stood still, waiting for the moon to come out. As the clouds sailed on, the light revealed a couple in a clinch. The man stood with his back to us, but I recognised the girl – Pippa.

'Wonder if she has a baby-sitter.'

'She wouldn't leave Pip alone, would she?' asked Liz.

'Too many young mothers do. We keep reading about children dying in fires while the parents are out . . . At least Pip won't be entirely alone in the house. The Blairs wouldn't leave Jamaica on her own. I'm going to speak to Pippa.'

'You can't!'

'Not now. I'll be seeing her in any case.'

'Anything the matter with Pip?'

'Nothing like that. No more beads in his orifices.'

'It can't be easy for Pippa. How old is she?'

'Rising seventeen.'

'I hope her new boyfriend's more responsible than Pip's father . . . Let's go, Jack.'

'Still worried about Earl?'

'I *would* like to see a light on in his cabin.'

We'd reached the High Street when the silence was burst by the crash of church bells. It was too late for bell-ringing practice. Besides, there was no pattern to the noise.

We suddenly found ourselves in a crowd, all making for the church. There were even more people in the graveyard, all staring at the steeple.

'Man up top,' said Mac Curran. 'And no sign of our police. Typical.'

'See anyone?' asked the postmaster.

The ringing had stopped. A figure appeared astride an open window of the bell tower, one leg swinging in mid-air.

'Earl!' Liz gripped my hand. 'I knew it. Jack, what are we going to do?'

'Come down, you bloody idiot!' shouted his father.

'You heard him!' Earl yelled back. 'I'm an idiot . . . and I want my rights! Put me away! Take me to The Close, or I'll jump!'

'Earl!' I called, 'This is Dr Mason. I'll come up and . . .'

'I'm not coming down, doc.'

'What is it you want?'

'My rights! I'm a psychiatric case and I want into The Close!'

'Earl, we've been into it. You're not a psychiatric case . . .'

'If I weren't I wouldn't be up here, would I?'

'There's no room at The Close!'

'There is, in the private block! My dad will pay! Ask him!'

'What about the log cabin? You don't want to leave your home, do you?'

'If you don't get me into The Close I'll jump!'

'Stay where you are!' I dreaded he'd fall by accident. 'I'll call The Close.' In the circumstances they'd have to admit him.

Plum-Ascot was surrounded by people who demanded that he send his son to the private block of the psychiatric unit. Wasn't he in charge of the money Earl's mother had left for him? Wasn't it his duty . . .

'What can I do?' whined Plum-Ascot. 'Earl's spent most of the money on the log cabin. I'm not a wealthy man. The boy's ruining me.'

'Call an ambulance.'

'You get him down!' Plum-Ascot turned on Sergeant Tripp, who had just arrived. 'It's your job. I want my son brought down.'

'Can't take the risk, sir.' Tripp shook his head. 'Nasty mess if he jumped. We don't want to upset people, do we? Seeing that you are his father . . .'

'I'm not legally responsible for Earl,' snapped Plum-Ascot. 'Hadn't you better arrest him for a breach of the peace?'

'Got to get him down first, sir. Doctor, you said get an ambulance. That's what I'll do then.' Tripp pushed through the crowd. 'Go home everybody. You're encouraging him. An audience is just what Earl wants. You leave him to me.'

'That'll be the end of Earl,' sneered Mac.

'Earl!' shouted Tripp, 'I'm calling an ambulance. We'll have you in The Close in no time. So you come down!'

'Want to see the ambulance first . . . Don't want to go to your lousy jail.'

'You're going to The Close, man!'

'Don't trust the fuzz. Is the doc there?'

'I'm here,' I assured him.

'You promise they'll take me into The Close?'

'Yes, I promise. I'll help you down. Okay?'

'Ambulance first. Send everybody away. You stay!'

People drifted away down the High Street, from where they could see the last act without being seen. There was a horrible fascination about the lone figure perched on the church steeple. Within ten minutes an ambulance drew up much to my relief.

'I see it!' called Earl. 'You there, doc?'

'Yes.'

'Don't come up. I'll make it on my own . . . no sweat.' He disappeared inside the bell tower.

Ten anxious minutes later he showed in the porch, his arms jerking nervously. 'Keep away from me,' he instructed Sergeant Tripp.

Liz and I followed him down to the ambulance. As he hauled himself in, Liz reproached him, 'Earl, how could you? We were relying on you . . .'

'Sorry.' He looked almost contrite. 'Sorry about the walls in the dining room. I meant to do the job, but my work-application's gone again; and I can't carry on when the work-application goes. That's the trouble with me. Doc, you tell my father he's got to pay. He's got my mum's money, less the five thousand the court made him give me for the log cabin. Tell him the five thousand's gone. I'm not fooling.'

'Not fooling,' I said, 'but behaving like a fool, wasting your inheritance on hospital bills. Think what you could do with that money.'

'Can't. Dr Bradley said I'm suffering a malfunction of my thought-processes.'

'That was years ago.'

Earl waved a hand. 'Be seeing you, doc.'

'Not at The Close. You're putting yourself in the hands of the psychiatrists; that lets me out.'

When the ambulance had gone I walked Liz to her rented cottage, went home and called Dr Bradley. He'd just returned, he said, from the Medical Staff Committee and he was going to bed, 'Unless you're worried about Earl.'

'I'd have been more worried if he'd jumped off the steeple.'

'Like that, is it? All right, he can wait until the morning. Has he been on drugs? Tranquillisers?'

'Nothing. He's tranquil enough.'

'I see.' Bradley was puzzled. 'Why should he want to come back to us after all this time? He's never been nutty enough to like electric shock treatment.'

'He's heard about your new indoor swimming pool.'

Bradley laughed. 'Hard luck, he's boobed. The pool's not for potential suicides. It won't take us long to get rid of Earl.'

'Don't bank on it.'

Ten

Jamaica dropped from the tree like a ripe plum. 'Can I be Liz's bridesmaid, Dr Jack?'

'Ask her.'

'She said to ask your mother.'

'Ask my mother.'

'Mrs Mason said she hasn't thought about bridesmaids yet.'

'Then you'll have to wait until she has.'

'Everybody's always making me wait, even at school.'

'How do you like your new school?'

'It's all right . . . better than Cuthbert's. We're allowed sex.'

St Anne's, an exclusive private school, was renowned for its advanced teaching methods. 'Jamie, what is it you're allowed?'

She looked at me pityingly. 'Don't you know what sex is?'

'Well . . .'

'Secs . . . second helpings, of course. Daddy didn't know either,' she added generously. 'I think daddy got it mixed up with the other kind of sex.'

'Which?'

'The kind Pippa had for getting Pip . . . But I don't know about it. It's sort of secret. Even Pippa won't tell me. I think it's something you buy at the post office, in the evening.'

'How do you know?'

'That's when Pippa goes out.' Jamie climbed up the garden gate and swung on it. 'I know when she does, 'cause she leaves Pip in the hall so we can hear if he cries. And she always says she's going to the post office.'

'Jamie!' Pippa, neat in a green overall, came out into the garden. She picked the child off the gate. 'Your tea's ready.'

Jamaica didn't have to be told twice. She went racing indoors, banging the door behind her.

'That child!' Pippa smiled. 'A Jack-in-the-box, that's what she is. And talk about food! I don't know where she puts it all . . . and Pip's going to be just as greedy.'

'How is he?'

'Ever so good, bless him. He sleeps all night; never gets me up until seven.'

'So Mrs Blair doesn't mind looking after him when you go out in the evening?'

'I get time off.' Pippa blushed. 'I don't go to the disco or anything like that . . . but I got to go out a bit.'

'You still have friends at the convent, haven't you?'

Pippa looked uneasy. 'Mother Superior said I could go and see her . . . I mean . . . I liked it at the convent . . . Sister Claudine and the girls . . . I mean . . .'

'You've been visiting the convent, but not Sister Claudine or Mother Superior. Pippa, I want you to help me. I need to know the truth about your friend Katie.'

The story began much as I'd expected. Katie had been *going out with this boy*, a sixth-former from the nearby public school. There was discipline at the convent but it was not so strict that the senior girls weren't allowed to cycle to the village. Katie had been meeting the boy on the playing field or in the teashop. When he'd left school and gone home to Bedfordshire they'd written to one another, but they hadn't met again.

Some three months ago Katie had phoned Pippa in great distress, asking her to go to the convent after lights-out.

I said, 'You didn't go alone.'

'No . . .' Pippa hesitated. 'I've got a boyfriend. He doesn't like me going out on my own after dark.'

'What happened?'

'Well, Katie told me all about Steve . . . She thought she was pregnant. I told her she couldn't be. I mean, she and Steve . . . they hadn't done anything. I mean, you don't get pregnant just kissing and cuddling. I said, missing her periods didn't mean anything; mine used to be irregular . . . Then somebody came out and Katie had to go.'

'You had another meeting with Katie.'

'Yes. She phoned me again. Dr Jack, she can't be pregnant . . . not if she's told me everything, and I think she has. But she made me feel her tummy, and it feels big . . . like a baby inside her. I told her she must see a doctor; but she'd have to ask Mother Superior first and she won't do it. My boyfriend was ever so good. He talked to her for ages . . . about his bitch who had a phantom pregnancy; she never had pups. It was no good. Katie made us promise not to tell anyone. And now . . .' Pippa had tears in her eyes. 'I didn't mean to . . .'

'It would have been very wrong to keep this to yourself. Whether Katie is pregnant or not, she needs help . . . medical attention.'

'I don't know what my boyfriend will say . . .'

'He'll be as relieved as you are.'

'Dr Jack . . . we want to get married.'

'Congratulations.'

'We're not engaged . . . not yet. He's got to be careful because of Pip . . . I mean he'll have to get his family used to the idea that he wants to marry a girl with a child . . . I don't mind waiting. He knows what he's doing.'

'Good. Thanks for your help, Pippa.'

'About Katie . . . Dr Jack, will she find out that I

told you? I mean . . . she hasn't got anybody except Steve and me.'

'It seems unlikely that she's pregnant, so I should be able to keep Steve and you out of it.'

I'd have to invent a simple, undramatic reason that would persuade Katie to submit to a medical examination.

'She's never been what you'd call a friendly child,' declared Mrs Walker. 'I tried to warn her father that she is . . . I suppose, devious is the word. Unfortunately he had this fashionable idea of never punishing his little darling . . . I had trouble with her in her first year at school. She stole a twenty-pound note . . .'

'I did not,' Katie spoke up at last. Perched on the examination couch, at the far end of my consulting room, she'd endured her mother's monologue stoically. 'I found the note inside a school book. I kept it because I didn't know that it had any value.'

'Of course the teachers gave her the benefit of the doubt,' Mrs Walker rattled on. 'But she didn't pull the wool over my eyes. If her father had been any help . . .'

The Mother Superior had been right in hesitating over calling in Katie's mother. And here she was, so sure that she'd always seen through her daughter's personality; a woman in her early forties with a curiously immobile face that owed everything to expensive cosmetics. I doubted that she'd ever been a natural blonde like her daughter, or possessed Katie's quiet good looks.

'. . . no more than I expected,' Mrs Walker pressed on, 'When I found out that she was sneaking off to the discotheque . . .'

'Only once,' murmured Katie. 'I wanted to see what it's like.'

'Quiet, Catherine! I said I'd rather keep her at the convent all summer than put up with her lies and deceit. I hoped the nuns would see to it . . .'

Enough was enough. I picked up the telephone and asked Mrs Cherry to come to the surgery.

Mrs Walker had obviously resented the interruption. 'As I was saying, doctor . . .'

'You have said enough. I want you to wait outside. My health visitor will be present while I examine your daughter.'

'I've never heard such . . .'

Mrs Cherry came in, took in the situation at a glance, and held open the door. 'It won't take long. You'll find a new *Homes and Gardens* in the waiting room.'

'I have a right,' protested Mrs Walker, 'I want . . .'

'Thank you,' Mrs Cherry slapped her down. 'Doctor will see you later.'

With her mother out of the room, I asked Katie to take a chair. Mrs Cherry was putting a disposable sheet on the couch.

The girl faced me. 'You think I'm pregnant.'

'I don't. Mother Superior thinks you might be developing appendicitis.'

'My mother . . . everybody believes I'm pregnant.'

'There's no reason why you should be, is there?'

'I don't know . . . I've been out with a boy.'

'What's special about that?'

'We went to the disco at Millers Common. We didn't stay long. Steve hated the noise,' she smiled. 'He said it made his ears ache. I didn't like it either.'

'Where else did you go?'

'For walks . . . He kissed me. I have a girlfriend . . . she has a baby. Well . . . she knows about things. She says, we didn't . . .'

'All right, Katie,' I was going to take a chance. 'We're going to prove to your mother, and anyone else who's been silly, how wrong they've been.'

Katie willingly submitted to the examination – inevitably an embarrassing one for a young girl – her eyes on Mrs Cherry's kindly face. I found a large swelling in her lower abdomen, but unlike a pregnancy it was well off centre. It also felt much harder than a pregnant womb. Not unexpectedly I was able to confirm that Katie was a virgin.

While she got dressed I took a physiology textbook from the shelf and opened it at a picture of the female sex organs.

'We can rule out pregnancy,' I told her.

She gave an audible sigh of relief. 'Thanks.'

'But there is a bit of trouble . . . nothing to be frightened about. Let me show you. This is a picture of a girl's inside. Have you seen something like this before?'

'No.'

I explained to her the parts and their functions. 'Do you know what a cyst is?'

She thought for a while. 'Daddy had one on his neck. It's a sort of lump, isn't it?'

'That's right.'

'Was your father's cyst treated?'

'Yes . . . he went into hospital and they cut it out.'

'Well now . . . you have developed a cyst, here.' I pointed to the ovaries on the picture. 'It's not an unusual thing. Many girls and women have such cysts without even knowing it. But sometimes they grow big, like yours . . .'

'Will it have to be cut out?' Katie looked unworried.

'Yes, I think so. You won't know much about it. It'll be done under a general anaesthetic, so you'll be asleep.'

'I don't mind, doctor.'

'Good. First you'll be seeing a specialist at the hospital . . .'

'Not with my mother. I don't want her to go with me.'

'What do you suggest?'

'Please . . . will you speak to Mother Superior? They won't let me go on my own. I wouldn't mind Sister Mary or Sister Claudine. Only . . . not my mother.'

'Katie, I can't interfere between you and your family. I'm sure your mother's anxious . . .'

111

'I don't want her.' For a moment I saw a family likeness between mother and daughter.

'She came with you today.'

'You heard what she said about me. I won't go anywhere with her. Never. I have friends in Dayton . . .'

'The girl with the baby?'

'Yes . . . Pippa. And her boyfriend . . . He's been really kind.'

'Well . . . I must have a word with your mother. Mrs Cherry will take you to her office and give you a cup of tea.'

'At least Catherine isn't pregnant,' said Mrs Walker. 'Something to be grateful for, I suppose. It's a nuisance, all the same.'

'It won't cause you any pain or discomfort.'

'No.' My irony was lost on her. 'But I'll have to take her home. She'd better have the operation in London . . . my uncle is governor of one of the teaching hospitals . . . It's all so inconvenient just now. My husband wants me to accompany him on a business trip to Hong Kong and Singapore . . . We haven't been married long, so naturally . . . We also have a rather full autumn programme; my husband adores the theatre. We were going to spend Christmas in California . . .'

'Don't let your daughter disrupt your plans. I daresay the nuns will be perfectly happy to keep her.'

'There's the operation.'

'We have good surgeons at our local hospital.'

'It might look rather odd . . . people don't understand that mothers are entitled to *some* life of their own. Catherine's done nothing to deserve my sacrificing myself. My husband's been more than generous to her – paying for her riding lessons and a music centre – and she's shown no appreciation whatever. Now this cyst, or whatever it is, coming at the worst possible time. I meant to have some clothes made in Hong Kong . . .'

'Do,' I almost shouted at her.

'I beg your pardon?'

'Go ahead. Do what you want. Katie *wants* to stay here.'

'What she wants doesn't come into it . . .'

I realised my mistake. 'Mrs Walker . . . as you said, there's no reason why you should sacrifice yourself for your daughter. I'll phone Mother Superior . . .'

She looked at her watch. 'My taxi's waiting. If I don't take Catherine back to the convent I'll miss my train. We're going to the National Theatre to-night . . .'

'Let's settle your problem here and now.' I dialled the convent number and asked for Mother Superior. I explained briefly what was wrong with Katie. The dear old nun, who'd entertained no illusions about the girl's family background, immediately offered to take care of her. Such a relief that Katie's condition would have no . . . permanent consequences. Now there really was no need to disturb the mother's rather busy social life. There was no condemnation in Mother Superior's attitude to Mrs Walker; I admired her charity.

'It's settled,' I told Katie's mother. 'You'll have gathered that there's no problem about your daughter being looked after here. My health visitor will drive Katie back to the convent. Don't miss your train, Mrs Walker.'

On Saturday a pall of smoke had hung over the village. The farmers, making use of the windless day, had been burning the stubble. That night Liz had stayed at the Old Mill and we'd watched the creeping fires lap at the foot of the Downs. An eerie sight.

On Sunday morning the whole valley lay transformed in a cool autumn sun, the sweep of yellow fields turned hazelnut brown. We put on jeans and sweaters and went out. On the public footpath to Kirby's farm the last of the blackberries had shrivelled, oaks and ash were beginning to shed

113

russet leaves. Before long bare, black branches would vein the skies, the land tighten its belt for winter.

If I hadn't known that Len had been laid up I'd have been sure that he'd done all the necessary work with his usual thoroughness. The roof of the barn had been mended, the hedgerows trimmed back, the pens set up for sheep-dipping. Even the heavy branches of a sycamore, cracked in the last gale, had been taken down and sawn into logs.

April and Len were writing at the refectory table in the kitchen. April said she was glad we'd come and given her an excuse for stopping the tedious paperwork. What with the stream of Common Market regulations, ministry forms and VAT calculations, she and Len were being turned into civil servants.

I said, 'All the same, you're keeping the farm up to scratch.'

Len stacked the box files. 'Don't ask me how. It's none of my doing. I've been obeying doctor's orders. Couldn't help it. The bloody leg's as stiff as a poker.'

'It's doing well enough.' April put on the kettle. 'Don't be ungrateful. He's getting around, Jack.'

'Like a snail,' grumbled Len. 'But . . . yes, it's mending. I'd just like to move fast enough to find out what's going on here.'

'Your sons have been doing a good job,' said April.

'I dursay.' Len took cups and saucers off the Dutch dresser and put them on the table. 'But you can't con me. Our kids couldn't have done it all . . . not even if they'd missed school.'

'You mind your own business, Len Kirby.' April filled the teapot.

'This farm *is* my business. And I don't like it when things happen here that I know nothing about.'

'It's results that count. And that's what you're getting.'

'I suppose the winter feed will walk into the barn on its own . . . There's three truckloads out in the lane and . . .'

'If it rains,' I continued his tune, 'the dryer will have to be brought in. Len, stop belly-aching. So far April's managed – as she said she would – and the weather forecast couldn't be better . . . Lavinia's asked me whether you'll be fit to act in the Christmas play. You will be.'

'That's a mercy.' April poured our tea. 'Be glad when he's out from under my feet.'

'We'll unload the trucks,' offered Liz. 'Jack and I should be able to shift a lot in an afternoon.'

'You'll do no such thing.' Having let off steam, Len looked happier. 'Don't want you two out of commission. Can't have you hobbling to the altar on crutches. No, we have no problems here. April's got fairies at the bottom of the garden . . . but, by God, I'd like to meet them.'

Still thinking of Len's winter feed we took a short-cut through the orchard to the lane. For the past months Liz and I had done such hard physical work at our Old Mill that we'd managed to unload the feed without crippling ourselves. As we came to the barn we saw that one of the loads had been considerably reduced. But there was no one about.

We stood and listened. No sound. Inside the barn it was dark, though not too dark to see something red on top of a bale, an anorak which was surreptitiously creeping out of sight. Squeezing through a gap we came face to face with Ken Morris and Pippa, Pip in a pushchair behind them.

They were looking furtive but they were laughing.

'Kirby isn't outside, is he?' asked Ken.

'You're safe. Have *you* been doing all the chores?'

'No. The Kirby kids have been working like stink. We've just given them a hand.'

'Like mending the barn roof? Isn't it time April told Len who's been keeping the farm in order?'

'We didn't want her to,' said Pippa. 'Not until we've finished shifting the feed. Then she'll tell him . . . I mean, about Ken, not me.'

Ken took Pippa's hand. 'This has to stop. I don't

115

mind if the whole village knows that I'm going to marry you.'

'Let it be,' pleaded Pippa. 'We're all right as we are.'

So it was Pippa, not Ken, who felt apprehensive that his family would be against her.

'I've heard from Katie,' Pippa rushed on. 'She'll be all right, won't she, Dr Jack?'

'Yes. She'll be in hospital next week. Visitors after Tuesday.'

Ken smiled. 'Better than visiting the convent at night.'

We were back at the Old Mill before Liz voiced her thoughts. 'Pippa could be right. Ken's mother might prefer a farmer's daughter.'

'Pippa's grandparents were farmers. She's a local girl.'

'With an illegitimate baby.'

'Mary Morris isn't a Victorian lady.'

'Her experience of marriage hasn't been that good, has it?'

'That could make her more sympathetic to Ken's choice.'

'Some hope.' Liz stopped on the doorstep and kissed me. 'You're an optimist.'

'Up to a point.'

There were reasons why Mary Morris would think twice about laying down the law to her son, the most obvious explained in a note in my father's diary. *Mary has given birth to her first child, a daughter. The baby weighs 8 lb 6 oz. A whopper. I don't know how she'll convince the village that the baby has arrived pre-maturely. I hope the birth won't revive the old rumour that she dropped Arthur Kirby to marry the man who seduced her.*

Seduce. It struck me that it was a word long out of use in connection with sex. Seduction, in my father's day, had implied that girls were innocent or – at least – given the benefit of the doubt. Not any more; and Mary Morris would be aware of that. A lot of water

116

had flowed under the bridge betwen the birth of her whopper and her husband's untimely death from an overdose of her sleeping tablets.

I believed that thirty years of an unhappy marriage had taught Mary Morris something about the dangers of *doing the right thing* and about human relationships.

Eleven

'Darling,' my mother had reproved me, 'I simply cannot break my principles, not even for you.'

Lavinia had developed a set of principles on becoming a widow – never to cook for anyone, except for Liz and me on unavoidable occasions, never to revert to her housewife-role in life or on stage, never to prepare food for parties beyond opening packets of nuts or potato crisps.

As her customary Sunday noon party wouldn't have served my purposes she'd used her ingenuity in organising an evening barbecue on the Bunting-Standings' terrace. She'd recruited Cyril and Tim, her theatrical producer friends, as cooks, a relay from the Young Farmers as barmen, and a team from the Dayton Players for clearing the debris and washing up. Days before the party Liz had made puddings from chocolate mousse to apple pies, filled my car with the dishes and made me deliver them to Standing Hall.

Up to the guests' arrival I'd felt concerned that such a mob would be too much for Bunny. He certainly wouldn't keep out of it. Yet, as the terrace filled with people, Bunny wandered among them – glass in one hand, a walking stick in the other – giving few signs of his physical deterioration. Dot, I noticed, kept out of his way. It was their daughter, Muriel, who shadowed him. Muriel, who'd exchanged the usual riding gear for a vast scarlet caftan, looked as powerful as the savage flowers in her paintings.

Lavinia scrutinised Muriel's stately figure. 'She wants Geoff Joseph to sell her Tommyrot.'

'How do you feel about it?' I asked her.

Lavinia shrugged. 'She can handle most horses . . . provided they're not too sensitive.'

'Tommyrot is.'

'Darling, I've warned her that he hates brute force. I can't do more. Of course, it's possible that the sheer weight of Muriel will quieten him down. But I'd rather she didn't break bones just now; Bunny and Dot might need her.'

'Do I persuade her to lay off Tommyrot?'

'Darling, how clever of you!' Lavinia sniffed the air and made for the scent of roasting pork.

Liz watched her with open admiration. 'Some mother-in-law!' Lavinia, in black velvet knee breeches and white lace shirt, was presenting the back-view of an Elizabethan page-boy. 'The things she gets away with . . . and she does.'

A few minutes later we saw her seated on the low wall of the terrace, an indecently large plate of food on her lap, in deep conversation with Colonel Maverick.

'So unfair,' she was commiserating with him. 'Expecting local committee chairmen to put forward *all* the plans for civil defence.'

'Absolutely,' Maverick downed a glass of wine. 'As I've said in my report, it's unfortunate that we have no previous experience of a nuclear attack. I mean, what is one up against? One doesn't know. Actually I didn't mention your son's views in my report; one doesn't want to discourage government efforts too much. Bad for morale, the idea that there's no defence at all.'

'Yes, Jack does rather call a spade a spade. Tiresome of him.'

'I'm the first to give a realist his due, don't you know. But civil defence – nowadays – is a matter in which realism won't get us anywhere . . .'

'I see what you mean, Colonel.' Lavinia dissected

the last of her pork chops. 'What's required is a more imaginative approach to civil defence.'

'Exactly . . . As a matter of fact I've been trying to work out why the defence boys recommended brown paper last time. Blessed if I know.'

'Sometimes one can make people believe in simple solutions. There was carrots . . .'

'Carrots, Mrs Mason?'

'Yes. We were told to eat them because they improved one's eyesight in the black-out.'

'I remember. That's when we first used radar. Score of Jerry planes we shot down went up and up. Quite possible that the carrot story foxed the Germans . . . Difference is, now the government wants civil defence to fox our own people. All the same, I did make a few enquiries about brown paper. Ran into a snag. What with the plastic bags people use these days, there's a shortage of brown paper in the country. It's a supply problem. Imagine how much it would take if the whole population wanted to wrap up in brown paper.'

'Colonel, have you considered another colour? Actually brown looks ghastly on me. I never wear it . . .'

Bunny, his hand heavy on my shoulder, was dragging himself along the path which skirted a patch of woodland to his greenhouses. 'Damned good binge, Jack. Am I paying for it?'

'No. You're lending us your terrace.'

'Pleasure, m'boy . . . What's your mob going to do if it rains? Bit muggy tonight.'

'Muriel and the Young Farmers have made room in the stable-block.'

'Lavinia's organisation, I shouldn't wonder. Y'know your mother's wasted on horses and acting. Should take over my committees.'

'Nothing would induce her. Hasn't she given you the definition of her ideal committee?'

'Yes, come to think of it. It's a committee of two with one member permanently absent. Oh well, I dare say Dot will be asked to step into my shoes. Little woman with a lot of spunk, my wife . . . I say!' Bunny came to a halt.

Somewhere among the trees was the boundary between his land and mine. The animal that was peering from the undergrowth was definitely on his side.

'Fox?' Bunny asked himself. 'Must be a rabbit. Anyway, not a hare. Damned poacher, your man Earl, gets my hares. Don't suppose you know anything about it.'

'Earl's retired into The Close.'

'Residing in a nuthouse won't stop him. Thieving lot, the Plum-Ascots.' He stopped at the door of his newest greenhouse, took a key from his pocket and gave it to me. 'Unlock it for me; there's a good chap.'

While I dealt with the outsized padlock he held on to the door-frame and his stick. He was out of breath. The walk had exhausted him. I hoped he wouldn't have to be carried back to the house; he'd hate it.

'Damned piles,' he muttered. 'Goat's milk isn't helping any.'

'I think you should go to bed.'

'Not a bad idea.' He switched on the light and shuffled into the greenhouse. 'Well, what do you say?' His eyes went bright with excitement. 'Ever seen anything like it?'

On the slatted shelves stood the most exotic collection of chrysanthemums I'd ever seen. Most of them were not yet in bloom, but the few flowers which had opened were of unusual colours and shapes – shades of dark lilac, coral red and cream; petals narrow, almost spidery, and splayed out in beautifully delicate shapes.

'They're fantastic.' I meant it.

Bunny chuckled. 'Can tell you this . . . they're a damned sight better than their Japanese ancestors. Japan . . . that's where I got them. Didn't pay for them either. Reckoned the Japs owed me. Didn't get within miles of them when I was a prisoner, not even when they repatriated me. Went back to Japan fifteen

121

years later. Did all the best gardens. Developed the plants . . . the colours.'

'They'd surely get the first prize at the Royal Horticultural Show.'

'Dayton's good enough for me.' He gazed at a plant of perfect shape. 'I'll have this honey ready for the show – blooms open – if it's the last thing I do.'

'Better start treatment,' I thought aloud.

'What? Got a new wonder-drug for me?'

'Nothing like that. Blood transfusions would put energy into you.'

'It's the anaemia, is it? Admit I'm feeling damned tired. Sometimes bothered about going to sleep, in case I don't wake up again. Will a blood transfusion do the trick?'

'It'll help. You might need more than one transfusion.'

'Fair enough . . . leave it to you, m'boy. You know, if my chrysanths go to the top of the pops it'll be one in the eye for Dot. Great little woman, but if she'd had her way I'd have grown nothing but vegetables. Cabbages, indeed! That's what Plum-Ascot grew before he stole my plants . . . I say; sure I'm not paying for the binge on the terrace? Lot of tax on hooch these days.'

Dot made her way through the dancing couples, the goat Cordelia following her like a dog. 'Silly old idiot.' She stared at a dimly lit window above the terrace. 'Weak as a pup, but he won't go to bed.'

'Not to worry, mums,' boomed Muriel. 'I've wrapped him in a blanket.'

'Do you know what he's up to?' Dot asked me. 'Believe it or not, he's set up his grandfather's old ship's telescope to watch us.'

'No harm in it,' I tried to reassure her. 'Let him enjoy the party.'

'Party, my eye! Jack, Bunny's policing the Plum-Ascots from up there . . . with a shotgun beside his chair.'

122

'Where are they?'

'They've just arrived. He said they'd come. If Plum-Ascot moves one inch beyond the rosebed Bunny'll pepper him. Would you have a word with them, Jack? You'll be more tactful than me.'

'Tact,' snorted Muriel, 'Tact's lost on tricky Dickie. Tell him straight . . . if he goes anywhere near the greenhouses there'll be bloody murder.'

I found Earl's father and Maisie at the barbecue, holding out plates for roast lamb. Tall, bony Plum-Ascot had a face as lined and hard as an old prune. Maisie, as Mrs Cherry had told me, wasn't nearly as plump as she had been when she'd served behind the bar, but the style of her towering hair-do hadn't changed. Maisie had always exhibited her state of mind by the colour of her hair – black for dissatisfaction with her lot, platinum blond for happy times. At the moment her piled-up tresses were black.

Plum-Ascot pushed his plate under Cyril's nose. 'I don't want all this fat. Give me meat.'

'It's all good English lamb,' said Cyril, peaceably, 'cooked with thyme and rosemary and . . .'

'Trouble with you is, you don't know how to cut meat. Here, give me the knife.'

I took it from Cyril. 'I'll carve.'

Maisie glared at her husband. 'I apologise for Dick. He's behaving like he was in a restaurant . . . Not used to private parties, Dr Jack; and that's not surprising, is it? Seeing the way he carries on.'

'Belt up,' snarled Plum-Ascot. 'You've got a stomach like a dustbin . . . Sorry, doctor, I have to be a bit careful about rich food.'

I took the chop off his plate and replaced it with a paper-thin sliver from the rump. 'I haven't seen you at my surgery.'

'No,' he gazed at the small portion I'd given him, realised I wasn't going to add to it, and made way for Maisie. 'I don't want to waste your time, Dr Jack. If I watch what I'm eating I manage quite well on milk of magnesia. In fact, I never worry about my health. It's

123

madam who reckons she's delicate.'

'You know I had tubercle.'

'Donkeys' years ago.'

I put a couple of chops on Maisie's plate. 'You're going to have a check-up, aren't you? Has Mrs Cherry given you an appointment?'

'She has. I'll be seeing you next week . . . if my dear husband hasn't worked me to death.'

'Delicate creatures, barmaids,' needled Plum-Ascot, 'to be handled with kid-gloves.'

'Right. It's how one's treated when one's dealing with gentlemen.' Maisie put a baked potato on her plate and marched off.

Plum-Ascot shook his head. 'We're both on edge, I suppose. It's the Horticultural Society show. We can't neglect our normal business – we're sending seeds and bulbs all over Europe – at the same time we've got to prepare for the show. As a professional nurseryman one's got to do better than the amateurs. Maisie could be a lot more help if she put her mind to it, instead of going to the hairdressers'. Says she's doing enough, keeping house and cooking, and she isn't going to run the office as well. Plenty of women nowadays who're housewives *and* business girls. Money's what she's after. Would you believe it? She wants me to pay her for the office work.'

'That seems like a good idea.'

'Pay my own wife? No way. I'm forking out enough for Earl.'

'According to Earl, his mother's legacy's paying the hospital bills.'

'It's . . . a complicated arrangement, doctor. What his mother had in mind was that Earl would go into partnership with me . . . invest his money in the business. But no, my son has his own ideas . . . like bumming around, playing the village idiot. I want him out of The Close, doctor.'

'Enjoy your supper, Mr Plum-Ascot. Find a chair.'

'I think I'll stroll around.'

'Do, but keep away from Sir Lionel's greenhouses.

124

Someone's guarding them . . . with a gun.'

'If someone had guarded them years ago, Earl might now be with his sainted mother, instead of living it up in that expensive nuthouse.'

In the centre of the terrace our guests were experimenting with the latest rave, an American dance, the *quake*. The idea was, Liz explained to me, to stay in one spot and tremorise from the soles of one's feet to the neck. It was, perhaps, not quite as hazardous to the spine as hoola-hooping but I could foresee disc trouble in the not-so-young, the over thirties.

Mary Morris, sitting at the table beside me, watched – her mobile eyebrows flickering with amusement. 'Whoever started this in Dayton?'

'Charlie Wellington,' I guessed.

'But he's Canadian.'

'He says he's American-orientated.'

'Never mind, he's a nice boy. I'll always remember how kind he was to his grandfather . . . Mr Wellington was such a lonely old man until Charlie turned up and gave him fun.'

Charlie had given him more than that. Unlike Mr Wellington's son, who hadn't written to his father in years, the grandson had arrived from Canada in search of his *roots*. He'd created a job for himself in London, settled in Dayton, married Maggie Donaldson – Dayton's most spirited one-parent family, and taken Mr Wellington out of the old people's home. Mr Wellington had spent a happy last year with the young people in the house he'd bought them with his life's savings.

Maggie, quaking away to the beat of drums, was in the last stages of pregnancy. Her circumference was vast. Her second fatherless child had almost been born in my surgery. I hoped the third, legitimate infant wouldn't enter the world on Bunny's terrace. Obviously no such thought had entered Charlie's mind. Dressed in stretch jeans, a shirt with a peacocks pattern and a formal black tie, he was quaking all around Maggie like a courting live peacock.

Mary was smiling. 'What a character he is! So un-inhibited compared to my son.'

'We were expecting Ken. Where is he?'

'I don't ask questions, but I expect Ken's with one of his girlfriends. When he's got a new flame I don't see much of him. Luckily these involvements are short-lived.'

'Luckily?' I asked.

'Well . . . yes. This time, he says, he wants to marry the girl.' Mary's pretence at feeling unconcerned was not successful.

'Do you know her?'

'Oh yes. Who doesn't know all about Pippa.'

'I know her, Mrs Morris, and I think that she's shown a lot of guts and character.'

'Because she refused to have Pip adopted? That doesn't mean much nowadays . . . with a social service eager to take responsibility for unwanted children . . .'

'Pip is not unwanted. His father was someone Pippa decided to do without.'

'Wasn't that irresponsible of Pippa?'

'No.' I thought of my father's opinion of Mary Morris's ill-fated marriage, her efforts at hiding the fact that her daughter was conceived out of wedlock. 'There's nothing new about sex outside marriage, Mrs Morris. The only difference about past and present is that girls like Maggie Wellington and Pippa don't try to conceal the results.'

I saw Mary stiffen, yet in a moment she had herself in hand. 'I have nothing against Pippa. I just don't want her to take Ken too seriously . . . for her own good. At Ken's age boys get hooked on every girl they meet. He knew quite a few when he was at college; they still phone.'

'There's something you haven't said, Mrs Morris.'

Her eyebrows jumped. 'What's that?'

'*I never interfere in my son's affairs.*'

'But I do.' She smiled. 'I suggested how he should deal with Len Kirby. Believe me, my son was furious.

126

The very idea of attacking someone from behind! Len did write a sort of apology . . . but it wasn't very convincing . . .'

'So you advised Ken to help the Kirbys.'

'I thought it best.'

'Are you sure your plan hasn't misfired? Len might be embarrassed at being beholden to someone he falsely accused. And embarrassment isn't the best foundation for good neighbourliness.'

'Maybe not. But I've known Len most of his life. He's got a temper, but he isn't mean. And April's been on our side. Anyway . . . I'll tell you the latest. April's told Len who did his work while he was laid up. My son didn't expect thanks, and he didn't get any. But Len now passes the time of day with Ken, and the two of them have got as far as speculating whether or not there's going to be a night-frost.'

'That's progress.'

'There's more to come, doctor. You know our blue cupressus . . . the trees we planted to keep the sou'wester off the orchard?'

'Yes.'

'Well, they've shot up in the past couple of years. I mentioned it to April . . . said I'd like about six feet of the centres cut out. I thought she might offer to lend us Len's tree-shears, but she didn't say a word. Yesterday I went down to pick up the windfalls, and there was Len knee-deep in cupressus tops. He's made a lovely job of it. Do you know what he said when I thanked him? Our trees were spoiling his view and he didn't think a college boy like my son would know how to cut the cupressus without ruining their shape.'

Liz and I joined in the most dangerous of the dances – the charleston, dangerous because it required navigational skills to avoid kicks from flying heels, but a lot of fun. Oldies, such as Colonel and Mrs Maverick, were dancing like professionals, giving the impression of speed and liveliness without really exerting themselves. Then there was Lavinia – who'd learned the charleston from her father – and the mob she'd taught, which included Liz and me. We certainly were exerting ourselves. Most lethal of the dancers were those who'd never heard of the charleston and were doing their own thing – Charlie and Maggie, and the disco brigade.

Liz said, 'Maggie's going to have twins.'

'Great,' I saw Charlie swing her round and round under his arm, 'provided she doesn't drop them here.' Maggie was my senior partner's patient and I had no wish to intervene.

'Wonder where Charlie gets his shirts.'

'I reckon the peacocks are out of his Canadian-American-orientated past.'

'They're super . . . I suppose you can get that sort of thing in London.'

'Liz, if you buy me a shirt like Charlie's I'll divorce you.'

'Your clothes are too conservative, Jack.'

'That's how my patients like me.'

'You could wear something more exciting at home.'

'Kinky.'

'Nothing of the kind.'

'Puritan.'

'Stockton-on-Tees.' Liz laughed. 'My folk will have naught to do with fancy shirts and kinky ideas . . . maybe that's why I wouldn't mind you in Charlie-style gear.'

'Not having it.'

'All right, all right, I'll knit you a grey sweater for Christmas.' The music had stopped and Liz detached herself. 'I'd better ask Cyril to put on something slow – for Maggie's sake, and yours.'

On the way back to our table Charlie stopped me. 'Great party, doc. It kinda scales down the stress.'

'You're not worrying about Maggie, are you?'

'No. She's earthy. Maggie feels real good when she's pregnant.' Charlie gazed into the dark trees beyond the terrace. 'The stress situation's connected with my work. The redundancies are escalating. I didn't figure it would happen in the civil service.'

'You haven't been made redundant, have you?'

'No, though it could happen any day.'

'But you have . . .' I almost said *invented*, 'built up a department from scratch.'

'Sure, but the Prime Minister's getting kinda tough on the information services. My Minister says she's ordered cut-backs. I guess APES is right on the elimination line.'

'APES?'

'Yeah . . . the *Anti Pollution Education Section*. I've been thinking, doc, Should I reconstitute the format? Say I retitle it DECENT. The P.M. would like that. It's a concept she's really hooked on. She's always talking of ordinary decent people; that's the kind who vote for her.'

'What does DECENT mean in *your* . . . field of work?'

'Isn't it obvious? Well . . . I guess it isn't your line of business. DECENT stands for *Department of the Environment, Conservation, Energy and Nutritional Trials*. The government's keen on people keeping fit, on account of saving Health Service money. And *Trials* implies research. The P.M. respects research. Of course I'd have to recast the teasers; you know, the information flashes we put on television – like the government warnings; *he'd be alive now if he'd given up cigarettes* . . . Sir John played a great corpse. Or, *check your shoes, check your tyres. Banana skins aren't funny and death is so permanent.* We hired the best stuntman in the business for that one.'

'Perhaps you've been spending too much on your television advertising.'

'Yeah. I've been thinking more in terms of cost-effectiveness. Doc, your party's super; I'm feeling real creative. Well, as I was saying, my new teasers would be a lot cheaper. How's this? *Save hot water, save energy. You don't need hankies, but if you use tissues always carry a plastic disposal bag.* Yeah, that's good.

It covers expenditure right across the board . . . health-hygiene to savings on street-cleaning. Or, *germs attack in the most unlikely places; so don't wear your tights or Y-fronts more than once*. Get it, doc?'

'A plug for tights and Y-fronts manufacturers?'

'I'm not in commercials.' Charlie looked hurt. 'I'm concerned with an energy-health-hygiene boost for the manufacturing industries – without a government subsidy – which would create new jobs . . . Okay, doc, I'm not kidding. Fact is, I'm preparing for the worst. I've applied for another couple of secretaries . . .'

'Surely that would increase the cost of your department.'

'Yeah, but if I get them I'll have enough staff for a cut-back. Secondly – in case I'm made redundant – we've let a couple of rooms at the going rate.'

'To Maggie's sister?'

'Right. And her boyfriend. Sybil and Jasper can afford the rent. They're in public relations.'

'I've met your sister-in-law.'

'Sure. Maggie told her to see you. Now Sybil's got it all together. She's pregnant . . . Hey! I've just thought of another DECENT imager for television. But I'll have to think some more about it . . . in case there's too much of a counter-productive element in it. There's a major factor I mustn't lose sight of; the Prime Minister's dead against what she calls *pampering the British people*. My Minister told me how she put it: *I do believe in individual private enterprise. People simply must learn to become responsible for themselves. I feel very strongly that our civil servants must not be called upon to wipe their bottoms for them.*'

'Strong words.'

'Yeah . . . Look here, doc, I'll talk to you later.' Charlie turned and made a beeline for Sir Frederick Ambler, who was something in a Royal Commission on something.

'Got him into bed, the old fool,' said Dot.

We were walking up the wide oak stairs side by side. 'First this party caper . . . Oh, don't worry, Jack; Bunny was dead keen on Lavinia having the party here. Nothing like a crowd to make him feel in top form. What's done him in is sitting at the telescope for hours, all set to shoot at anyone going near the greenhouses.'

'He wouldn't have done it.'

'Well, if he had hit someone it would have been the most unlikely accident. If nothing else, Bunny's a good shot . . . Sorry to bother you, Jack, but when Muriel took up his supper she found him more dead than alive.'

'Was he conscious?'

'You bet. Just too weak to move out of his chair, not that he wanted to. Thank God my daughter can handle him. She won't stand any nonsense.' Dot led me into the bedroom.

Muriel, who was sitting beside her father, had managed to get him into pyjamas. 'He's alive all right,' she announced, 'though not kicking any more. Jack, what are we going to do with him?'

'Get him into hospital tomorrow.'

'He'll die,' said Dot.

'I've already told him that he needs a blood transfusion. He's accepted it. He won't mind going into a day-bed.'

'What did he say to you?' asked Muriel.

'*Fair enough*. He means to have that cup for his chrysanthemums. I'll arrange for an ambulance to pick him up in the morning and bring him back a few hours later.'

Bunny didn't wake up when I took his wrist. His pulse was soft and rapid. I decided to ask Helena Tate for packed cells rather than ordinary blood for Bunny's transfusion. I'd have to avoid pumping in surplus fluid, which would overload Bunny's heart. Packed cells, blood from which some of the fluid had been removed, would be safer – though even the best treatment couldn't be better than a stopgap.

131

'Will it be all right to give him breakfast?' asked Dot.

'Yes.'

'Goat's milk.'

'Why not give him whatever he likes?'

'Goat's milk's good for him – he thinks – because he hates it. If I suddenly gave him what he likes he'd believe that he's seriously ill.'

Bunny opened one eye. It scrutinised each of us in turn, then wandered. 'What's the time?'

'Past midnight,' Dot told him.

'Why aren't you in bed?'

'The party isn't over yet.'

'Party!' Bunny raised his head. 'Damned nearly forgot.' He moved feebly to the edge of the bed. 'Plum-Ascot . . .'

'Daddy,' Muriel put a big hand on her father's shoulder. 'The Plum-Ascots went ages ago. Lie down and go to sleep.'

Bunny lay back on the pillows. 'Claudine . . .' His head rolled restlessly from side to side. 'Claudine . . . must see her . . . must . . .'

Back on the terrace, Lavinia was watching our guests dance the last waltz. She didn't like slow music; dancing to it – she maintained – made her leg muscles ache because it made her put the brakes on. The effect was the same as driving a car at speed and slamming on the brakes – unpleasant.

'Darling,' she linked arms with me, 'it worked. Are you pleased?'

'Thanks for all you've done. I am pleased. What worked?'

'Everything. Darling, perhaps you should go private.'

'I'm the wrong type for private patients.'

'But you behave like a doctor who collects nice fat fees.'

'Hope I don't.'

'Take this party, darling. It'll cost you a bomb.

132

Your Health Service patients won't pay for it.'

'Never mind. Any GP can afford a party once in a while.'

'As a last resort. Your father always regarded parties as a last resort . . . when he simply didn't have a clue what his patients were suffering from. He used to say, *let's put them under the microscope*. So we invited them and jammed them close together. My cooking was a waste; at the end of the evening your father didn't know what he'd eaten . . . he was so busy watching his *specimen*. The method worked, for him.'

'Lavinia, what is it that worked tonight?'

'You missed a few things. You spent too much time on the supporting cast.'

'Bunny?'

'No, Charlie for one. Darling, Joclyn Runciman had a perfectly lovely time.'

'Good. He's new in the village . . . the idea was to introduce him to a few people.'

'I don't know about *people*. He spent the entire evening with Martha Goldstern. He doesn't just train horses for Brian Runciman. Did you know he was a publisher?'

'Yes.'

'Why didn't you tell me? Liz and I got stiff necks trying to listen to him and Martha Goldstern.'

'Give.'

Lavinia laughed. 'What's in it for me?' she mimicked a gangster's moll in a George Raft movie.

'Box of chocolates.'

'Droste from Fortnum's or nothing.'

'Okay, Droste.'

'Don't get the wrong kind . . . bitter chocolate.'

'You're on.'

'Well . . . Joclyn once published a book with Sandor Goldstern's illustrations. He said it was Goldstern's artwork that made it a bestseller. I don't think he was just chatting up Martha. He sounded as if he meant it. Then Martha told him about the books her husband had worked on – which she wants to

133

complete . . . and a great time was had by both of them.'

'Fine. But did she eat?'

'Like a horse. No more trouble swallowing than I have. So now you know.'

'Yes, now I know . . . considering the amounts you can swallow.'

'Poor darling . . . it's a shame. But if you ate as much as I do you'd get fat.'

'Not a chance, Lavinia. The whole county feeds you. Nobody takes me to Wheeler's or The Ship or Ockenden Manor.'

'That's why you're getting married.'

'Not quite.'

'Liz is a gorgeous cook.'

'Liz is gorgeous. I'm not exactly helpless in the kitchen.'

'True. You're an improvement on your father, domestically speaking.'

'Did Martha Goldstern eat pork or lamb?'

'Both. She definitely cut, chewed and swallowed. Oh Lord! that reminds me; I promised Bunny I'd make him a game pie. Dot's such a ghastly cook. Now I'll have to do it. I must be mad.'

'What are you going to put in the pie?'

'Beef, of course . . . flavoured with bay leaves and anything else I can lay my hands on. What with Earl in purdah I just haven't got the real thing.'

'No pheasants committing suicide against your car?'

'None. Darling, you're such a marvellous driver . . . and the road to Millers Common's full of pheasants. If you . . .'

'I'm not going to hit and run, mother. My job's to cure, not to kill.'

'Beautifully put, darling . . . *cure, not kill*. But – you know – pheasants are such careless birds. No? Poor Bunny; he's painfully thin. I shouldn't have neglected Earl. I'd better visit him.'

134

Twelve

It was a typical Sussex October morning. One moment sun, as strong as footlights, setting the autumn trees ablaze and creating a vivid backdrop to farmhouses and fields; next, black clouds bowling before the sou'wester and blotting out all colour. A dangerous morning too. Driving along the road from Dayton to Millers Common I'd suddenly run into swathes of mist so dense that even the cats' eyes turned invisible.

Coming out of such a witches' cauldron, to the crest of Stoke Hill, a couple of pheasants rose from the verge and flew low and leisurely over my car, almost touching it. No doubt the birds belonged to the consortium of London businessmen who had bought the Griffin estate for the fishing and shooting. Bunny hadn't had the money to keep up such sport on his land for years, according to my father's diary.

Pop Bridger's quite a gardener. His produce, this morning, consisted of two onions, a basket of cooking apples from our neighbour's tree (they happened to hang over our fence), the last of the autumn roses, parsley (from the wild crop which is choking the flowers in the herbacious border) – and no less than seven pheasants. We don't have to worry about shot, Pop told Lavinia; the stupid birds had trapped themselves in our fruit cage. Needless to say Pop delivered his offerings during morning surgery so that I missed

the opportunity of questioning his story of the foolish
pheasants. Too late now; there is a delicious smell
emanating from the kitchen. I don't know what Lavinia
will do if Bunny carries out his threat of sacking his
gamekeeper and giving up the hatchery, though she is
no mean hunter in her own right. If I don't like her
techniques I have only myself to blame. She wanted the
dreadful old car as a wedding present, but I was crazy
to give it to her. Well, pheasant for dinner it is (I really
will have to teach her to hang birds) and – on balance –
I prefer Pop's methods of procuring such delicacies.
P.S. Just had a call from Clifford. Bunny's game-
keeper has gone to the Griffin estate and the Bunting-
Standings are definitely giving up the shoot.

I had just negotiated another patch of mist and was
turning right into the hospital's road when an out-
standingly fat pheasant, hampered by his weight, rose
slowly from the grass verge. I put my foot gently on
the accelerator. The bird was almost upon me when a
goat came capering from the undergrowth. I jammed
on the brakes. The car stopped within an inch of the
animal. I got out and confronted the goat – un-
mistakably Bunny's Cordelia. She stood still, as
shaken as I was.

Bunny must have been taken to hospital. Presumably the goat had followed the ambulance. I got the
tow-rope out of my boot and approached Cordelia,
watching those vicious horns. She was still trembling
when I slipped the rope over her head, followed me
meekly to the nearest tree and gazed at me limpidly
while I tied her to the sycamore.

At the hospital I went straight to reception and
called the police.

'Yes doctor. I've had a report in,' said Sergeant
Tripp complacently. 'Parked on a corner, weren't
you?'

'Who's been complaining?'

'Give you three guesses.'

'Mac Curran. I didn't see him.'

'He was lurking, as usual; on the other side of the

hedge. Bet he wasn't alone. He's quite a goat, is our traffic warden. And one of these days I'll catch him with his pants down. When I do . . .'

'Sergeant,' I stopped him. 'The goat would have been a traffic hazard. For all I know she's chewing through the rope right now.'

'Not to worry, sir. I'll go over in the van and take her home.'

'Watch her horns.'

'Dangerous, is she?'

'Don't know. She hasn't attacked me.'

'Right, sir. I'll put a blanket over her head. Better safe than sorry.'

'Her name's Cordelia, by the way.'

'Thank you, sir. Always easier to deal with a delinquent when you know her name.'

Helena Tate was at the bench in her laboratory. She said, 'The blood's ready for you. Shall I set up the drip?'

'Thanks, I'll do it.'

'Olive will take the stuff over for you. How is Sir Lionel?'

'Weak but determined.'

'Bless him.'

'I saw his chrysanthemums yesterday. They're quite spectacular.'

'Good enough for the Lady Corbett cup?'

'I think so.'

'More than two weeks . . . the cup within his reach, and the presidency of the Horticultural Society. Will he make it, Jack?'

'If he doesn't it won't be for want of trying. I'll keep checking his haemoglobin. If necessary I'd be prepared to give him another blood transfusion. How do you feel about it?'

'He's getting the equivalent of two pints today. He might well need the same amount before the show,' Helena speculated uneasily. 'I'll give you the blood whenever you ask for it. Let's hope his heart stands up to it.'

I was walking the long corridor to Bunny's side-room when someone in Juniper Ward called me. It was Katie, sitting in a chair, with a young nun perched on her bed.

'Doctor, look!' Katie stretched, displaying her flat stomach.

'Feeling good?'

'Super . . . It's still hurting a bit, like after I had my wisdom tooth out; but it's nothing . . . a sort of healing-up pain. Mr Chailey says I can go back to the convent next Friday.'

'You have done well.'

'It was a big cyst. Mr Chailey's going to show it to me.'

The nun laughed. 'I wouldn't want to see it. Katie has more courage than I.' Sister Claudine – it was the nun who'd been dancing with the lawn mower – took a diary from her pocket. 'What Katie would like to know is when she'll be fit to play hockey again. She's our best girl in the senior team.'

'You should ask Mr Chailey.'

'I did,' said Katie. 'He wants to see me again in a month; then he'll tell me.'

'When do you want to play?'

'She won't have to train before January,' said Sister Claudine. 'Our big match against Hillborough School is in March.' She consulted the diary, 'Eighteenth of March . . . If Katie is ready by . . . about the last week in January . . .'

'I think Mr Chailey will let you play by then.'

'Oh good! Doctor, will you come to the match?'

'Yes, if I'm invited.'

'You are,' said Sister Claudine. 'Katie will send you the details. Doctor, I heard the nurse say that Sir Lionel's in the hospital . . .'

'Only for a few hours.'

'May I see him?'

'Well . . . he's about to receive treatment.'

'I can wait.'

138

This was an unexpected embarrassment. Bunny had expressed his feelings for Claudine in no uncertain terms. Was I to give him the opportunity of seeing her? I had a vision of a headline in the *News of the World*, TITLED SCHOOL GOVERNOR IN HOSPITAL-BED WITH GAMES MISTRESS NUN. Yet such a situation was unlikely to arise, with Bunny hitched up to the transfusion machine.

'You won't be able to see him for an hour or so,' I stalled.

'I don't mind, doctor.'

'Very well, but ask the ward sister whether you may visit him.'

'What's this contraption?' asked Bunny. He looked comfortable on the high hospital bed, and more alert than the night before.

'It's a giving set.'

'Blood in the container?'

'That's right.'

'How are you going to get it into me, m'boy?'

I took up the needle attached to a fine tube. 'This'll feed into you.'

'Can't stand things in my nose.'

'It's not going into your nose.' I took his arm and rolled up his sleeve. 'The needle will go in here.' I wiped the inside of his elbow and put it into the vein.

'Where?'

'It's in, Bunny.'

'Bless m'soul . . . Fast worker, aren't you? Is the thing in my artery?'

'No, in the antecubital vein.'

'Didn't know I had one. Antecubital? Fascinating . . . What's next?'

'That's all. You lie back, relax and – in the afternoon – you go home. Tomorrow you'll be feeling more energetic.'

'Fair enough. Just like to know the mechanics of things. Always wanted to be an engineer, y'know. War messed it up. Afterwards . . . well, we couldn't bring ourselves to sell the land and old Standing Hall. Dot and I come from a long line of peasants . . . always believed that land's the best asset, no matter what the state of the world. Not true any longer. Nuclear war's likely to poison everything . . . including the soil. Glad I won't have to see it. Hear you're on the Civil Defence Committee. Load of bullshit, isn't it?'

'Just about.'

'Muriel's talking about those demonstrations against nuclear missiles. What do you make of them?'

'I'd be impressed if they were taking place in Russia.'

'Not likely.'

'Not yet. But there are murmurs even in Russia. I've just read in a medical journal that President Brezhnev's personal doctor – Yevgeny Chazov – attended an international medical meeting in Berkshire. There's now a medical organisation which is teaching people throughout the world how and why nuclear war would end life on this planet. Dr Chazov did a programme on Soviet TV which was watched by a hundred and fifty million Russians.'

'Is that what he claims?'

'It seems to be true. The programme was monitored by the Americans.' I checked the drip. The blood was going steadily into Bunny's vein. 'It's not all gloom.'

'Fly in the ointment,' said Bunny. 'What's to stop the Russians starting a nuclear war . . . then telling their people that the Yanks fired first? Know what I would do if I were a world leader? Go isolationist . . . make every country look after its own *at home*; send every Yank back to America, every Russian to Russia. See that every country grows its own food and keep trading to a minimum.'

'Hasn't it been tried?'

'What if it has? No reason why one shouldn't try twice. Thing you learn when you're developing a new strain of chrysanthemum . . . must allow for failures. Oh, I say!' Bunny pulled the sheet up to his chin, a

140

strangely self-conscious gesture.

I turned and saw Sister Claudine in the doorway.

'Sorry,' she apologised to me. 'I did ask the nurse. She said . . . she thought it would be all right for me to call on Sir Lionel.'

'Oh . . . er . . . come in, dear lady,' said Bunny. 'Wasn't expecting . . . visitors. Just staying for a few hours, y'know. How's Reverend Mother?'

'Very well; thank you Sir Lionel.'

The two of them seemed to have no more to say to one another. Sister Claudine was regarding Bunny with a sweet smile, Bunny looked as if he wanted to jump out of bed and run.

'You don't remember?' asked the nun.

'What . . . er . . . course I do. Course. Not likely to forget a thing like that.'

I thought I'd better relieve Bunny of the constraint. 'The ward sister will look in presently.' I picked up my bag and went to the door. 'I'll be seeing you at home.'

'Thank you, m'boy . . . Wonder, would you call Dot for me? Ask her to tie up Cordelia. Wretched goat's taken to following me around . . . spends half her time in the morning room. Trouble with Cordelia, dogs don't bother her any more. Real devil . . . Cordelia.'

As I walked out I saw Sister Claudine cross herself. And Bunny still looked as if he'd like to cut and run. What had happened to his dream of Claudine?

Thirteen

I recognised the child in the waiting room before I noticed his companions. Jimmy, aged seven, was Maggie Wellington's younger offspring, a souvenir of the flower-children period when Maggie had lived in a commune at Millers Common. Though he'd had a chaotic start in life, Jimmy had somehow learned to read and write at the age of five. I had treated him twice, for measles and bronchitis; each time he'd put up with the discomfort with stoic good temper.

On second thoughts I realised that the woman, dressed in pink layers and a flowing scarf, was his broody aunt, Sybil Dawn. The young man on the floor, who was making matchstick pictures with Jimmy, had to be the man she'd chosen for fathering her child.

I glanced through the telephone messages Angela had left on the consulting room desk. Nothing there that couldn't wait until after evening surgery, so I pressed the button for the waiting room light.

Jimmy came in, followed by his aunt. He put a toy house on the table. 'This is my railway station,' he announced. 'I've got trains and engines and signals and . . .'

'That'll do, Jimmy,' Miss Dawn cut him short. 'Doctor, he cut his hand on a cat-food tin. The nurse has dressed it, but she said he should have a tetanus injection.'

At the word injection Jimmy backed into the far corner of the surgery and began to cry.

'What's the matter, Jimmy,' I asked.

Jimmy's sobs turned into piercing screams.

'Don't be silly,' snapped his aunt. 'Really. Doctor . . . I don't understand it. I told him it wouldn't hurt. I warned him, if he made a fuss you'd send him to hospital and they'd cut off his hand.'

'How stupid!' I was angry and I didn't mind if it showed. 'Jimmy wouldn't have expected to get hurt if you hadn't put the idea in his head.'

'But the injection . . .'

'Children don't worry about injections. What's Jimmy going to think of hospitals, now that you've told him they cut off the hands of naughty boys?' Jimmy was paying no attention to us. He was howling, trapped in his private misery. 'Miss Dawn, most seven-year-old children are perfectly happy to go into hospital . . . they've seen it all on TV.'

'I didn't think . . .'

'Then you'd better start thinking about others, not just yourself . . . and you can begin by trying to work out how to get Jimmy to have confidence in you again. Now you can wait for him outside.'

'Sorry, doctor.' Much to my surprise the outrage in Sybil Dawn's heavily made-up eyes subsided and she meekly left the room.

'Jimmy,' I did not approach the child. He was watching me under his brows. 'Have you got a lamp for your railway station? You know, a tall lamp like the one at Millers Common.'

Jimmy sniffed and shook his head.

'I'll make one for you, but you'll have to help.'

The boy edged out of the corner, still wary.

'Remember when I came to your house?'

'You gave me a lolly.'

'That's right. Your aunt's been very silly. You know I wouldn't hurt you, don't you?'

Jimmy nodded. 'Are we going to make the lamp?'

'Yes. Come and watch.' I took out a syringe and a

143

rubber-capped vial. 'Now I'll put the needle on this syringe . . . like this . . . and then we put it into the little bottle. It's a sort of water pistol . . .'

Jimmy watched, fascinated, as I drew the liquid into the syringe.

'Let's see whether it works.' I pressed lightly on the plunger and a fine squirt of liquid shot out.

Jimmy jumped up and down. 'There's a hole in the needle.'

'That's right. It's like the barrel in a water pistol.'

'But the needle's thin. How do you make a hole in it?'

'I didn't make it. You don't make water pistols, do you? So we'll have to find out how the hole is made. I tell you what . . . let's ask your aunt to find out. And next time you see me you'll be able to tell me how it's done.'

'All right.'

'Now, I'll give your arm a little wash . . . That's it. Now . . . I'll fire the pistol.'

'It's gone in my arm.' Jimmy watched unperturbed as I pumped in the fluid.

'That's right. I can take it out now. That didn't hurt, did it?'

'Where's my lamp?'

'Here.' I gave him the plastic needle-cover which did look somewhat like a modern street light.

'Thanks.' He looked pleased. 'Can I have another one?' He picked up his railway station and held the *lamp* to it. 'There's one on this side and on that side, at Millers Common.'

'You're right. I haven't got another lamp now, but I'll get you one. I'll put it through your letter-box.'

'In an envelope?'

'All right.'

'Will you put my name on it? Then everybody will know it's *my* letter. I'm called Wellington now 'cause I've got a real dad.'

The man who'd been with Jimmy and Miss Dawn

looked ill at ease in my consulting room. He had a carefully styled Londoner's haircut, a pleasant face with a firm mouth and lively dark eyes.

'I'm here under false pretences,' he told me. 'I'm Jasper Hanbury . . . and there's nothing wrong with me . . . I wonder whether I may have a word with you about Sybil.'

'Yes.'

'We've been living together for two years. Now she's pregnant . . . I think Charlie mentioned it to you.'

'He did.'

'Sybil's been on the pill.'

'You didn't want her to get pregnant?'

'It isn't me. Sybil didn't want to give up her career . . . we're in advertising. I don't mind one way or another . . . only, now that we're expecting a child she shouldn't take it all upon herself.'

'What do you suggest?'

'I want her to marry me. She's got a lot of silly ideas about one-parent families, but I think a child needs both parents. I should know. My parents were divorced. I was eighteen before I got to know my father. Then I realised how much I'd missed. There's no reason why our child shouldn't have a more settled life.'

'I don't see how I can help you. It's something you'll have to work out with Miss Dawn.'

'What's putting her off – I'm certain – is the age difference. I'm ten years younger than her . . . Sybil will be attending your ante-natal clinics. If you could give her reasons . . . I mean, scientific and medical reasons why the age-gap's unimportant . . .'

'There are pros and cons, Mr Hanbury. If you think in terms of a whole family . . . yes, it's better for a child to have two parents, provided there are no quarrels and tensions. From your point of view, you should consider that Miss Dawn will be sixty when you are fifty. The older you both get the more you're likely to become aware of the age-gap.'

'What about Sybil's position? Won't it be good for her to have a younger husband? Sorry . . . I don't suppose you can answer that. Perhaps you can make her consider the child first. Or am I being unreasonable?'

'Up to a point. I can't act as marriage broker. But if I get an opportunity I'll certainly point out to her the advantages of a child with both parents.'

'I've been wondering . . . Maggie, Sybil's sister, used to know someone in the social services; a Miss Vivienne . . .'

'Vivienne Allen.'

'You know her?'

'Yes, our paths keep crossing.'

'Could she help?'

'In what way?'

'Maggie got sick and tired of her, before she married Charlie. On her doorstep day in, day out. I gather Miss Allen has a thing about one-parent families. Some people might consider her helpful, but Maggie didn't like being treated like Miss Allen's property . . .'

I began to see the drift of Jasper Hanbury's thoughts and they weren't by any means stupid. I could imagine Vivienne at her most Joan-of-Arc-like rushing to the aid of Miss Dawn and advertising-executive Miss Dawn's reaction to being turned into a worthy cause.

'This has got to be handled as a hard sell,' urged Jasper.

'You are to be sold in matrimony.'

'It's how I see it. And I can't do it for myself . . . not entirely. I know Sybil. She's pigheaded, but certain people do influence her . . . usually outsiders.'

'Is Miss Dawn still going to London?'

'No, she's given up work . . . She's suffering from morning sickness.'

'I suppose I could ask Vivienne Allen to call on her.'

'Doctor, I really would appreciate it. If there's anything I can do for you . . . I do a lot of promotion for

146

the new Ritz range of cars. I'm sure – if I suggested it – Ritz Company would let you have the Omega Model under a special-arrangement-discount.'

The Shastris had trooped into my surgery in force. Now the six of them had formed a group which would have looked perfect on a Victorian family photograph – Mr and Mrs Shastri sitting side by side, hands in laps; behind them their four children, arranged in a descending line. Not for the first time I wondered why the shirts of Pakistanis and Indians always looked so much better laundered than mine.

There was a remark in my father's diary about what he'd called His Majesty's exotic subjects: *My first visit to London in several months. I was struck by the unusual aspects at Victoria Station. It was crowded with families, dressed in vibrant colours and in the lightest of materials despite the winter cold. They were sitting on bundles and suitcases, trembling like beautiful butterflies which had accidentally survived the summer. They looked so lost, and yet expectant, that I felt like hiring a coach and taking them somewhere warm. But where? I also felt peculiarly guilty. What promise had England given them to make them come in such numbers? What were they expecting? How would they feel walking urban streets under grey skies?*

Mr Shastri seemed self-possessed rather than lost. He put an elegant visiting card on my desk, printed gold on black. *Mr Nanda Shastri, B.Sc.Econ. Belfast (failed). The Shastri Chain of Restaurants, London Road, Millers Common, Sussex.*

'I have now introduced myself to you, doctor,' he stated.

'Thank you.'

'My family and I have taken up residence with my cousin, the owner of restaurants. According to proper regulations we have registered with you . . . to give you the opportunity to look after our health, as required by Dr Patrick Low, the Community Physician.'

'Thank you, Mr Shastri.'

'I wish to lodge a complaint, doctor.'

'Yes?'

'My eldest son, Kumar is a very good boy . . . a clean boy. Do you not agree?'

'I'm sure he is.'

'Please look at him. You behold a blemish on his right cheek.'

'A pimple, Mr Shastri. How old are you, Kumar?'

'Fifteen years and three months, doctor.'

'Do you know what puberty is?'

'The interval,' answered his father, 'between boy and manhood.'

'That's right. During . . . this interval it's perfectly normal for boys to develop spots.'

Mr Shastri shook his head. 'Far be it from me to dispute your learning, doctor, but in Pakistan no member of my family displays pimples. I too have learning . . . I have attended a famous university and it is my considered conviction that the blemish on my son is due to the undesirability of our accommodation.'

'Mr Shastri . . .' I knew what he was leading up to.

'Please,' Mr Shastri raised his hand, 'may I complete my in-depth researched observations. It showed proper family spirit that my cousin – the owner of the Shastri chain of restaurants – imported us from Pakistan. For this my family and I work sixteen hours a day; that too shows proper family feeling. But it is not proper that we have only one room to live in. My cousin – the owner of the Shastri chain of restaurants – quite agrees. He has advised me to adopt the proper procedure . . . my son has a pimple, you write a certificate and we are given a council house with a garden and three bedrooms.'

'Sorry, Mr Shastri, it's out of the question. According to Dr Low's report you and your family are in good health and . . .'

'My eldest son is blemished . . .'

'And there is a shortage of council houses. There

148

are many families who have waited for years . . .'

'Doctor,' Mr Shastri leaned forward confidentially. 'There are six very fine new council houses in Laburnum Road. They are empty . . .'

'They won't be empty for long . . .'

Shastri turned to his wife. 'Pushpam, take the children out. The doctor and I have a matter to discuss in confidence.'

'I can't justify . . .' My protest was lost in the exodus of the tribe.

Left alone with me, Mr Shastri approached my desk. By some slight of hand he produced a small red flannel bag which he emptied into his palm. 'Doctor, these coins are pure South African gold. I will give them to you with very good grace in exchange for the certificate.'

'Sorry, Mr Shastri. Your cousin should have told you that things don't work like this in England.'

'My cousin said that in England one can trade, as one can do business in the whole world. Doctor, my wife Pushpam would be very happy with number one in Laburnum Road. The lady social-service would be very happy for my wife and children to have the number one Laburnum Road.'

'You have spoken to Miss Allen?'

'Miss Allen called upon us and explained the importance of the certificate.'

I knew now why Vivienne was hanging around the reception desk. 'I'll speak to Miss Allen.'

'You're displeased?' Mr Shastri had picked up my tone. 'But, please, it is all very uncomplicated. You take the gold as a token of my esteem . . . not payment, you understand. I tell you, as a Belfast economist, that gold goes up and down but not as up and down as poor dirty pound notes . . .'

'Let me give you some advice, Mr Shastri. Use your gold as down-payment on a house . . . a house on the commercial market. If you don't have enough, tell your cousin to show proper family spirit and lend you more. Then get a loan from a building society . . . a

149

mortgage. If it's any comfort to you, the majority of house-owners have mortgages. I have a mortgage.'

'You, doctor?' Shastri looked astonished. 'You have a medical degree?'

'Of course.'

'You did not fail your final examinations?'

'No.'

'Then why did you have to borrow money to buy your house?' He shook his head in sorrow. 'The English economy must be wrong. Perhaps you should go and work in Pakistan . . . where proper doctors don't have to borrow for a house. You could rent a council house perhaps?'

'I wouldn't get it. I don't earn enough to buy a house outright, but too much to get a council house.'

'I am sad for you, doctor.'

'I'm not complaining . . . Just trying to explain to you why I can't give you the certificate you want.'

'You'd lose your position if you gave me the certificate?'

'I'd certainly deserve to lose it.'

'My cousin did not properly explain to me the economic ins and outs.' Mr Shastri looked thoughtful. 'Doctor, is there an Indian restaurant in Dayton?'

'No.'

'You know this nice village very well?'

'I think so.'

'My cousin, who owns the Shastri chain of restaurants, is not the only Shastri who can cook. A family man like me should work for himself perhaps . . . Doctor, do you have a fish and chips business in Dayton?'

'No.'

'You know this nice village very well indeed?'

'Yes.'

'Ah! so you know all . . . You are good friends with everybody. Very excellent. I think, doctor, I will proposition you . . . Yes, I will think economics, and then you and I will do good business together . . . I am

150

happy to know you, as my cousin in New York always says.'

'Look at it, Dr Jack!'
Maisie Plum-Ascot gave me no option. Her net-stockings were down, her head – with its tall edifice of black curls – bent mournfully over shapely but muscular legs.

'See them bruises?' she demanded.
'Blotches.'
'What?'
'They don't look like bruises to me, Maisie.'
'I'm black and blue, I am.'
'Red and blue would be more accurate.'
'What's the difference then?'
'Just trying to find out what caused the marks.'
'What do you think? Him . . . Richard Plum-Ascot esquire.' A whiff of whisky travelled from her frosted-pink lips to my nose.

'What did he do to you?' I asked.
'He's always pushing me around.'
'He couldn't have made these marks without tying up your shins and hanging you from the ceiling upside down.'

'Go on!' She almost giggled. 'Give me a certificate.'
'What for?'
'Well, I want it in writing don't I? I got to have *something* to make him pay me the rate for the job. All the office work I'm doing for him . . . beside acting as secretary to the horticultural show for free. *I'll get my wife to do it*, said his nibs. Didn't even ask me. When he told me about the office work - after we was married – I said to him I'd do it if he paid me the rate for the job. Three or four thousand's what part-time secretaries get now. It's not true that I'm not trained. You know, I wasn't a barmaid . . . My job-description was bar-manageress.'

'Maisie, I can't give you a certificate to make your husband pay. Be honest now. When did you first notice these marks?'

'Must be about a week ago . . . Dr Jack, I'm not as strong as I look. I had TB, you know.'

'I do know. That's why Mrs Cherry arranged for you to have X-rays. There's no sign of TB now.'

'I'm not strong,' Maisie insisted, 'Not really.'

'Have you had a sore throat recently?'

'My throat was awful,' she assured me. 'Cough, cough, day and night. I couldn't hardly swallow.'

'Why didn't you let me know?'

'Well . . . it was only a cough.'

'I see.'

'It was bad, mind you.'

The chances were that Maisie's sore throat had been due to a streptococcus which had caused erythema nodosum – the blotches on her shins. It would be as well to take a blood sample and see whether the hospital laboratory could find strep-tococci.

'What's my throat got to do with my legs?' She watched me draw her blood into a syringe.

'If you have an infection it can show up in different parts of your body.'

'You going to give me some cream for me legs then?'

'No. The marks will go without treatment.'

'What am I going to say to his nibs? He won't believe I've got something wrong with me if you don't give me a tonic or something. I mean, he's got to know that I'm not all that strong . . . and if he wants me to do all this extra work he's got to pay for it. I mean, he could be my father.'

'You married him.'

'Well, he was lonely – the bastard. But what's in it for me? now that he's spending all this money on Earl's hospital bills. Like Vivienne says . . . I'm en-titled to *something*.'

I'd had enough of the social service who was un-doubtedly still hanging around reception. I called Angela, who confirmed it, and asked her to send Vivienne in. She appeared, tottering on tiny heels – which were her acknowledgement of fashion. The rest

152

of her, enveloped in dingy quilted cotton, looked as scruffy as ever.

'May I ask what you've been doing at the Health Centre all day?' I asked her.

She tossed her greasy hair. 'Gathering data . . . since you have failed in giving me the information I require . . . When a disadvantaged family arrives in the country I'd expect you to . . .'

'I'd expect *you* to use some discretion. Here we don't discuss one patient in front of another. However, I'll say this; the family I've just seen is healthy and far from disadvantaged. I'm sure the father will soon have a flourishing business, not a hundred miles from here . . . What I wanted to see you about is Mrs Plum-Ascot. You've told her that she's entitled to something?'

'That's right.' Maisie nodded contentedly.

'Well . . .' Vivienne faltered, 'my department does have a small budget for battered wives . . .'

'You see.' Maisie rolled up a net-stocking and hitched it on to a scarlet suspender. 'Like I said.'

'Let me get this straight, Miss Allen. You pay out money to women whose husbands knock them about?'

'Not really. What I suggested to Maisie was that she should make her husband pay for the office work. She's entitled to it.'

'Legally?'

'Well . . . no. But she could sue her husband.'

'Hey!' Maisie turned on her. 'I don't need you to tell me that. I thought *you* could get me something on account of him bashing me.'

'We've got a house for battered wives. I could get you in there if . . .'

'Me, mucking in with all *them* girls! And what's going to happen to my husband?'

'You've got to leave him, of course.'

'Leave Dickie! Not bloody likely.'

'He beat you up,' pleaded Vivienne. 'Wives must preserve *some* human dignity.'

153

'You bet. Last time he lost his temper with me his face wasn't a pretty sight, I can tell you. He didn't go out for two weeks . . .'

'Maisie, you shouldn't talk like that,' warned Vivienne.

'Why ever not? I've got dignity all right. If the bastard raises his hand to me again I'll kill him.'

'You'd be better off without him.'

'Who says?' Maisie had fixed her other stocking. She pulled down her skirt, fastened her coat and marched to the door. 'Thanks Dr Jack . . . And you, Miss Allen, I'll tell you straight: If you can't get my old man to pay me the rate for the job, and you can't even get me money for being a battered wife, I don't need nothing from you. My husband and I don't mind Mrs Cherry dropping in for a cup of tea, but I don't want you interfering between Dickie and me.' She walked out, piled curls held high.

I felt almost sorry for Vivienne, who'd slumped into the armchair and was contemplating her shoes. 'If only I was given the resources,' she complained. 'There are so many people who need looking after . . .'

'Not by the state. As you've heard, Maisie refuses to be classified *battered wife*.'

'Did she show you her legs?'

'Obviously. The marks are not due to ill treatment.'

'But she said her husband . . .'

'She has an overdeveloped imagination. Never mind. I've got something for you.'

'A case?' Vivienne unwilted herself.

'Let's say a potential case . . . though I doubt whether it'll turn out satisfactory from your point of view, for your survey.'

'What is it?' Now she was sitting bolt upright.

'An unmarried mother-to-be.'

'Who, doctor?'

'You may have seen her around the village . . . Maggie Wellington's sister, a Miss Sybil Dawn.'

'Pregnant? How incredible! She looks such a smart

154

woman.'

'She is, I believe. She's just had to give up her job. She was an advertising executive.'

'Can I see her notes?'

'I have no notes on her yet. All I can tell you at the moment is that she's unmarried, about eight weeks pregnant, and that she's living with the Wellingtons at the moment. I understand she's looking for a cottage to buy.'

'So she's got money.' Vivienne sounded almost disappointed.

'I'm sure she has some money.'

'Never mind. One-parent families usually have more than one problem . . . Thanks for the information anyway. Oh . . . there's one other thing. I spent an awful lot of time trying to find a psychiatric unit for Earl. Do you remember? He badly wanted to be admitted, and no one would have him . . . not even when he appeared in church in the altogether.'

'Sure I remember. He's in The Close now, as you probably know . . . in a private room.'

'Would you mind if I went to see him?'

'You'll have to ask Dr Bradley, who's looking after him. Why do you want to see him?'

'I wonder whether I couldn't have him transferred to a Health Service bed. Private beds are so expensive. Earl won't have any money left if he stays for some time.'

'Then he'll have to earn a living, won't he?'

'He's never held down a job for long . . . not even with you. I'm sure you made allowances for his difficulties.'

'He hasn't left the Old Mill. He's just . . . resting.'

'I know he's quite handy, but what's the use if he can't concentrate on work for more than a few weeks?'

'Earl's my cross, Miss Allen. But he's improved. I'm beginning to understand his case.'

'Then why did he finish up on the church spire?'

'An episode. I expect there'll be more before he

settles down.'

'You take this kind of thing much too calmly. I'm going to discuss the matter with Dr Bradley.'

'You do that. But don't forget the unmarried mother. By the way, she's living with her boyfriend.'

'Men,' snorted Vivienne. 'Irresponsible; every one of them.'

Fourteen

Though the windows of my surgery were closed I heard my mother's whistle loud and clear. I'd never seen Lavinia do it, but I guessed that she produced this penetrating noise by putting her fingers in her mouth. I dived for the side door where I found her mounted on Tommyrot.

'Good,' she looked gratified, 'you heard me.'

'So did the combined staff of the Health Centre. Where's the fire?'

'At The Close, I think.'

'You've seen Earl?'

'Yes . . . and Dr Bradley. It's a puzzlement, Jack. Apparently Earl was extremely depressed until recently. So, naturally, Dr Bradley barred him from the pool . . . in case he was a potential suicide. Suddenly, a few days ago, Earl changed completely. He certainly struck me as placid . . . almost happy. I warned Dr Bradley; there's something fishy about it.'

'What was his reaction?'

'That Earl's improving. But he doesn't know Earl as well as I do. I told Bradley the boy's up to no good.'

'What did Earl have to say for himself?'

'He admits that he's missing his log cabin and the Old Mill, but he doesn't want to leave The Close. That's the trouble; you do see, don't you? The pie I made for Bunny – I put in plenty of beef and spices – was just not good enough. Bunny did no more than taste it; and he told Dot that pheasants aren't what they used to be . . . *if* I had put in pheasants. Bunny's become terribly hard to please . . .'

'He's a very sick man.'

'I know. Dot's having an awful job feeding him. Darling, I simply must make him the real thing. And I've got to make a pie for the raffle.'

'Which one?'

'Don't say you've forgotten! When have I not made a game pie for the horticultural show? The society relies on the proceeds.'

'Lavinia, Earl can't be the only procurer of pheasants. Why don't you try the Griffin estate?'

'Darling, don't you think I've tried? I even let Norman Griffin take me out to dinner. It's no good. The birds left over from his shoot go to London. And I'm damned if I'll buy our local pheasants in town . . . at Harrods prices.'

'I see your point.'

'I'd be gravely disturbed, as Billy Whitelaw'd say, if you didn't see my point.'

'You know, I almost hit a pheasant on my way to the hospital.'

Lavinia frowned, 'What happened?'

'Bunny's goat intervened.'

'Pity.'

'It wasn't. I'm not going to butcher birds for you or anyone else.'

'It's not the ideal way,' Lavinia agreed mildly. 'It tends to bruise them rather badly . . . though if you use them in a pie it doesn't really matter.'

'Have you no conscience!'

'Too much conscience, darling . . . That's why I'm worried about the damned pies.'

'I suppose you've come here – trampling our grass – for a purpose. What do you want me to do?'

'That's my boy! I don't want you to do anything criminal or revolutionary, darling. Just go to The Close.'

'Is that all?'

'Well it's not just a matter of visiting Earl. I had a chat with one or two people on the staff . . . just to get some idea of the routines. There's one period when the private patients are virtually unsupervised . . . before dinner, between six and seven. That would be the best time for you to go. And you'd better go to the pool first.'

'Why?'

'Just a hunch, darling.' Tommyrot was getting restive and Lavinia patted his neck. 'One other thing, Jack . . . About the raffle. Will you be seeing Martha Goldstern?'

'Yes.'

'Good. Try and get a nice painting out of her. It would make people spend real money on tickets. I read that Goldstern's birds and flowers – originals that is – are becoming quite valuable.'

It was about a quarter past six when I drove into the grounds of the county's major psychiatric hospital. I left the car in the doctors' parking lot and walked to the pool. The glass and oak structure, which included table tennis and snooker rooms, provided by the League of Hospital Friends, lay in darkness, except for a pearly blue night-watchman's light.

After a while my eyes adjusted to the dim glow and I was able to survey the pool area. It looked as deserted as I'd expected until I became aware that the water was not entirely still. Presently a shape broke the surface, as elegantly and smoothly as a playful seal. It dived again, swam under water the length of the pool, turned and rose in a perfect butterfly stroke. Who else but Earl?

I walked all round the building, checking windows and doors, without discovering how Earl had managed to get in. Clearly he'd found some way of laying his hands on a key. But for my mother's remarkable shrewdness, Earl might have remained undetected for a very long time.

I watched him for half an hour or more before he

came out of the water, rubbed himself down and put on his clothes. By the time he reached the service door at the back I was waiting for him. I let him lock the door on the outside before I grabbed him by the arm. I immediately regretted it. Earl began to shake, and it wasn't from the cold.

'What's Dr Bradley going to say?' I asked him.

'It's you, doc.' He breathed an audible sigh of relief, but he was still trembling with shock. 'You wouldn't tell him . . . would you?'

'Why not. You've broken the rules. In a mental institution the rules have to be strictly enforced, as you should know.'

'I haven't done any damage. I haven't.'

'That's beside the point.'

'Doc . . . look . . . I need to swim. If I swim every day I'm no trouble. It's the only thing I've got.'

It was sad that the combined medical services hadn't realised before that Earl's passion for water was, in fact, all he had . . . apart from drinking bottles of milk. His mother, the one person close to him, had died; his father had always despised him; and the village had treated him as the local idiot and taken it for granted that he was an unpredictable layabout. Yet Earl, when he did not feel lethargic, had skills in the country crafts – as Lavinia had recognised – apart from poaching.

'Let's work something out,' I suggested. 'Wouldn't you like to be back in your own home, Earl?'

'Yes . . . but the pond's too dirty. And, come winter, I can't swim in it anyroad. It's too cold.'

'There's a perfectly good public indoor pool at Millers Common.'

'Doc, it's three miles from the Old Mill. There are no buses any more. If I had a motor-bike I'd go around noon . . . that's when it's quiet . . . no kids. I used to have a Vespa.'

'What happened to it?'

'Wore out. I'd like a new motor-bike, but the old devil won't give me the money.'

160

'So you're wasting money on a private room here, where you're not even allowed to use the pool.'

'I'm using it, aren't I?'

'Dr Bradley will put a stop to that, I promise you.'

'You won't tell him?' Earl sounded desperate. 'You can't, doc. Mrs Mason and you . . . you're the only ones that haven't got it in for me.'

'Nobody's got it in for you, unless you behave like a hooligan.'

'I haven't behaved like a hooligan with you or your mother, have I? Look here, doc . . . I get bored here. I'd rather be home. There's always things to do, like watching hares, grouse, pheasants . . .'

'Watching, you call it?'

'You've got to watch or you never get near them,' he said ingenuously. 'Your mother wants me to go home. She said it . . . Now you've given me an idea, doc; I'll leave The Close tomorrow if the old devil gives me a cheque for a motor-bike.'

'I suppose you want me to haggle with him.'

'There's no other way, doc. My father's got a head for business. A bike . . . no, I'd rather have a car . . . will cost him less of my mum's money than if I stay on at The Close. Will you tell him?'

'First, let's get things straight. How did you get into the pool?'

'With a key.'

'How did you get it?'

'I paid good money for it.'

'Come on, Earl.'

'It's true, doc. I asked a nurse to buy a honeycomb for me. Then I made an impression of the key. Then I got Allister to have a duplicate made.'

'Who's Allister?'

'A nutter,' said Earl pityingly. 'Nice enough chap, but he's as crazy as a coot. Harmless though. Dr Bradley lets him go to Brighton once a week . . . it's part of his treatment. You see, Allister has no self-confidence; it makes him talk all the time, whether there's anyone around or not. It's girls he's talking about; he's a nutter all right.'

'Unlike you, Earl.'

'Well, you know I'm different. I couldn't see the point of going to a university or into the army, or into a polytechnic, or make a business out of our land just because I'm a Plum-Ascot. What for? If I want to know how to do a job I go to the public library and get out some books.'

It was perfectly true that Earl, with the help of the scouts, had built his house on my land from what he'd learned by reading . . . built it well enough to pass building regulations. An eccentric he was, but not a fool.

'Doc,' he was accompanying me to the car park. 'I've been reading books on swimming pool construction . . . I've been thinking . . .'

'Oh no!'

'There's plenty of water at the Old Mill. We have the pond, and the stream. All we'd need is . . .'

'Money, which I can't afford.'

'Doc, labour's the expensive part. And when you've got me . . .'

'Materials aren't cheap either. As to you, Earl . . . I've had you for quite a while. When you don't feel like work you announce that you've lost your *work-application*, and that's the end of . . .'

'That's because I had nowhere to swim.'

'You used the pond all summer.'

'Mud-baths, that's what I had. I don't call that swimming. I need a pool I can use all the year round, doc . . . I really do.'

'All right, I'll have a word with your father.'

'He'll say that I need a driving licence . . . Don't let the old devil fool you. I've got one that covers cars . . . and I've kept it up to date . . . Building a covered pool for you at the Old Mill might take me two or three years.'

'Building a pool for yourself, you mean. Earl, it's a pipedream. I can't afford it.'

'You'd like a pool, wouldn't you?'

162

'Forget it.'

'Don't worry, doc, I haven't yet read all the books . . . and there are new ones coming out. Tell my father if he brings me the cheque tomorrow I'll get myself discharged right away. I don't think Dr Bradley wants me here. I don't know why.'

'I do, Earl.'

'It's unreasonable . . . I don't want to drown myself. I don't want to jump off the church. I just want . . .'

'Your own way.'

'Doesn't everybody?' asked Earl.

There was no answer to it. I unlocked my car and got in.

Earl leaned on it and I had to open the window. 'I'll do what I can,' I promised.

'Horticulture show coming up,' he said.

'I know.'

'Your mother will need birds for her pie, won't she?'

It was Joclyn Runciman who let me into Martha Goldstern's house. He was so obviously at home in her studio, I could see that they'd come to know each other well since my party at Bunny's.

'Martha's in the kitchen. She'll be along presently. Thing is . . .' he smiled, 'she's an artist in everything she does, so she doesn't like being interrupted. Right now she's making a béarnaise sauce.'

'No need to disturb her. How is she?'

'Fine,' he looked surprised. 'Is this a professional visit?'

'Partly.'

'Has she been unwell?' He looked concerned.

'No . . . just a bit undernourished.'

'Undernourished?'

'No appetite.'

'But she enjoys her food. We've been out to dinner, and she's invited me here . . .'

'No difficulty in swallowing?'

'None at all. What's all this about, doctor?'

'No reason why I shouldn't tell you . . . in confidence.'

'I'd appreciate it.'

'Mrs Goldstern had various tests because she was unable to swallow solids. We found no medical reason for her trouble . . . She ate well at the party, when you met her, didn't she? That confirmed my theory that her difficulty in swallowing was due to her living alone . . . not *having* to cook proper meals.'

'Is that why you invited her to your party, doctor?'

'Well . . . I did want to see whether she'd eat in company.'

Joclyn laughed. 'An original method of making a diagnosis.'

'I couldn't think of any other. Normally, Mr Runciman, I wouldn't discuss a patient with an outsider. But in this case . . . you seem to have become part of her recovery.'

'That's something of a bonus for me, on top of the super food I've had here; and on top of the privilege of working with such a great artist.'

'Working?'

'Martha's working. I'm just making suggestions.'

'Publishing advice?'

'I'm trying to put together a package for selling her books worldwide. Publishing's changed a lot since her last book came out. A good many individual publishers, who relied on their own flair, good taste and marketing ability for success, have been absorbed into big commercial companies who sell anything from cosmetics to TV sets. In turn these companies have become dependent on two or three wholesalers who have a virtual monopoly on markets. Unless the wholesalers buy and distribute a certain book it doesn't reach the bookshops . . . not even the public libraries, which are being given less and less money for buying new books. Many readers don't get the books they want. So there are more and more books – many of them rubbish – chasing a diminishing readership.'

'I've heard of *packagers*.'

'They're people like me, who're trying to make fine art books – for instance – bestsellers by selling the same book in a number of countries. Whatever the mess publishing makes of its business, there are still many people who want to own genuinely beautiful books. If I find publishers in America, France, Germany, Japan, etc., then my firm will be able to bring out the book in this country at an economic price . . . because all firms will be sharing the cost of production and artwork. It seems my best way of assisting Martha's work.'

'You talk of *her* books. I thought they were her husband's.'

Joclyn walked along the walls of the studio. 'You can see his work. You can see hers . . . and draw your own conclusions. Martha's your patient. Perhaps I should tell you a bit about the Goldsterns . . . in confidence.'

'I'd like to know.'

'Drink?'

'Thanks . . . a gin and tonic, mainly tonic.'

He poured the drinks and sat down on the couch beside me, facing an easel with a superb painting of a green woodpecker on a silver birch. When Martha was a schoolgirl in Germany – in Dresden – Sandor Goldstern was her art teacher. In 'thirty-eight, shortly before the war, each became a refugee in this country. The Jews who could not escape Hitler's Germany were killed in the concentration camps – including Martha's parents and brothers. Martha eventually won a scholarship to an art college. That's where she met Sandor again.'

'She told me he taught her all she knows.'

'Perhaps. What he never told her was that he was a mediocre technician, she . . . an artist of genuine imagination and talent. After they married he played the great master. He treated her as a perpetual apprentice . . . She hasn't said a word against him, but it's perfectly clear to me that he exploited her

165

shamelessly. She painted most of the illustrations for his famous nature books, acted as his secretary, housekeeper, mother of his son. His nurse too, at the end. He was twenty years older than she.'

'Aren't you biased?' I asked Joclyn.

'I don't think so. Martha became a recluse because that's how Sandor wanted to live, except for his business trips. Their son couldn't get out of this house fast enough . . . He and his father didn't hit it off. When Sandor died Martha continued to live like a recluse. Do you know why? She told me it was so wonderful to have the days to herself . . . to catch up on the pictures she'd always wanted to paint . . . to walk out into her garden and have the time to watch the changing light over the Downs . . . to have no one calling her and telling her what to do. Martha didn't put it quite like that; she hasn't complained about her husband. Not once. But I've come to understand how much it meant to her to be free of him . . . to be alone, at last.'

'And now she's no longer alone.'

'No. But she's got her appetite back.' A smile passed through his gentle grey eyes, then he was serious again. 'I don't call Martha, and I don't come here unless she asks me. Look . . .' He went and fetched a folder full of watercolour studies. They were so good that I coveted them. 'Martha's painted all this since we met. I'm not distracting her, doctor . . . At least, I hope I'm not.'

'You seem to be an important part of her recovery.'

'I hope so.'

'How's your rider's bone?'

'No trouble.'

'Liar.' Martha stood in the doorway, regarding Joclyn with an affectionate smile.

'He says it's nothing,' she told me. 'But I know when he's in pain.'

'It hurts a bit after I've been riding, only because I don't want to keep swallowing paracetamol. I'm training myself to do without.'

166

'Should he?' Martha sat down on the stool at her easel.

'Yes,' I told her, 'if he can manage without. The human body and mind have considerable resources for fighting and suppressing pain. Most of us don't make the best use of our built-in resistance to pain.'

'You see.' Joclyn got up and poured a sherry for Martha. 'It's only a little pain . . . two inches by one. Forget it. I do.'

'I've come here for a non-professional purpose,' I told Martha. 'My mother's sent me on a begging mission . . . Will you be going to the horticultural show?'

'I wouldn't miss it for anything. I'll be there with my sketchbook.'

'Good. There's always a raffle at the end of the first day.'

'Of course . . . you're welcome to one of Sandor's pictures. Let's see . . .'

'Would you part with one of your own?'

'Mine?' She looked confused and pleased; not as young as Lavinia, but attractive. 'Joclyn, what do you think?'

'Why not, if the doctor wants a painting of yours?'

'The signature's the same,' she said, shyly.

Joclyn picked up the folder. 'Martha had the job of finishing her husband's pictures and signing them . . . Just *Goldstern*. She wishes to keep it that way.'

'Do you mind?' she asked.

'Certainly not.' Perhaps she didn't care for making a name of her own, perhaps it was loyalty to her husband. I guessed that what mattered to her was the act of creating her pictures, not the name.

'What shall I give you?' she glanced at the folder. 'You've seen this lot?'

'Yes . . . a beautiful lot.'

'Will one of them do?'

'It'll raise a lot of money for the society.'

'I hope so . . . Doctor, thanks for all you've done for me.'

167

'Luckily there was nothing wrong with you.'

'No?'

'You're looking . . . much better.'

'Doctor, I'm very fit . . . thanks to your party and those indecently large chunks of meat from your barbecue.'

Fifteen

The discussion with Richard Plum-Ascot had been
time-consuming, but in the end he'd come to terms
with the fact that a car for Earl would use up less of his
first wife's money than Earl's continued stay at The
Close. He'd given me a three-thousand-pound
cheque, sufficient for a decent second-hand car, not
without reminding me that Earl would be *my*
headache once again.

By the look of the well-kept tree nurseries and
greenhouses it was obvious that Plum-Ascot's
business was flourishing. In one of them, full of
flowering chrysanthemums, I saw Mr Bright. He came
to the door, beer-belly wobbling, blue pop-eyes
friendly.

'Morning, doc. Is the old devil sick?'

'If you mean Mr Plum-Ascot, he's blooming like his
flowers. What are you doing here? The strike at
Jones's is over, isn't it?'

''S right. Gave me the push, they did.'

'Are you on the dole?'

'In a manner of speaking . . .' he had a quick think,
'I mean, I had to go on the dole like. Now the old . . .
I mean, Mr Plum-Ascot and me have come to an
arrangement like. Today, that is. I been helping out
like . . . seeing as we're neighbours. Didn't want to
take on a heavy job like, on account of me back . . .'

'I remember your back, Mr Bright. There was

nothing wrong with it.'

'Me discs, doc.'

'Nothing wrong with your discs.'

'Not when you saw me. Buggered up me discs after like . . . The wife made me work in the garden. Cruel it was. So Mr Plum-Ascot, he says to me why don't I do a bit for him and make a few pounds on the side. Didn't make nothing out of him . . . honest. Today he says to me, why don't I do a job for him like. Mind you, doc, it's not as good as a storeman's job. I'm taking a cut in pay, see. Leastways it'll get me off the dole.'

'Good.'

'Honest, doc, the dole's not for me. My car packed up, so I had to fetch me money by bus when me mates didn't give me a lift. Who wants to hang around bus stops in the winter?'

'Heated greenhouses will be more comfortable.'

'That's what I said to the wife . . . Mind you, what she's after are cuttings. Mad on them little button chrysanths, she is. Got her plants all ready for the horti-show. She'll win the class too if Maisie Plum-Ascot doesn't change her mind. I said to her it wasn't right her putting in exhibits, with her a nurseryman's wife. So she said, it was the old devil who wants her to show the plants and she wasn't going to do it . . . Here he comes.' Mr Bright, amazingly nimble for his weight, went on his knees before an Azalea and I walked on.

Plum-Ascot caught up with me at my car. 'Doctor, you've seen Sir Lionel's show-plants, haven't you? I saw him take you to the greenhouse.'

'Well?'

'I've been thinking . . . My wife doesn't wish to compete with him.'

'Good. I don't think the committee's too keen on exhibits from the wives and families of professional growers.'

'There's no rule against it.'

'Didn't you say your wife doesn't want to compete?'

170

'I never know what Maisie will or won't do. But if I could tell her what Bunny's showing . . . If you gave me some idea . . .'

'Why not ask him?'

'We haven't always seen eye to eye . . . I'm not prying or anything like that. It just occurred to me that Maisie needn't necessarily compete with Sir Lionel.'

'I don't quite understand, Mr Plum-Ascot. Surely the question doesn't arise if your wife doesn't enter plants.'

'You know what women are, doctor . . . My feeling is that Maisie hasn't made her final decision.'

'Thanks for your information.' I unlocked my car.

He frowned, 'What information?'

'Maisie, as everyone knows, wants to be paid for the office work that saves you a secretary. If you were giving her a salary she'd probably do as you ask and enter your plants for the show . . .'

'*Her* plants.'

'She's not renowned for her interest in plants, Mr Plum-Ascot. What you have just told me is that you're still not paying Maisie for doing your office work.'

'Why should I? Damn it. She's my wife.'

'When the wife is working as your secretary you can claim tax-relief, can't you? I wonder whether you could possibly have overlooked such a useful saving.'

I turned my back on a bewildered Plum-Ascot, none too sure that I should have squeezed him so hard. Yet tricky Dickie's peace of mind seemed less important than the fulfilment of Bunny's modest ambitions. People would soon enough forget Bunny's unstinting service to his country and his community, though the Royal Horticultural Society might one day remember the former prisoner-of-war who'd developed a Japanese plant into a superb English flower.

'Why do I always have to get involved?' asked Dot. She was standing at her gas cooker, stirring an enormous copper pan. There was a distinctive scent in the kitchen. Dot was making the traditional quince cheese which had been popular in the Horticultural Society raffle ever since I could remember. 'It's not as if the society appreciated Bunny.'

'He's had some prizes, surely.'

'For pumpkins and onions . . . never for his flowers.'

'It'll be different this year. He's got the most unusual chrysanthemums.'

'That's what I'm afraid of; his plants *are* unusual.' Dot whipped the wooden spoon around the pan. 'What they like – the old ladies of both sexes – is stuff that can be neatly pigeon-holed into the various categories. The Dayton worthies on the committee have no ruddy imagination. Who's on the committee this year?'

'Bunny, for one.'

'He's got no talent for influencing judges. Who else?'

'The vicar.'

'Canon Crispin's an old humbug.'

'Toby Jugg.'

'Well, as an undertaker he at least has some knowledge of flowers. Trouble is, he can't make up his mind . . . not even on what he *is*. One day he goes around in overalls, doing plumbing jobs, the next he's driving a coffin in that depressing Rolls of his. You look at his shop window, Jack . . . An advert of *sincere and efficient services to the bereaved* next to a paddle-pool of rubber ducks advising potential customers not to wait until the water pours through the ceiling.'

'Our traffic warden and Sergeant Tripp are on the committee.'

'The arch-enemies . . . Well they cancel each other out.'

'And Lavinia.'

'Of course . . . Lavinia. Has she seen Bunny's chrysanths?'

'I don't know.'

'I'd love to show them to her.'

'Don't bother.'

'True, she's pro-Bunny,' reflected Dot. 'No one like her for charming the pants off judges and adjudicators. Well, it's all in the lap of the gods. I'll be thankful if Bunny makes the show.'

'How is he?'

'Crawling around like his granny at a hundred; grousing to me about your treatment, though he won't complain to you.'

'I'll provoke him. Where is he?'

'Usual place.'

He was dozing on the horsehair sofa in the morning room, attended by two of the dogs – who paid no attention to me – and the goat Cordelia, who pointed her horns at me and appeared to resent my intrusion. Pretending not to notice her, I thumped my bag on the table.

'What?' Bunny opened one eye, 'What? Oh . . . it's you Jack.' He struggled into a sitting position, which caused him obvious distress. 'Don't understand it,' he glanced at the papers on the floor, 'minutes of committee meetings put me to sleep every time. Dot says it's normal. Don't agree. Still chairman of a few committees; can't do a decent job without studying the minutes . . . make sure they're accurate. Haven't yet thanked you for the blood treatment.'

'Did it make you feel better?'

'Can't say it didn't. Felt as fit as a fiddle for a few days. Even managed to go and see Claudine. Then . . . flop, down I go again. Been trying to work it out. Sure you didn't give me the blood of some female? Inferior quality and all that.'

'Better not mention this to Dot.'

'Quite right, m'boy. Touchy subject since she went to that women's lib meeting with Muriel.'

'Bunny you got the right blood . . . the type that matches yours.'

'Didn't give me enough, I reckon.'

'I promised you more, if necessary.'

'It is.'

'I'm going to check your blood again.'

'Needle?'

'Just a prick.'

'Don't mind. Go ahead m'boy.'

I took a sample knowing that it would be low in haemoglobin and that a second transfusion would have to be carefully timed to produce the best effect when it was most needed.

Bunny looked at the folder beside my bag. 'Yours?'

'I've brought it for you to look at. Martha Goldstern's giving a picture for the raffle. She'd like you to choose the one you like best.'

'I say! That's civil of her.'

I untied the tapes and gave him the ten watercolours I had picked. He turned them over slowly and with great care. 'Goldstern was a fine artist, m'boy. Odd character . . . unsociable . . . foreigner y'know. Fine artist though. Look at this wagtail by the water. Lovely little bird. Want to touch it, it looks so much alive. And these chrysanthemums . . .' He looked up at the flower painting on the wall opposite. 'M'daughter's done this. Powerful, don't you think?'

'So it is.'

'Asked Muriel once why she painted like that. Know what she said? She wanted her flowers to look vibrant . . . a burst of creation . . . creatures – creatures, mind you – to whom something had happened. I said they looked like creatures to whom *everything* had happened. It just slipped out, d'you see? Felt a bit mean afterwards . . . That's why we have Muriel's bloody flowers and horses all over the house.' He gazed back at Martha Goldstern's wagtail. 'Give me this kind of painting every time.'

'Is this your choice?'

'Yes, I think so. Keen on this spray of chrysanthemum. Better not, though. Might put my plants in the shade. Couldn't risk that, eh?'

Back in the kitchen, Dot had poured the quince mixture into jelly-moulds and was lining them up on the windowsill with some satisfaction. 'This is one of my more useless talents. Wish I could boil an egg the

174

way my old idiot likes it. Hopeless cook . . . always have been. Wonder he hasn't left me long ago. Well, Dr Jack, what do you make of him?'

'He isn't doing too badly.'

'Considering . . .'

'Considering. He's chosen a raffle prize for the show.' I took out Martha's picture of the wagtail.

'It's a charmer. Wouldn't mind winning it.' Dot bent over the folder on the kitchen table. 'I didn't know Mr Goldstern also painted flowers.' She lifted out the painting of the chrysanthemums. 'If only Muriel could do something as true and delicate! Bunny would love it . . . Wish I'd known; I'd have asked Mr Goldstern to paint Bunny's best.'

'You could ask Martha Goldstern. Don't broadcast this, Dot . . . it's not generally known that some of the famous Goldstern studies were painted by her. She's always been too modest to make it known . . . This wagtail, and the rest, are her work.'

Dot beamed. 'You've given me the nicest news I've heard for a long time. I want Mrs Goldstern to paint Bunny's show-plant, his best. Jack, will you persuade her? I'll get her into the greenhouse *somehow*. I'll make sure Bunny's gun's out of reach.'

The lab report showed that Bunny undoubtedly needed another blood transfusion though – with luck – he'd manage without for the moment. I was none too happy about the gamble of trying to judge the best time before the show. It was certainly necessary to keep a close watch on him, to keep dropping in at Standing Hall.

A few days after he'd chosen Mrs Goldstern's raffle prize I found him seated at the morning room window, staring out towards his greenhouses. An autumn mist was swirling some ten feet above the ground, blotting out the trunks of trees so that the spread-out branches looked like sailing-frigates on a becalmed ocean. The goat was sitting beside his chair, head bent, submitting to Bunny's caresses.

'Oh, it's you m'boy.' He didn't turn round. Somehow he just knew who had entered the room. 'Much appreciate your visits . . . No one else keeping me posted about the show. Dot's haring around collecting raffle prizes; Muriel's gone up north to look at a show-jumper with a name like Harakiri.'

'Isn't she buying Tommyrot?'

'No. Blasted horse tried to roll on her. Not on, I told her. Can't trust a brute that throws tantrums every time it rains . . . I say! Look at this!' The sun had come out and was diffusing the mist with shimmering light. 'That's how it looked yesterday, when I saw the black lady.'

'Claudine?'

'Funny, I hadn't thought of her. Maybe it *was* . . . her spirit, so to speak. Imagined it was dear old Pam, the first Lady Bunting . . . sixteenth century. Didn't know we had a ghost, did you, m'boy?'

'It rings a bell.'

'Ah, yes . . . suppose Lavinia told you. Mind you, our Lady Pam's been no trouble. Never appears unless one of us is dying. Conventional sort of ghost . . . no originality. All the same, decent of her to give us warning.' He caressed the goat's neck. 'That's why I'm keeping Cordelia indoors. Reckon she's off colour. Too docile all of a sudden. Devil by nature, don't you know. Vet's coming to look at her . . . Last time Lady Pam appeared Muriel's budgie almost bit the dust. Would have done too if old Pam hadn't put in one of her hauntings. Vet managed to save the bird.'

'Is Cordelia giving milk?'

'Plenty, and bloody awful. Keep drinking the damned stuff . . . good for m'piles . . . Funny you should think of Claudine. Known stranger things when I was a prisoner-of-war. Come to think of it the – er – lady I saw yesterday didn't look like old Pam. My ancestor was a fine figure of a woman, six-footer like Muriel. The . . . apparition was a little titch, like Dot.'

'Perhaps it was Dot.'

'No . . . no, Dot doesn't float, if you know what I

176

mean. Dot, small as she is, thunders and bays like a pack of hounds. Been wondering . . . got any blood for me, m'boy?'

'It's organised.'

'Could do with it. Low on energy, don't you know. Still . . . so long as you've got it under control. Now, tell me what's doing at the village hall.'

'They've managed to put up the new curtains for the show. The trestle tables have been delivered. Some five hundred pounds' worth of raffle tickets have been sold . . .'

'Well, it's early days. We'll double or treble the sales once the prizes are on display.'

'In a day or two. Mac Curran will be doing his night-watchman stint, as usual.'

'Damned sight more useful than sticking parking tickets on farm tractors. Did your young lady get us a prize from the chemists?'

'Yes, perfume.'

'Hope it's less dangerous than the aerosol last year. Almost choked the winner. Dot says the perfume-makers are putting in some pretty lethal chemicals to make it squirt out faster. Too many synthetics nowadays . . . too much profiteering. I say . . . are you a member of the Chrysanthemum Club by any chance?'

'No.'

'Thought you might be. Took quite an interest in my plants, didn't you?'

'They're unusual.'

'Certainly are. Club's meeting tonight, at The Crown. Perhaps you could drop in later . . . half past nine, ten.'

'I'll try.'

'Won't be going meself. Bit whacked. Keep me posted, eh? Would be interested to know what kind of plants the Plum-Ascots are going to show . . . *if* they're exhibiting. Nothing against Maisie showing button chrysanths; any fool can grow them . . . Oh yes. Tell Lavinia I'll be dropping her a line . . . thank her for the pie. Not her fault I couldn't wolf it as usual; pheasants aren't what they used to be . . . probably fed on synthetics.'

Between the end of evening surgery and nine o'clock, Liz and I had finished painting the bedside cupboards and dressing table we'd picked up at a charity auction. I'd been doubtful when Liz had chosen a light grey colour and decreed that we'd put bunches of purple and yellow pansies on the drawers – it seemed an aggressively ethnic idea, but the end-result was unusual and attractive.

'Well?' asked Liz.

I kissed her. She smelled of turpentine, like our shed. 'I think we'll be able to live with this junk.'

'Is that all?'

'No. It's *inspired* junk and it'll accommodate all our beauty-creams and hairbrushes. Let's get some fresh air.'

'Better eat first, I'm starving.'

'Bunny's asked me to spy on the Chrysanthemum Club. Beer and sausage rolls at The Crown?'

'I'd like that. Do we have to change?'

'All right as we are.'

We washed the turps off our hands, decided it was too late to walk and took Liz's Mini. Driving with the windows down, I heard the bark of a dog-fox, the call of a nightjar. Liz stretched, relaxed and contented. All the work we'd put into our Old Mill was showing results; it wouldn't take much more to make it comfortable for the winter.

The mullioned windows of The Crown shone like a beacon. The low-ceilinged saloon bar was awash with voices. We made our way through the crowd and got our elbows down beside Len Kirby and Ken Morris.

'How's the leg?' I asked Len.

'Quite useful again.'

'He managed the sheep-dipping,' said Ken.

Len glanced at his neighbour. 'He gave me a hand.'

'We did the job together,' said Ken. 'His sheep and

178

mine, in one go.'

'Sort of thing boys learn in college,' Len paid for the beer and gave Ken a tankard without looking at him, 'time-and-motion operation. Something to be said for it. We whistled through the two lots of sheep in record time. Wouldn't be surprised if he had a new system for the lambing too.'

'When it comes to lambing,' Ken told us, 'it's the experience that counts. Don't get enough of it at college.'

I said, 'You'll pick up a trick or two from Len.'

'I dursay,' agreed Len.

All very satisfactory. Though the two *enemies* still seemed to prefer communicating via a third party they had progressed beyond exchanging observations on the weather.

Ron, the landlord, served us beer and home-made sausage rolls at the far side of the bar. A few minutes later we heard applause in the room next door and the members of the Chrysanthemum Club came trooping into the saloon, Mary Morris together with Pippa.

While Pippa joined Ken, Mary came over to us. 'How's Bunny?' she asked me.

'Looking forward to the show,' I dodged the question.

'Will you be seeing him, Dr Jack?'

'I think so.'

'Would you mind telling him that his number has won a prominent display area. Until he introduced the system of drawing for positions our meetings were rather less amicable. I used to think that our beautiful flowers brought out the worst in their growers.'

'I'll give him your message.'

'Thanks. We've recruited Pippa to help me set up the displays . . . You'll be pleased to know your – I'm not sure whether it was blackmail or not – has succeeded.'

'Blackmail, Mrs Morris?'

'You said something about girls nowadays being more open and honest than my generation . . .'

179

'Surely not.'

'Words to that effect. Afterwards I wondered who'd been telling you about . . . my past.'

'No one. I've been going through my father's notes.'

'Mrs Cherry once mentioned that he kept a diary.'

'I let Ken see it . . . to show him how the feud between the Kirbys and the Morrises began.'

Mary Morris thought for a while. 'What else did you show my son?' she asked at last.

'Nothing that need concern you.'

'No . . . neither your father nor you,' she faltered, 'You wouldn't use your father's information destructively. He didn't mince words . . . and he didn't tolerate hypocrisy. You're like him in many ways. What you said to me at the party made me think.'

'Is that why you've *recruited* Pippa?'

'I'm getting to know her . . . and the little boy. They're so young, Ken and Pippa.'

'Are you holding that against them?'

'I just want them to know their own minds. Come next year, if they still want to marry, I won't stand in their way.'

Sybil Dawn came pushing between us, long turquoise silk scarf floating from her neck. 'Doctor, let me buy you a drink . . . Your fiancée? Liz, isn't it? I've seen you in the chemist. What will you have?' She seemed more than anxious to get into our group. I spotted the reason for her frenetic rush – Vivienne, elbowing through Chrysanthemum Club members and farmers.

'We're just going,' I told her.

'Oh please . . .' she looked desperate, 'a soft drink if you prefer it.'

'Apple juice, thanks,' Liz accepted.

Mary Morris was drifting away. I accepted half a pint of bitter.

'I'm waiting for Jasper,' said Sybil. 'He must be coming on the next train.' She turned her back on Vivienne. 'When one's in public relations one can't always keep office hours. Jasper's got a super new account . . . the Ritz Company . . . you know, the firm that's marketing the new Omega Model. It's a fabulous car. Doctor, it would suit you . . .'

I wondered what Sybil would think if she knew that her boyfriend had already offered to bribe me with a cut-price Omega for my good services in bringing her to heel. She paid for the drinks, still with her back to the looming social service.

'You really shouldn't,' Vivienne addressed the back. 'Drinking in your condition . . .'

'Miss Allen,' Sybil whipped round, 'as it happens, I'm having apple juice. But even if I were drinking double gins it would be none of your flocking business.'

'I beg to differ,' said Vivienne stiffly, and rather foolishly. 'You are unemployed, and in my experience of one-parent families certain preventive measures . . .'

'Doctor,' Sybil appealed to me. 'I haven't applied for any money or help. I don't want to have anything to do with the social services. Do I have to put up with this . . . persecution?'

'That's putting it a bit strongly,' I said. 'Surely it's kind of Miss Allen to show such concern.'

Vivienne seemed unsure whether to be suspicious of me or grateful for my support. 'Miss Dawn, I honestly think we should get together, as soon as possible, and consider contingencies . . . plan ahead . . .'

'Thank you. I am planning.'

'Good . . . well, I'll call in tomorrow morning . . .'

'No!' Sybil shouted. She suddenly caught sight of Jasper and bulldozed through into his arms.

'You see my difficulties,' Vivienne appealed to me. 'Women like her are so impossible. Because she's been in business she thinks she knows it all . . . I've seen it so often. She'll get some sort of a home together and make ends meet until the baby arrives. By that time she'll realise what a single-parent household

181

costs. She'll look for part-time work . . . try to dump the baby on her sister . . . cause friction in the family. And then she'll expect me to help her at twenty-four hours' notice.'

'She's not alone,' said Liz.

'Not yet. But the affair won't last. The man's much younger than her. Wait until she *looks* pregnant. She won't see him for dust . . . that young man.'

'Keep at it,' I advised Vivienne. 'You're doing very well.'

'Thanks.' She glowered distrustfully. At the other side of the bar Jasper had put a protective arm around Sybil's shoulders. 'It's pathetic.'

'Persevere. She'll be grateful to you one day. Have a drink, Vivienne.'

'No. I want to take a look at Hazel Road before I go home.' She stepped back, trod on the traffic warden's toes, apologised and fled.

Liz said, 'I'd be sorry for her, if she weren't going to Hazel Road.'

'What's she doing there?'

'What isn't she! Nancy's been crying on my shoulder. She says she's scared of having her own brother staying with her.'

Nancy, a woman with three children, had been deserted by her husband several years ago. He'd drifted to Eire, where he seemed to be safe from having to maintain his family, and Vivienne had been providing social security payments and suplementary benefits for the family. Vivienne, in common with the whole village, was aware that Nancy received a good many male visitors from Millers Common.

'Nancy says that Vivienne's trying to establish that her friends are giving her money . . . One man's been staying in the house for a few weeks . . .'

'Her brother?'

'A cousin. Jack, whether he's a cousin or not it must be awful to have your house watched.'

'Why should the social services keep paying if Nancy's found herself a common-law husband?'

182

'Do you think she has?' asked Liz.

'I shouldn't be surprised. Nancy's got a good head for figures.'

'All the same . . .' Liz stopped. 'I don't believe it!'

I didn't either. The apparition, about to leave the saloon, was a figure from another age. Lavinia . . . in an ankle-length tweed skirt and a cape with a fur-lined hood. Even on stage she'd never looked less like my mother.

Sixteen

I'd taken Liz home and was walking along the public footpath, happy in the thought that she'd soon be vacating Duck Cottage, to come and live with me at the Old Mill. It was a curiously unquiet night. The bracken on the perimeter of the Griffin estate seemed more agitated than I'd have expected at eleven. Sounds of flapping wings. Crackling in the undergrowth. And when a cloud shut out the moon I imagined seeing a moving light weave in and out of the trees.

The light I saw in my own copse was not imaginary. It was burning, steady and clear, in Earl's log cabin. As I approached I saw that it came from the lantern in the porch. The living room, lit by a candle on the table, was far from bright. It took me a while to recognise the figure on the floor.

'Tha's got such a nice tail on thee,' she murmured in a low sexy voice. 'Tha's got the nicest arse of anybody . . .'

'Mother, what on earth . . .' She was reclining on a blanket. At her feet lay a heap of petticoats and antique bloomers. Golden glints flashed from her towsled hair. 'Get up.'

'In a minute, darling. I've got to work this out.' She turned on her side and arched her back. Her right hand caressed an invisible object, the left pulled up her tweed skirt and then – with an impatient tug –

slipped off a pair of grandmotherly knickers. It was done with a conjurer's grace and dexterity. 'How was that?' she asked.

'I'll tell you, if you tell me what you're supposed to be doing . . . rolling on the floor in this ridiculous get-up, close to midnight, in Earl's house.'

'Log cabin.'

'All right, log cabin. What's the difference?'

'The difference is all important, darling. It's so rustic . . . absolutely Mellors's kind of place.'

'Lady Chatterley, is it?'

'Of course.'

'I didn't know you'd started rehearsing.'

'We haven't, Jack. It's just me doing a bit of research. This place would make an ideal location. I know Cyril will agree.'

'It's Earl's place.'

'He will be thrilled. I'm sure the BBC will pay him for the use of the cabin.' Lavinia got up, collected petticoats and bloomers and put them into a plastic bag. 'I felt I *had* to solve a technical problem before we start rehearsals. Lady Chatterley *was* a lady. On certain occasions she had to divest herself of those cumbersome knickers. Right?'

'Right.'

'Obviously I simply had to find out how it's done . . . in a ladylike manner. The briefs I usually wear are no problem; they're stretchy. You just hook in a finger and pull. If Lady Chatterley were a modern script I could wear tights; then Mellors could tear them to bits – in his passion. But those bulky old knickers present quite a problem. I'd absolutely ruin the love-scenes if I fumbled.'

'You didn't fumble, mother.'

'No . . . Actually I think I've just about got the hang of it. Of course, I'll have to practise . . .'

'Not here, not now . . . please.'

'At home then. It shouldn't be a problem, now that I've got the feel of Mellors's cottage.'

'Earl's cottage, Lavinia. How did you get in?'

185

'Earl's back. I fetched him this morning . . . and not before time.' She went to the window-seat and lifted a bunch of five or six pheasants.

'One of these days he'll be caught and charged . . .'

'Darling, have you looked at your holly recently?'

'What's my holly got to do with it?'

'Everything! By Christmas you won't have a single berry on your trees. It's criminal how the wood pigeons are gorging themselves. The wretched birds are so fat now, they sit on your lawn flapping their wings, unable to take off.'

'Your birds aren't wood pigeons.'

'Did I say they are? No . . . you see, it was absolutely essential to get rid of the worst offenders.'

'With father's gun, I suppose.'

'It's the kindest way, Jack.'

'So . . . the pheasants attracted by the shooting came rushing to the Old Mill. Or did they fly to the defence of the wood pigeons?'

'Darling, pheasants are lovely wild things. They fly where they please . . . all over the countryside.'

'They don't sign contracts with their owners. Lavinia, when you present your pie for the raffle the whole village – knowing that Earl's out – will be aware . . .'

'Rubbish. The whole village knows that I have an account at Harrods.'

'Mother, the whole village, knowing you, will be aware that you don't buy your pheasants at Harrods.'

'Idle speculations, darling. The members of the Horticultural Society are too keen on raising funds to worry about minor details . . . such as where the contents of my pie come from. And dear Bunny . . . Well, *he* never asked any questions before he sold his shoot to the ghastly Norman Griffin.'

'Where's Earl?'

'I think I can hear him.'

As Earl walked in I stepped back into the shadows of a cupboard. He was wearing a black track suit, running shoes, and carrying a flashlight. Slung over his

186

shoulders were a coil of wire and a sack.

'That's it then, Mrs Mason.' Earl dumped the sack on the table and pulled out a large hare. 'He's a real champion. Come morning his mate will be in the bag too.'

'Lovely.'

'Are you sure you've got all you need?'

'Positive,' my mother assured him. 'Plenty for the pie. Sir Lionel, I've discovered, has gone off pheasants. But since he's mentioned jugged hare, that's what I'll make for him. Earl, will you prepare the game for me?'

'Don't mind skinning the hares, Mrs Mason, but the birds . . . I don't like feathers. I think I'm allergic to them. When I did your birds last year I passed out. They found me on the cold kitchen floor.'

'Who?' asked Lavinia.

'The scouts did.'

'Lucky. They always know what to do.'

'Yes, but I dislocated my stomach.'

'You've got it wrong, Earl. Stomachs can't be dislocated.'

'It was twisted. I mean, I could feel it.'

'I'll tell you what, Earl. You prepare these gorgeous creatures for the pot and I'll take you to Millers Common.'

'For a swim?'

'Of course.'

'How will I get back?'

'I'll do my shopping at the supermarket . . .'

'You don't like the supermarket.'

'Never mind. It'll save time. I'll take you at ten and pick you up about noon. How's that?'

'That'll do nicely, Mrs Mason. Will you want the feathers?'

'Good idea, Earl. Mrs Morris might make a hat. Just the thing to wear if the Players put on *Separate Tables* next year.'

'Waste not, want not, as my sainted mother used to say. That's why I want to use the pond and the stream for our swimming pool. Don't see why the doc should pay water rates . . .'

'Thoughtful of you, Earl.' I left my corner. 'You can save yourself the trouble . . .'

'Doc, you made me jump.'

'Sorry.'

'Not doing any harm, thinking about the pool, am I? You get newspapers don't you? Well . . . you shouldn't waste money on papers that don't go in for bingo. If you got the *Express* . . .'

'Win money for your swimming pool? Not a hope. I've always had to work for my money.'

'It'll be your pool too. If you're too busy I'll fill in the bingo book for you. Mrs Mason's doing it too.'

'Are you?' I asked Lavinia. 'You haven't given up *The Times*?'

'Darling, it's become so expensive. Of course, if *The Times* decided to be practical and introduce bingo . . .'

'What next!'

'If *The Times* can be quite socialist I don't see why it shouldn't update itself with bingo. If you want it you'll have to buy it yourself.'

'I will.'

'Good. When you've read it you'll put it through my letter-box, won't you?'

'Can't win, can I?'

'Why not?' asked Earl. 'In bingo you've got the same chance as Mrs Mason and me. Now . . . I've got a pool-plan . . .'

'Earl, do you know what time it is? I'm going.'

'Tomorrow then, doc. I'll be back from Millers Common in time for your morning surgery.'

'Don't you dare! I'm not going to see you at the surgery.'

'But, doc,' Earl looked hurt, 'I'm just out of hospital.'

'That's why. You're as fit as a flea, especially after your day's *work*.'

'I was only obliging your lady-mother, doc. It

wasn't work . . . not like planning your pool.'

Earl did not turn up at the surgery. I congratulated myself on having made some impression on him. I sailed through some twenty patients; nothing serious, mainly seasonal coughs and wheezes.

About half past twelve I called the last patient in the waiting room, a man of around forty whom I hadn't seen before. He had a greyhound face with darting black eyes, and he was dressed in tartan trousers and a tight-waisted green leather jacket.

'Sit down, Mr . . .'

He did. 'Ian McKenzie's the name. I've registered with ye. I've always been attended by private physicians. But my partner pointed out that I've been very remiss in not registering with a National Health doctor. Apparently I'm entitled to treatment under the National Health Service; but if I fail to register, some poor doctor misses out on my capitation fee. Ye'll be glad I've come to ye. Now, be guid enough to take doon my history . . .'

'Are you ill, Mr McKenzie?'

'Ach no.'

'In that case I don't need your medical history now.'

'You wouldna like to be prepared? Ach well . . . I've been nae trouble to my physicians, give or take a broken bone or two. I'm a construction engineer . . .'

I began to smell a rat. Had Earl wished this new patient on me? I said, 'There's no need to register with a doctor unless you've come to live here.'

'Aye, I have. I'm looking for a hoose.'

'Where are you staying now?'

'In Hazel Road. For the noo Mrs Fish has kindly accommodated me.'

Nancy's lodger, the man who had attracted Vivienne's official or officious attention.

'A very nice lady,' Mr McKenzie assured me, 'with three bairns who've been deserted by their faither. Some men have nae conscience. Take me now . . . I've worked all over the world . . . India, South

189

America, Middle East; you name it, I've been there. That's why I never married. I couldna countenance leaving a wife and bairns withoot their father. It's irresponsible. But now my travelling days are done. I'm going to settle down in your beautiful county while I'm young enough to build up my own business.'

'Good luck.'

'I *have* a business, doctor . . . a construction firm. My partner and I are negotiating for premises in Millers Common. For the noo I'm working from Hazel Road.'

'There can't be much room for a construction firm.'

'We have clients, doctor. While we're waiting for premises I'm using sub-contractors. I know fine I'm taking a risk, starting in a time of recession. But I'm not daunted. The McKenzie family motto is *faint heart never won . . .*'

'A swimming pool contract, Mr McKenzie?'

'Aye, ye're a man of perception, doctor. It's what I told myself the moment I stepped into your surgery.'

'Is my perception telling me that your partner is one Earl Plum-Ascot?'

'Ach no. If I understand aright that young man's your factor.'

'I have no estate, hence no factor.'

'Don't be modest, doctor. The Old Mill will require much work, but it is – what we call in the trade – a pocket estate with potential. And now . . .'

'Sorry, I can't give you any more time. I must go.' I got up, Mr McKenzie remained seated.

'I'll no detain ye.' He unbuttoned his leather jacket, fished out a paper and unfolded it. 'Here's the plan for your swimming pool. We'll sink the grids here . . . They're a series of filters which will – at the same time – screen off this section of your pond. We then sink the concrete . . .'

'And flood the orchard. Good day, Mr McKenzie.'

'Bide a while, doctor. Ye'll no regret it. My partner's worked out a discount, an introductory offer . . .'

'If Earl isn't your partner, who is?'

'A very guid man, doctor. Mr Ernie Bright who . . .'

'Is working at Plum-Ascot's nurseries.'

'Merely a temporary job, pending his recovery from a slipped disc; and, of course, an appointment more in line with his considerable abilities. Mr Bright has handed in his resignation. Now, as I've said . . .'

'You have, Mr McKenzie. I'm not building a swimming pool. Sorry if you've been misinformed.'

'Doctor, ye're entitled to changing your mind, as the great John Knox said to the virgin. When you've studied my plan . . .'

I grabbed my bag. 'My health visitor will see you out.'

'Doctor, ye're a practical man . . .'

'That's right. Goodbye Mr McKenzie.'

I decided to skip my ploughman's lunch at the Old Mill. I was in no mood for facing Earl and a post-mortem on Mr McKenzie's visit. The convent seemed my best bet. Mother Superior could be relied upon to offer me anything from scones to Scotch.

Though the convent and school was an enormous complex of thick Sussex flint walls the bush-telegraph worked remarkably fast. Within minutes of visiting Katie, who was able to do all but play hockey, a little nun came to summon me to Mother Superior.

The food on her table looked delectable – quiche lorraine, an assortment of salads and cheeses, three bottles of Veuve Clicquot.

'You will join us for lunch, doctor, won't you? Our convent of Maria Oscura is about to receive important visitors.' Mother Superior was solemn, yet excited. 'I'd appreciate your moral support.' Without waiting for my answer she opened a bottle of the champagne, with practised ease, and poured two glasses. 'What is your opinion of this wine, doctor?'

'Excellent.'

'I am glad.' She took her glass to the alcove that overlooked the drive and the playing fields. 'I am expecting Mr Corrigan ... the gentleman who's sponsoring the visit.'

'The visit, Reverend Mother?'

'Of His Holiness, the Pope. It's in the spring, doctor.'

'Yes, of course.' I knew nothing about Tondo Corrigan except that he went in for sponsoring events from pop concerts and boxing to motor racing. So far it hadn't occurred to me that somebody – inevitably outside our government – was investing money in the Pope's visit and organising His Holiness's timetable.

'Lord Briefman will be with him ... Such a talented man.'

Briefman's accomplishments were public knowledge. He was a broadcaster on almost any subject. He regularly appeared on television. His book *The Economics of the Cross* had been in the bestseller lists for several months. More recently he'd hit the headlines as the guardian of good taste in the marketing of the souvenirs which would be sold in honour of Pope John Paul II, before, during and after his visit. There had been warnings in the newspapers already that any souvenir which was not authorised by Lord Briefman's Ultimate Cross Souvenirs Corporation would not appreciate in value and would not – in God's good time – rate as an antique.

Mother Superior, sipping her champagne, made a visible effort at controlling the turbulence in her mind. 'How did you find Katie, doctor?'

'She's recovering very well.'

'The child is much happier now. Her father's returned from abroad and is buying a house in London.'

We watched the hockey team in training. The girls, in shorts and bulky stockings were playing with zest, but none moved with greater enthusiasm and speed than the sports mistress. Even the Mother Superior was smiling at Sister Claudine, her habit tucked into voluminous black bloomers, rushing along the field – legs, in scarlet and white striped stockings, flashing in and out among the players.

'Once Katie's allowed to play games again,' said Mother Superior, 'she'll be as happy as a lark . . . She's rather a physical young lady.'

Sister Claudine, too, was undoubtedly a physical young lady.

'Doctor, our dear Claudine is quite distressed about Sir Lionel's illness. How is he?'

'Bearing up.'

'Good. He was most generous, helping Claudine with her propagation.'

'What . . . kind of propagation?'

'Claudine grows our chrysanthemums, doctor. Sir Lionel gave her such valuable advice. Last year our convent was awarded the prize for the biggest bloom.'

'Two hundred pounds, wasn't it?'

'Yes indeed. It made all the difference to our entertainment fund . . . which is not allowed for in our accounts. Unfortunately alcoholic beverages are expensive nowadays.'

'Veuve Clicquot, for instance.'

'We don't indulge unless we have important guests. I feel that the visit of Lord Briefman and Mr Corrigan might influence the whole future of our convent and school. What weighs heavily on the entertainment fund is malt whisky. But there it is; Father Augustin won't touch a drop of anything else. He's so splendid and patient at confession that we mustn't grudge him his little luxury . . . May I replenish your glass?'

'No, thank you. You've already made me break my rule of not drinking before I've finished work for the day.'

'Your father once accused me of the same sin. In fact, he claimed that I deliberately left him alone with a bottle of Chivas Regal in order to cloud his medical judgement. I had so much work, you see, and he made me stay in bed after pneumonia.'

'You wanted him to let you get up.'

'He did . . . though I refuse to believe that the Chivas Regal had anything to do with it. But as it was a borderline question, I did impose penance on myself.

193

A little more champagne, doctor?'

'No more. I'm sure you have more important things to do than to impose penance on yourself.'

'Very true. The preparations for the horticultural show are keeping us busy. But it's all so worthwhile.'

'Seeking to top up the entertainment fund again?'

'God willing, we'll again have the largest bloom in the show.' A dreamy expression came into her gentle old eyes. 'Imagine, doctor; we might achieve a double . . . with the largest *and* best bloom. Four hundred pounds' worth of Chivas Regal, Napoleon Brandy . . . a few bottles of Drambuie perhaps . . . a case or two of Veuve Clicquot . . . and claret of a vintage that even the Bishop would appreciate. But, God forgive me, I mustn't lose sight of our immediate aim. This year the whole purpose of our entering white chrysanthemums in the show – an entirely new plant for us – is to provide the perfect English flower for the Pope . . . the *authorised* flower, doctor.'

'You mean, the top winner in the show?'

'It could be a winner provided it's granted authorisation to be included in the flower arrangements for His Holiness.'

'Lord Briefman's authorisation?'

'Well . . . yes, he is the Chairman of the Ultimate Cross Souvenirs Corporation. He must have some say in the promoters' plans. But I am hoping that he'll give me . . . more active help. I've had information which indicates that the Griffin estate is posing a serious threat to our white chrysanthemum.'

'Surely not. Norman Griffin's interest is his shoot.'

'He has three gardeners, doctor . . . all Dayton men. Besides, Mr Griffin is competitive by nature.'

'I doubt that you can change Griffin's nature over-night.'

'Doctor, in a few months time His Holiness will visit England. Already there are many, many almost lapsed Catholics crawling out of the woodwork . . .'

'Is Norman Griffin an almost lapsed Catholic?'

'I have reason to believe so . . . Lord Briefman

knows Mr Griffin personally. A Pope John Paul II Blessing Committee is about to be formed. It makes sense. His Holiness cannot be expected to bless everyone in the multitudes individually. If Lord Briefman offered Mr Griffin the chairmanship of the Blessing Committee . . .'

Down below a Rolls-Royce had driven up and was spilling Lord Briefman, whose crumpled tweeds and academic stoop were unmistakable, and a beefy red-headed man who fitted the name Corrigan.

'Reverend Mother,' I interrupted the nun's reverie. 'Your politics are too devious for a simple country doctor like me.'

'You're no simpler than your father, Dr Jack. And I'm relying on your support . . . Ah yes, there's another little matter I meant to mention. Mr Griffin's advertising his lambs on television . . . it must be costing him a lot of money.'

'I see. You think he wants to provide *authorised* lambs for the Pope's table?'

'I think God sent you to us, today of all days. I know you'll be a great help to me.'

'Well . . . I'll be happy to uncork the champagne for you.'

'Dear doctor; how very thoughtful of you!'

'I don't have your skill . . .'

'Never mind. I mustn't give our guests the wrong impression.'

On the way to the hospital I tried to sort out my impressions. Corrigan had been no surprise; he was the kind of man I would have expected to make huge profits from putting on shows for the masses – essentially an entrepreneur and showman. Lord Briefman was another kettle of fish, apparently erudite, seemingly possessed of a deep religious faith and firm principles – not to mention his charm. Which of the two had prevailed upon the Pope's *cabinet* to bring about *the visit*? Corrigan, I'd have said, if I hadn't discovered the extent of the monopoly Lord

Briefman had established. In the course of our lunch it had become quite clear that he'd make a fortune from the *authorisations* of all articles manufactured for the Pope's visit – souvenir programmes and potted papal histories, picture cards, papal pennants, beer glasses, ashtrays, lambs and even flowers.

Yes, even chrysanthemums. I suddenly recognised the Mother Superior as a formidable adversary of any plant with a winning chance. She was certainly using Lord Briefman in dissuading Norman Griffin from entering his plants for the show. For all I knew there were others on whom she'd exert pressures. And yet . . . even if her convent did capture the prizes she coveted, the convent's gain would not amount to much – a few hundred pounds in the liquor-kitty and an authorised flower for His Holiness. The Convent of Maria Oscura would be unable to supply all the flowers required throughout the Pope's tour; therefore many professional growers would seek *authorisation*, and the ultimate winner would be Lord Briefman.

The Pope's visit apart, the horticultural show was beginning to affect people in no uncertain manner. I passed several cars with stickers on their rear windows, some advertising the show, others displaying prints of technicolour chrysanths with the caption, *Dayton will beat 'em all*. Cars which normally seethed with agitated dogs' tails and barking heads carried boxes of plants and were being driven well below the speed limits.

My father had recorded his reflections on past shows in his diary. Little had changed since the early sixties:

Our horticulturists are sharpening their knives for the show. Pop Bridger tells me that there are more chrysanthemum entries than ever before, chiefly from the farmers' wives, county squires and retired politicians. The convent, which is always hard up for booze-money, will also have a go at the prizes. Jolly Paula Joseph has put a heavy padlock on her green-

house; our new postmistress – a real sweetie – is sleeping with a shotgun beside her bed; Plum-Ascot, who gave his wife an Alsatian pup after last year's show, lets the big brute patrol the nursery at night; Colonel Hapgood has electrified his fences; Ramsbotham – former labour member of parliament turned property developer – has installed an elaborate burglar alarm system. And so on. I suppose this outbreak of distrust in one's neighbours originates in the theft of Bunny's prize plant and the subsequent legal dispute.

Ever since the Dayton Horti Society won the national chrysanths award our village has become jealous of its status in the chrysanthemum stakes. In the run-up to the show submerged feelings rise to the surface. Plum-Ascot, not famed for his sense of humour, becomes positively morose and keeps plaguing me for a tonic. The Kirby and Morris families don't as much as pass the time of day. The council house growers turn paranoid to a man, suspecting that the 'gentry' is plotting against any of them winning a prize.

Lavinia is miffed because I don't want her to enter our chrysanths in the show. I have tried to explain to her, with little success, that the doctor shouldn't take part in such a free-for-all. For my patients' sake I must remain neutral, showing no political, religious, sexual or horticultural bias. Nor should I make grateful patients feel that the community owes me a prize for my plants. They are her plants, maintains Lavinia, and I'd better realise that she's not my chattel. I agree.

Interestingly enough Lavinia had never, to my knowledge, competed in the chrysanthemum show. I wondered what the odds were against Bunny's spectacular Japanese plants. There was the possibility that Maisie – with her husband's professional skills behind her – would put in something good. There was the convent, with Mother Superior admitting to owning indecently large blooms . . . thanks to Bunny's generous advice. And then there was Norman Griffin with his three expert gardeners. I couldn't see him give up his winning chances too easily.

Idle speculations. There really was nothing I could do for Bunny except increase his chances of making it to the platform at the show. Helena Tate, a good haematologist by any standard, would help me work out the best time for giving Bunny his second and all-important blood transfusion. I had carefully monitored the first, but there was no guarantee that the second would have exactly the same effect.

I had stopped at the hospital cross-roads when I noticed a couple of horses on the parallel bridle-path. Tommyrot's tossing head was instantly recognisable; so was Lavinia's flying blonde mane. Her companion baffled me somewhat. Why, of all the people who were eager to go riding with my mother, had she chosen Norman Griffin – the city man who had refused her the pheasants for her pies? As I watched him canter after Tommyrot I found myself pitying him as a member of an endangered species.

Seventeen

At the Old Mill there is one spot only, on the north side, where there is an uninterrupted view from my pond to the pastures of the Griffin estate. It was at dusk, in this clearing, that I saw the curious figure of what looked like a coolie carrying two buckets suspended from a pole resting on his shoulders. I jumped out of my car and sprinted in pursuit of the fast moving labourer. Eventually I closed the gap between us and recognised Earl's running boots.

I called him and he stopped with reluctance.

'Earl, what on earth are you up to?'

He bent his knees, put down the buckets and let the pole slide off his back. 'Easier to carry, this way.'

The buckets were packed with fish and topped up with water. 'What's this?'

'Roach. They're no good for eating. Even my cat won't touch 'em.'

'Are they out of our pond?'

'In a manner of speaking.'

'What's that supposed to mean, Earl?'

'Well, if they *are* our roach, I reckon they haven't always been our roach.'

'Come on, you can do better than that.'

'There was no roach in our pond when I came to work for you last year. If we don't keep the fish out of our water they'll get killed come spring . . . when we build the pool.'

'Once and for all: I'm not going to build a swimming pool.'

He looked surprised. 'Haven't you seen Ian McKenzie?'

'Yes. He finally made up my mind for me.'

'Ah . . . then he didn't show you the plans.'

'I didn't want to see his plans.'

'It's me who's done most of the work, doc . . . so Mr McKenzie won't cost you much.'

'McKenzie will cost me nothing because I'm not employing him.'

'I've got a copy of the plans. If you like . . .'

'I'm not going to argue with you Earl. Now what about this roach.'

He gazed at me, decided that he'd get nowhere, and picked a fish out of the water. 'Doc, you know the pond over at Mr Griffin's estate? Well . . . he's stocked it with all kinds of fancy fish, ornamental silver and gold things no use to man nor beast. I reckon the roach don't like the fancy stuff. Maybe they're attacking the goldfish.' He held up the squirming roach. 'See his mouth? It could do quite a bit of damage, I shouldn't wonder. That's why *we've* got all these roach.'

'They're not flying fish, are they?'

'You've put your finger on it, doc . . . To get into our pond they've got to be carried, like this. If you ask me, it's Mr Griffin's man – Terry, that is – who nets them, and tips them into our pond in the dead of night.'

'So you catch the fish in our pond and tip them back into Griffin's pond?'

'That's right . . . though not at night, because I don't trust that dog of Terry's. He's prowling at night.'

'Earl, how long has this been going on?'

'I suppose Terry put in the first lot in June or July. There were a lot more when I got back from the hospital.'

'Why didn't you tell me?'

'What would you've done about it? Mr Griffin

200

would have said you're dreaming or something; he wouldn't put his fish into our pond.'

'Maybe *you're* dreaming, Earl.'

'Not me. I know what's going on and I know what I'm doing.'

'So, one night Terry's going to tip the fish into our pond, the next night you're going to put them back into Griffin's. Is that it?'

'Terry comes over every week to ten days, I reckon. I don't go to his place oftener than that . . . I don't mind, doc. The way I see it, it's sport; like finding pheasants or hares when Mrs Mason needs them.'

'But you don't get anywhere with roach, do you? If even your cat won't eat it.'

'I'll carry on until I catch that Terry in the act.'

'Then what?'

'I'll see.'

'Earl, I'm not going to have a brawl.'

'Doc, you know me. I wouldn't hurt anybody . . . and Terry's twice my weight anyroad. Don't you worry about the fish. I'll get it sorted out one way or another.'

'What's the other way?'

He grinned. 'Mrs Mason.'

'It's got nothing to do with my mother.'

'Don't know.'

'I'm telling you.' I'd also told my mother that I didn't want a handyman, least of all Earl; but here was Earl, looking thoroughly at home between two buckets of roach.

'Mrs Mason could sort it out with Mr Griffin . . . in time . . . when she's got him trained.'

The health visitor, an experienced member of the Horticultural Society committee, had predicted that no one would turn up for evening surgery – not on the Thursday before the show. Anyone who felt ill, said Mrs Cherry, would ignore the aches and pains over the weekend. On Monday my surgery would be crowded. In living memory there hadn't been one

201

death during the horti-show – not in anyone's home.

I left the Health Centre earlier than usual, thinking I might get rid of the suckers which were sprouting from the roses. I went home, changed into clothes which had been shredded when I'd pruned the roses in the spring, and went down to the toolshed. Lavinia's car was parked in front, she was clattering inside.

'Hello darling,' she greeted me as if I were the visitor.

'What are *you* doing?'

'Just checking.'

She'd shifted my tools to one side of the shed and lined part of the roof and walls with plastic sheets. The workbench too had been cleared to make room for pots of flowering white chrysanthemums.

Lavinia surveyed the plants, head tilted to one side. 'Nice, aren't they?'

'What are they doing in my shed?'

'I think they'll be warm enough overnight, don't you?' She ignored my question. 'Be sure to lock up when you're finished in here.'

'Are these *your* plants?'

'Of course.'

'What are they doing here?'

'I have no room for them in my cottage. I knew you wouldn't mind.'

'Where do they come from?'

'Norman Griffin's given them to me. Isn't he a pet?'

'Is he? You didn't call him a pet when he wouldn't let you have pheasants.'

'Oh, he's come a long way since then.'

'I saw you ride with him.'

'I'm giving him lessons. Don't look at me like that, Jack. It wasn't my idea. I've been frank with him . . . I told him he's not a natural. On the other hand, one must grant that he has perseverance. He won't make the Dayton gymkhana, but by next year he should be . . . Well, he'll stay in the saddle anyway. The surprising thing is that he didn't break his collarbone when . . .'

'Mother.'

'Yes, darling?'

'You're not putting these plants into the show for him?'

'Certainly not. They're mine now.'

'*You* are not exhibiting, are you?'

'Do stop this inquisition.'

'Look, Lavinia . . . Griffin made you a present of the plants, right?'

'Absolutely.'

'He didn't give them away for the love of you.'

'Jack . . . he adores me, but that's not the reason why he gave them to me. You see, the convent didn't want his plants to compete with their plants. He was so upset about it, poor man. He was so keen on entering his chrysanths; on the other hand – what with the Pope's visit – he does want to earn grace. He's an almost lapsed Catholic.'

'So he decided to sacrifice his chrysanths to unlapse himself.'

'More or less. I persuaded him that it'll be better business for him in the long run if he doesn't enter his plants.'

'You know about the lambs?'

'I guessed. All the advertising on TV. He must have reasons for spending so much . . . Obviously, if the Pope is authorised to eat Griffin lamb in England . . .'

'No, Lavinia . . . if the promoters of the tour authorise Griffin lamb for consumption by the Pope . . .'

'Darling, don't be so complicated. What I mean is . . . Norman's lambs will be bigger business than his chrysanths. And by giving me his plants he'll earn this bonus of grace.'

'Fine. What about the chrysanths?'

'Well . . . they're mine, as I said.'

'What's the *but*?'

'Oh, he made a condition. Nothing important.'

Lavinia is a good actress, but I'd seen her act before. 'He gave you the plants on condition that *you* enter them in the show. Lavinia, you cannot do this to Bunny.'

'They can't be better than Bunny's.'

'I think Bunny's chrysanths are more unusual. But if just one of the judges prefers conventional blooms your blasted plants could defeat him.'

'Yes . . . I see your point.'

'Then you *won't* enter Griffin's plants.'

'Darling, I have twelve hours to think about it.'

'Surely, there's nothing to think about.'

'You mustn't rush me.'

'Bunny's dying, damn it.'

'Oh dear! He'll make the show, won't he?'

'He will, if I can help it.'

'That's all right then.'

'It's not all right!' I shouted at her. 'Don't you realise . . .'

'Darling Jack . . . ever since you've gone into long trousers – by the way, the one's you're wearing are hideous – I've felt that you're *my* son. But there are times when you behave exactly like your father . . . Now, *would* I hurt Bunny?'

'I just don't understand you, Lavinia.'

'Darling, you really don't have to understand me. You should concentrate on more important things. Forget me and the horti-show and do your job . . . keep Bunny alive.'

Eighteen

My Friday morning surgery was also patient-free. As Angela had taken the day off I dealt with the mail on my own, answering letters on my father's antique Underwood. Then, giving in to the holiday atmosphere, I took out my father's diary and looked through the early sixties entries, the part in which he'd written of the autumn horticulture shows.

I must admit, the new village hall has come into its own. When it was completed last year I was none too pleased with the mixture of fifteenth-century Sussex flint – the old hall – and the modern extension with its big picture windows facing the Downs. But what a showcase for Dayton's giant pumpkins and onions! And, above all, the blazing colours of the chrysanthemum display. For the first time the nurserymen of Dayton and Millers Common have been allowed to show their wares outside the hall. They have transformed the rather bare approach – which looked like a hurriedly tidied building site – into an arborium of tubbed acers and baytrees, maples, winter jasmine, escalonia and veronica.

The lay-out had remained much the same over the years, with the chrysanthemums, prominently displayed, visible from the road. The winners, on the other hand, had varied. In 1962 my father'd had something to say about it.

This time two of the judges were men who have

*earned national renown for their gardening pro-
grammes on radio. They chose the winners without fear
or favour. The Chrysanthemum of the Year prize has
gone to Wally Potter from the council estate (that'll larn
the bitchy lot of them). The biggest onion award has
gone to Sir Lionel Bunting-Standing. Bunny's tongue
has been hanging out for the chrysanths accolade, yet
he's philosophical about his failures. Considering his
heroic efforts – stealing from the famous Hiromotu
gardens, smuggling his loot into the country, trans-
forming the plants into something less bizarre and
unEnglish – I cannot help hoping that he'll make it to
the top one of these shows.*

There was a knock on my door. 'Mind if I come in?'

He *was* in – Sybil Dawn's young boyfriend.

'You don't seem too busy this morning, doctor.' He
looked over his shoulder, 'Just Vivienne Allen lurking
outside . . . I've brought your special-arrangement-
discount certificate . . . for Ritz's Omega Model.'

'What's that?' I looked at the scarlet and gold
folder, which looked like an expensive advertisement.

'Don't you remember? We made a deal. Sybil and I
got married yesterday.'

'Congratulations.'

'You managed her for me. I'm keeping my part of
the bargain . . . Now, this is how it works. You want
to get an Omega car. Right?'

'I don't.'

'All you do is, you send the voucher to the Ritz
agent in Belgium. Right? Then you or a friend picks
up the car in Ostende. By the time you get back to
Dover your Omega will be taxed and registered in
your name, and that's it. This voucher, or special
certificate, will save you about fifteen hundred
pounds.'

'That's very nice of you, but I've done nothing . . .'

'I wouldn't call Vivienne *nothing*. Sybil's handled
some tough businessmen in her time . . . not to
mention showbiz gussies. But one look at Vivienne – a
sort of red Indian squaw with Uncle Sam's briefcase

under her arm – and Sybil would fling herself into my willing arms.'

'It's no more than you expected,' I reminded Jasper.

'Hoped for.'

'You're obviously a good public relations man.'

'Private relations are different. Believe me, I needed your help.'

'Vivienne's. I think you should give this car voucher to her.'

Vivienne the social service had been a thorn in my flesh from the day we'd met. Yet when I saw her framed in my doorway, with the empty waiting room behind her, I felt sorry for her. With her big sandalled feet and ethnic dress she did rather look like a red Indian squaw with Uncle Sam's briefcase under her arm, but there was something lonely and vulnerable about the ungainly girl.

'I suppose you've already got a programme for the horticulture show?' She stood there, defeat in her posture and the greasy drooping hair.

'I want to buy one for Liz,' I told her.

She came in and put the briefcase on my desk. It contained a lot of unsold programmes. 'They're sixty pee each, and they're numbered. There'll be a draw at the end of the show.'

I gave her the money and she handed me a programme. 'Maybe Liz will be lucky. I never win . . . Have you heard? Sybil Dawn and Jasper are married. He's ten years younger . . .'

'Than Sybil. I know.'

'And Pippa and Ken Morris are engaged,' said Vivienne gloomily. 'You don't care, do you doctor? I think you believe in marriage.'

'On the whole it's better for children to have two parents.'

'You do believe in marriage,' she accused me.

'Why not? It's just a form of people living together, and that's rarely easy. It's not easy for an adult son or daughter to live with a parent, for female or male friends to live together, for unmarried couples, for children at school or for a touring cricket team. Being married or unmarried doesn't make for automatic harmony. You've got to work at it if you want to live happily with *anyone*. So don't be depressed because some of your chicks are taking off.'

'I've also got Hazel Road to contend with,' complained Vivienne. 'The man who's living with Nancy Fish is not related to her.'

'McKenzie? He's a lodger, isn't he?'

'So she says. I've taken five pounds off her social security benefits. It's all he gives her, she claims. I know it's a lie . . . I've seen her in a new outfit, a nice coat, leather boots . . . It makes one's job impossible.'

'Then don't try to do the impossible. How's your survey coming along, Vivienne?'

'It's finished. I've sent it to the Department . . . They've turned down my application for an assistant.'

'Do you need more staff?'

'Unemployment in Millers Common is still going up.'

'Then it's even less likely that you will be made redundant.'

'You don't have a high opinion of me, do you?'

'If I said that I haven't you'd be offended. If I told you that I respect what you're trying to do, you wouldn't believe me.'

'What I'm *trying* to do,' she snapped, 'not what I *am* doing.'

'Vivienne, I'm not going to play games.'

'No, not you doctor. You'll just go on blocking and frustrating me. How *can* I do a worthwhile job when you refuse me access to your records!'

'My *patients*' records, which are and will remain confidential. Once you understand that you'll be much happier in your work.'

'I'll call you; don't call me . . . it that your idea?'

'That's it.'

'I'm not to call on Lady Dorothy then?'

'What for?'

'I think she'll be entitled to benefits.'

'What *are* you talking about?'

'She'll be losing her husband, won't she?'

'You'll be able to ask the husband himself, to-morrow, at the show . . . I don't know who's been telling you what, but I promise you Sir Lionel will be there.'

On my way out I stopped at the waiting room desk, leaving a prescription which a patient's wife would collect later.

'Just the man I want to see,' said a voice I wasn't pleased to hear.

'Yes?' I made for the exit, but Adam Nutley hung on to my sleeve. I hadn't seen the administrator of the Health Centre in six months or more. I thought he'd shot his bolt after he'd increased the Centre's rent for the second time in eighteen months and let the dental suite.

'Quiet morning, eh?' His spongy face wore its benevolent expression. 'Everyone busy at the village hall. I must say, I'm looking forward to living here.'

'You've moved to Dayton?'

'We've installed ourselves in Fieldway Cottage . . . just in time for the show. My wife's exhibiting.'

'Chrysanthemum, I suppose.'

'Yes; best she's ever grown. Doctor, a word in your ear. There's an extraordinary committee meeting of the Horti Society tonight. A few loose ends to be tied up . . . a few things to be ironed out . . .'

'Are *you* on the committee?'

'I am, though – having lived in Brighton – I haven't been able to attend meetings too often. That'll change. From now on I'll be playing a more active part; which brings me to the point: Sir Lionel Bunting-Standing. He's the president elect.'

'I know.'

'It's rather awkward.'

'Why?'

'There's a rumour that Sir Lionel's a very sick man.'

'You shouldn't listen to rumours, Mr Nutley.'

'Are you telling me that there's nothing the matter with him, except piles?'

'I'm not telling you anything.'

'Professional ethics, eh? I quite understand, having been – so to speak – connected with medicine for more years than I care to remember. The point is . . . the show's on tomorrow. If Sir Lionel *were* unable to take the chair, it would leave the society in the air – so to speak. My feeling is, the committee should make alternative arrangements. Under Emergency Rule 7B we could appoint next year's president tonight. In the eventuality of Sir Lionel's inability . . . you understand, doctor . . . circumstances being what they are, I'd appreciate your giving me some indication of Sir Lionel's condition.'

'Mr Nutley, you just claimed that you understand professional ethics.'

'I do, my dear fellow. But extraordinary circumstances require extraordinary measures. I wouldn't expect you to give me Sir Lionel's medical history . . .'

'Good.'

'Just . . . let's say, a guideline.'

'Do I take it that the committee of *our* Horticultural Society has given you the task of questioning me on . . .'

'No, most certainly not.' Nutley, flushed, looked like an overfilled rubber hot-water bottle. 'Don't misunderstand me, doctor.'

'I don't, Mr Nutley. You want my advice? You're welcome to it . . .'

'Thank you . . . thank you.'

'Our Horticulture Society is one of the oldest, most distinguished in the country. The presidents have always been elected on merit . . . merit amounting to years of devoted service to the society; hard, consistent work, Mr Nutley . . .'

'Now that I live in the village, I should have

thought . . .'

'You'd be wise to keep your thoughts to yourself.'

'We do know that Sir Lionel won't be attending tonight's meeting. Surely *someone* should bring up the emergency situation in committee.'

'Why not have a word with the vicar about it? He's on the committee.'

'You mean, phone him before the meeting?'

'That's up to you.'

Nutley frowned. 'It's a thought . . . I suppose.'

'Canon Crispin advised someone in your position many years ago.' I took my father's diary from the bag and opened it at a page I'd marked. I'd put in the marker to remind myself not to underrate our some-what bumptious, bumbling man of God. 'Listen to this, Mr Nutley. *I must hand it to the vicar. He can function remarkably well when his dander is up; and up it was at last night's committee meeting. He warned Dick Plum-Ascot not to get above himself – warned him with deceptive mildness. He told that gentleman that he obviously had much to learn about our village. In Dayton, he said, we don't need a bulldozer to cut a straight furrow.'*

Nineteen

'Lavinia's quite right to call you a darling,' said Dot, on the way up to the bedroom. 'That's what you are. You have no idea how chuffed Bunny is about the blood transfusion . . . getting it at home instead of having to go to hospital. Jack . . . I know it's a bit silly, but will you let Cordelia stay with him?'

'You mean, he's keeping the goat in his bedroom now?'

'Well . . . sometimes. Cordelia's as good as gold. Really. Remember when we bought her . . . at the South of England Show? That's when I first realised that things were going wrong with the old idiot. It was so unlike him . . . wanting such an outlandish animal. We'd always been dog people.'

'I thought it was you who wanted to fill Bunny up with goat's milk.'

'Not me. I just played it Bunny's way. I am supposed to be the eccentric of the family, so it had to be me who *deep down* yearned for a nanny-goat. I think I know why he wanted Cordelia.'

'Why?' We'd stopped on the landing.

'It's to do with a Sussex superstition.' Dot lowered her voice. 'I found an old book about it in Bunny's mountain of committee minutes . . . In these parts, when someone was dying, neighbours or family would give him a goat, so that he could put all his sins upon her. Goats were considered creatures of the devil; so a few sins more or less didn't matter, and the sick man could die with his soul purged.'

'The scapegoat idea. Doesn't it go back to the Bible?'

'I don't know, though it wouldn't surprise me. But – of course – Sir Lionel's above superstition,' Dot smiled, 'a practical man is Bunny, a man of action and no nonsense. So, what with the fashion for organic foods, I adopted the lesser bit of folklore . . . that goat's milk is healthy. You know, Jack, every time I saw Bunny drink Cordelia's milk I dreaded the bugs he might be swallowing. And then I thought, to hell with it! Poor sod, a few extra bugs won't make any difference to his condition.' She turned away, sharply. 'In you go, Jack,' she bawled, 'you know the way. About time the silly old ass got some red blood into his lilywhite veins.'

'When's Muriel coming?' Bunny watched the tube which was carrying the blood into his body. 'No sense of time, m'daughter. Supposed to take my plants to the village hall and . . .'

'She's done it.'

'You sure?'

'We passed each other in the drive.'

'Didn't hear her car . . . noisy old wreck too. Must be dopey. Been taking one of your pills.'

'That's what they're for.'

'Doing without most of the time. Pain's not that bad . . . nothing like the wound I had when I was a prisoner. Taught me a lesson, that did. Human body can cope better than people think. Bit of faith in the way nature's constructed us . . . that's all we need,' he looked up at me, eyes suddenly alert, 'plus a pint or two of some generous fellow's blood . . . I say, you're not pumping female blood into me, are you?'

'No, you chauvinist.'

'Not that I don't admire the female of the species. No one like Dot . . . good little trooper.'

The goat had begun to prowl about the room. She

glared out of the window, then sank her teeth into the curtains which were already full of holes. I assumed that Cordelia was entitled to the chintz roses.

'Feel I can take it easy now.' Bunny stretched. 'Done m'best for Claudine. Been seeing her as often as I would have done if I hadn't been under the weather. Debudded her. Not easy, mind you, but I didn't fall down on the job. Wait until you see her. She's never looked more beautiful . . .'

I thought of Sister Claudine, her habit tucked into her bloomers, legs in those bulky red and white striped stockings. Beautiful was the last thing I would have called her.

'Saw her *before* Lady Pam appeared . . . y'know, the ancestor who ghosts around before somebody's about to die. Thought it was m'goat she was after. Had the vet in. Vet said she'd probably eaten something. The devil . . . she's always eating something. Right as rain now. Think it's me old Lady Pam's come for. Got nothing against it, mind you. Family affairs ship-shape. Done my damnedest for Claudine . . . Black Lady was here yesterday. Saw her walk . . .'

'Bloody old idiot!' Dot came bursting in, a fierce little Nemesis. 'The ghost of your flocking ancestor, was it! Let me tell you *who* you've been seeing before you make yourself utterly ridiculous . . . And you wouldn't have seen *her* if you weren't such a nosy bugger.' Dot thrust a framed picture at Bunny. 'I wasn't going to give it to you until tomorrow, but I can't allow you to make a fool of yourself.'

Bunny, clutching the painting in his free hand, gave a strange hoot. Then, still speechless, he held it out to me. It was a marvellous picture of his finest chrysanthemum – each petal so alive that it seemed to be opening in the sunlight.

I said, 'It's the best Goldstern I've seen.'

'Right,' said Dot. 'Get it into your fat head, Bunny; you liked the picture Martha Goldstern gave us for the raffle, so I asked her to paint this one for you. It's Mrs Goldstern you've been seeing, not bloody Lady

214

Pam . . .' She bent to take the painting from him, and suddenly froze. 'Jack! Look at him! Oh my God!'

Twenty

'Members only.' Sergeant Tripp, a red badge on his tunic, barred the way into the village hall.

'I *am*,' protested Jamaica.

'Show us your membership card then.'

'Junior members don't get cards.'

'That's right. You're not allowed in until we open the doors to the general public. Be a good girl now . . .'

'Juniors *are* allowed in,' Jamie stood her ground, 'if accompanied by an adulterer. I want to see the judge.'

'The judges? They don't have time for children.'

'Mr Curran let me in last year.'

'He *would*. He isn't the law.'

'Is so. Traffic wardens are the law too.'

'That's enough from you, young lady. You come back at eleven.'

Jamie turned, almost defeated, spotted me and slipped her hand into mine. 'I *am* accompanied by an adulterer.'

'Is she, doctor?' Sergeant Tripp grinned. 'Reckon she's right within the meaning of the rules.'

'I'll take her in.'

'Thanks Uncle Jack.' Jamie squeezed my fingers. 'I want his autograph. I've got Geoff Boycott and Penelope Keith and . . .'

'Jamie, whose autograph?'

'Giles Butt's, of course.'

'Is he a star?'

'What's a star, Uncle Jack?'

'Someone famous.'

'Giles Butt's ever so famous. He's on TV every week, in *Gardening for Children*. He's the judge for our show.'

'There'll be three other judges.'

'I don't need *them*. They're not on TV.'

Behind us Sergeant Tripp was turning away another gate-crasher 'Sorry . . . officials and members only.'

'Are you an official,' asked Jamie.

'I'm the duty doctor.'

'Can I have your badge afterwards?'

'I'll have to hand it back. Anyway, it wouldn't get you in next year.'

'Why not?'

'You're too little.'

'I know.' Jamie frowned, 'I'm a disadvantaged person.' She caught sight of the judge who was examining a long table with plates of apples, and tried to break free.

'Oh no you don't!' I held on to her hand. 'You're with me and you're going to behave. Giles Butt is busy. We'll ask for his autograph after the judging.'

I led her past the displays of fruit and vegetables to the main hall where the chrysanthemums were on show – between 100 and 150 feet of trestles covered in green cloth, a perfect background for the bewildering variety of flowers.

On the platform, facing the exhibits, stood a baize-covered table with silver pots and shields, among them the stately Lady Corbett cup for the winning chrysanthemum. Some chairs, in front of the platform, were already occupied but most members of the Chrysanth Society were wandering along the trestles, anxiously assessing their rivals' exhibits.

Still holding on to Jamie I studied the plants and the single blooms most likely to pose a threat to Bunny's superb flowers.

I dismissed – rightly or wrongly – the huge curly

217

heads of the convent's blooms, not caring for the dreary rust-coloured ones, and discounted the less than perfect foliage of the whites. I was neither an expert, like Giles Butt, nor unbiased. Yet – trying to be objective – I believed that Bunny's chances were good until I discovered the most serious contender for the Lady Corbett cup – Norman Griffin's blooms, blatantly displayed in my mother's name.

Lavinia stood at the far end of the hall, chatting with April Kirby and Mary Morris, a serene smile on her face. I could have strangled her. It was too late to make her withdraw her entry; the judges were in the hall, examining the miniature and button chrysanthemum classes.

Jamaica had managed to detach herself, but I no longer cared whether or not she disrupted the proceedings. Wild ideas shot through my mind. I could crash into the table and break Lavinia's pots; I'd pretend a brain-storm and tear them up. No good; I couldn't very well embarrass my patients. The hall was full of them. My father had committed some eccentric acts in his time – such as marrying a damned female twenty-four years his junior – but to my knowledge he'd never been guilty of vandalism. No, there was nothing I could do except watch the judges admire the flowers entered by my hypocrite mother.

The judges stayed a long time with the button chrysanths, making notes and talking among themselves. I was worrying about Bunny. Why wasn't he here? When I'd phoned Dot early in the morning she'd told me that he'd been up since six o'clock; he was fine; bloody fool wasn't going to use a walking stick; he was even up to his old trick – rocking back and forth on his feet, which always made her feel seasick. God only knew what he'd be like on the platform.

The members of the society had filled the seats when – to my immense relief – I saw the Bunting-Standings arrive. Dot, ignoring her husband, stopped for a word with Martha Goldstern and Joclyn

Runciman; Bunny walked with his arm imprisoned in Muriel's. I hadn't expected Bunny to appear other than frail, yet he looked alert and held himself gallantly upright.

There was a slight commotion behind him, but I was too intent on watching the judges to pay attention. The judges had begun to examine the full-sized flowers when I spotted Earl ahead of them. He looked bizarre in the kind of sack-like smock that farmers had worn centuries ago. Even more bizarre – he was leading Bunny's goat on a rope.

I fully expected our traffic warden or Sergeant Tripp to eject Earl and Cordelia – they were standing near enough – but, astonishingly, they were so engrossed in conversation as to seem totally unaware of the goat. Nor did anyone else pay attention. People had, of course, discovered long ago that the best way of stopping Earl's lunacies was to ignore them. Nonetheless, it surprised me that nobody made a move to get rid of the incongruous intruders.

Earl was strolling along the trestles, nose in the air, gazing into the middle distance. It dawned on me that he was not just sniffing the spicy scent of the flowers; he was keeping an eye on Lavinia. I saw her give an almost imperceptible nod, which brought Earl and Cordelia to a standstill, and then continue her animated conversation with Norman Griffin.

Suddenly Earl appeared to be in difficulties with the goat. While he was trying to disentangle the rope, which had somehow wound itself around his legs, the goat succeeded in burying her face in the nearest chrysanthemums. Without disturbing the pots and specimen vases, Cordelia daintily bit off bloom after bloom, each disappearing down her gullet with remarkable speed.

All at once people became aware of Earl's struggle. The goat was pulled clear of the plants, Earl freed of the rope. By the time the judges reached the scene Earl and Cordelia had disappeared. The incident might never have happened, except for the evidence –

the total absence of blooms on Lavinia's exhibits.

While the judges, the president, the secretary and the president elect took their seats on the platform my mother and I briefly brushed shoulders.

'Why?' I asked her.

'Darling, there was nothing for it.'

Of course. Norman Griffin was a business tycoon who drove hard bargains. He'd given his plants to Lavinia on condition that *she* would enter them in the show. It made sense.

'I keep my promises,' said Lavinia, angelically. 'In this village one simply has to play things straight.'

'Your timing was perfect.'

'Darling, I *am* an actress.'

The president's gavel silenced the audience. He thanked the committee and members of the Horticultural Society for their splendid support during his year of office, paid tribute to the hard-working and popular incoming president and then, ceremoniously, divested himself of the society's silver badge and pinned it on Bunny's coat.

Bunny, visibly moved by the prolonged applause, took over in the style we all knew – efficiency blended with warmth and humour. For the benefit of the few who'd failed to buy a programme, he announced, he'd quickly run through the sequence of the judges' awards from single-petalled sprays and category K button chrysanths to the premier prize, the Lady Corbett cup for the best bloom in the show. There was still time, he reminded us, to buy raffle tickets for a superb Goldstern painting, Mrs Mason's famous game pie, for bottles, perfume, flower arrangements and the many other prizes generously donated by Dayton's shops. He'd now call upon a much honoured and popular horticulturist – Mr Giles Butt – to speak of the Chrysanthemum Club's exhibits and to present the prizes.

'Friends,' Giles Butt rose to his feet, 'this is not my first visit to your beautiful village. I was privileged to be present, years ago, when you won the national award – and well deserved it was . . .'

I was listening to Giles Butt's pleasant north country voice without paying much attention to what he was saying. I was watching Bunny, aware of a change in his face which I hadn't consciously noticed before. He was looking twenty years younger, and I didn't like it. I'd seen the same phenomenon in other patients shortly before their death. I'd have to come to terms with the inevitable; I'd done all I could to preserve Bunny for the joy of this day, and if he lived through it he would have no regrets. He himself had acknowledged the miracle of nature that harmonised mind and body, bestowing on the dying a final gift of tranquillity. Bunny, sitting up there before the people he'd known all his life, was happy and unafraid.

The winners of the various categories, some flushed with pride, others shy of such public recognition, mounted the platform to receive their prizes and Bunny's handshake. Gradually the table became stripped of all but the flower arrangment in the centre and the one big silver cup – the Lady Corbett.

Giles Butt rose again. 'To tell you the truth, I've never been keen on judging the *best flower* in a show. What's best? The biggest? The littlest? Which shape? Curly and round? Straight and spiky? Which colour? We judges are supposed to be experts. But what's an expert? Except a person who's been lucky enough to be able to do his own thing a bit more intensively than a person who works at it as a mere job or the so-called amateur.

'Knowing the high standards down here, in Dayton, I wasn't looking forward to reaching a decision on which plant and flower is to be dubbed *best in the show* . . . not least because I don't like arguing with my fellow-judges. But this has been a special occasion; my fellow-judges and I arrived at a unanimous verdict in record time.

'All of us are happy about the winner, and I'll tell you why. It's a lovely English chrysanthemum. Like some of our most exciting plants in this country it reminds me that our great British botanists traditionally travelled the corners of the earth to discover new specimen and to bring them to the heart of what was once a great empire. Now, I know that *empire* has become a dirty word. I say to you, give it a couple of centuries and I daresay future historians will have some good to say of our work in far-flung lands . . . not least, of the gentle botanists who brought many plants to our country – often saving them from extinction – and integrated them in our own precious flora.

'As I've said, the winner is a lovely English flower, yet there's something that bit different about it.' Giles Butt stepped down from the platform, fetched a plant from the trestles and returned to his place.

'Here she is.' He held aloft Bunny's prize exhibit. 'And I don't think I need to tell you why it's the best flower in the show. Just look at this honey . . .'

The applause lasted for several minutes. Bunny, waiting to receive the cup, was rocking back and forth on his feet. I reckoned Dot wouldn't complain that he'd made her feel seasick.

Giles Butt lifted his hand, restoring silence. 'Before I present Sir Lionel with the cup there's a bit of tradition to be observed. In Dayton the winning flower has always been named by its grower, and the name will be registered by the Royal Horticultural Society . . . Well, Sir Lionel?'

'I should – er – explain, I suppose . . .' Bunny was less fluent than usual. 'Some years ago a young orphan came to our neck of the woods . . . shy girl . . . wouldn't say boo to a goose . . . Knew how she felt. Bit shy m'self. Wondered how she'd make out in a strict community. Outsider . . . much the same as my chrysanth. Tried for years to develop a flower as good as I saw in her country of origin . . . where I was in jail. Orphans, both of 'em . . . girl and plant. Girl was meek . . . definitely meek. Made me think of a bit in the Bible . . . *the meek shall inherit the earth* . . .

222

something like that.

'Fact is, the meek *don't* usually inherit the earth. But I thought I'd give it a try. My chrysanth . . . in alien earth, don't you know. Plant developed as slowly as the girl. My fault. Took me a long time to get the hang of her. Answer was, *debudding* . . . debudding on the right day . . . the right hour almost. Well, got my chrysanthemum debudded on time . . . it seems. Girl's well away too. Good at her job. Bright as a button. Been teaching her all I know about chrysanths. Wonder her plant hasn't pipped me at the post . . .'

'Bunny!' Dot's voice rose from the crowd, 'Get on with it, man. The *name*!'

He raised his blooms. 'Claudine.'

'There! Didn't he pick the perfect name?' Dot asked my mother. 'Delicate blooms, Bunny's chrysanths. Delicate girl, our Sister Claudine, until you see her wield a hockey stick.'